IN THE HANDS OF THE GODS

Also by
Frank F. Fiore

Cyberkill
The Oracle
Murran

The Chronicles of Jeremy Nash
A Taste of the Apocalypse
Seed
Black Sun

I j i n

Volume 1

IN THE HANDS OF THE GODS

a novel

FRANK F. FIORE

WordCrafts

To My Lovey Wife

on my obsession with World War Two documentaries,
who reminds me—
"You already know who won."

Author's Note

You may think that an American teenager as a kamikaze pilot is far-fetched, but not so. There was such a pilot—a Japanese/American by the name of Shigeo Imamura.

His book, *Shig: The True Story of an American Kamikaze,* tells the story of a boy growing up in America and returning to Japan, where he later became a kamikaze pilot. Shigeo Imamura, the oldest son of Japanese immigrants, was born in 1922 in San Jose, California, and grew up in San Francisco. At the age of ten he moved with his parents to Japan, where he quickly adapted in school and entered commercial college at eighteen. He graduated early so he could enter the naval flight training program in September 1943. Imamura advanced rapidly in the Japanese Navy, and he volunteered for and was put in charge of a kamikaze squadron of twelve planes in February 1945.

Many may wonder how a kamikaze pilot can survive to write his memoir. The kamikaze squadron of twelve pilots led by Imamura engaged in several weeks of night flight training and instrument flight training in preparation for their final mission. At dawn on July 30, 1945, his squadron got ready to make attacks on the invasion fleet thought to be off the Japanese coast near Tokyo, but the operation was called off as his men were at their planes making preparations to depart.

They later found out the blips on the radar screens were not Allied ships but rather tinfoil dropped as a diversion by B-29s on their way home from bombing the Japanese mainland. The war ended without his kamikaze squadron taking off on a mission.

So read on, and I believe you will find that this story is not nearly as far-fetched as it sounds.

Hiroshima

I think of death.

I sit in a cold, dank cell in the darkened bowels of a military prison in Hiroshima. As I await my execution, I think about another who is facing death. He was a remarkable young boy; an innocent soul that was coming of age against the backdrop of this ill-conceived war that my country has waged for these past nine dreadful years.

The story I'm about to tell is my recollection of that boy, maturing amidst this war, with whom I was thrown into contact over a period of years. It was a war that had cost the lives of millions of my fellow countrymen who bled in the belief of superiority, who burned in the cities that were built on false promises; men who did their duty but ultimately lost their humanity. It was a war of national suicide and the personal perversity of hundreds of thousands of people; a polite and cultured people gone mad—and that young boy, now a teenager, who was tormented by this war, placed himself in harm's way and was thrown into the turmoil of a plot to overthrow an Emperor.

Whether it was out of fear, revenge, honor, or personal salvation, I still cannot say. But this American teenager, Connor Williams, placed himself of his own free will in the pilot's seat of a Mitsubishi Zero, joining other young Kamikaze pilots hell-bent on attacking the powerful American fleet off our coast.

How did this young American teenage boy arrive at such a strange and startling fate? Perhaps I should start at the beginning.

—THE GATHERING STORM—

1936 to 1941

The Incident

I hurried through a deluge of pouring rain, my leather dress shoes clopping through standing puddles over the wet cobblestones of the ill-lit courtyard of the Tokyo Shibuya Military Prison. The water splashed around me like fireflies on a summer night clinging to the darkness.

It was the summer, July of 1936 to be exact, when most parts of Japan were visited by a rainy season called the *tsuyu*, literally meaning 'plum rain' because it coincides with the season of plum ripening. I was late, and if I missed the execution and returned without the story, my editor would surely fire me on the spot.

The newspaper I worked for, the *Tokyo Nichinichi Shimbun,* had a liberal reputation that didn't sit well with the ultra-nationalists in government. Did I say liberal? I jest. In reality, the paper traded in sensational news stories and borderline sex by using headlines that shouted the latest scandals from below the masthead.

Human-interest stories, as my editor referred to them.

The newspaper, which trafficked in scandalous news, had two editors. There was the real one—whose name was never published and known only to a few—and another, who publicly occupied the chair, and when it was necessary, went to prison or worse.

So, given our reputation, it was both a last-minute invitation and a surprise from the Imperial High Command that we were asked to witness the execution of the perpetrators of the attempted overthrow of the government.

Innocuously called the *February 26 Incident*, it included the assassination of several leading officials, including two former Prime Ministers and the occupation of the government center of Tokyo—even the attempted control of the Imperial Palace itself. A group of junior officers of a Tokyo regiment had murdered several liberal statesmen. One of them was Jōtarō Watanabe whose entire family and servants were mercilessly gunned down at his home.

The Emperor ordered the conspirators to return to their barracks, and the ringleaders were condemned to commit suicide. Those that refused were court-martialed.

My editor, who had the privilege of publicly occupying the publisher's chair, felt a first person perspective on the execution would prove the efficacy of our paper. "Good ink," my editor said.

"Koga, sell first, truth later," he added.

However, I, and some of the other reporters, believed our witness to this execution served as a subtle warning to toe the party line. However, not as subtle, was the vandalism of our newspaper's office during the incident.

As I hurried along, the towering brick walls that framed the courtyard taunted me, warning me of their power. My pace slowed as I was stopped by a frowning Imperial Marine sergeant. "Papers," he ordered." I produced my press credentials which elicited a gruff order, "Stand with the others." I then joined the other reporters present to witness the execution.

Taking my place amongst my colleagues, I leaned close enough to hear them mutter about the *Incident*, placing blame and laughing over the impending doom these men were facing. I turned and observed five Imperial Army officers behind us, standing in a line, backs pressed against a brick wall, silent.

Their hands were tied behind their backs. I could see one of the knock-kneed prisoners crouching downward as if the strain of his impending death was too much for his shoulders to bear. Perhaps it was simply dishonor. Perhaps he had resigned to his fate.

The young prisoners were stripped of rank, but I recognized

them as officers due to their tailored uniforms, single-breasted tunics with stand and fall collars, wool pantaloons, and leather ankle-boots.

Their complement faced them, rifles at the ready, and waited nervously for the command to fire. Though ordered to face straight ahead, one or two would periodically cast quick nervous glances to an Army major that was in charge of the firing squad.

I could see that the major was seized by barely contained distress. The man was on the brink. The Adam's apple in his throat bobbed with anguish; the spot between his eyebrows clinched with overwhelming emotional pain; but the major stood firm. His fear conquered his conscience—for the moment.

"Give the command to fire!" ordered a colonel off to the major's right. I recognized the Colonel's uniform and insignia immediately. He was a member of Kempeitai, the dreaded military secret police. There was another distinguishing factor on the man—a nasty scar half-closing his left eye running to the bottom of his cheek.

Next to the Colonel was an Imperial Army Lieutenant. He stood emotionless, stroking the handle of his service sword that hung by his side. This day was no different than any other in his book. He had grown accustomed to death. Killing was as innate to him as eating and drinking.

Through the curtain of water and under one of the eaves of the building that was protecting him from the *tsuyu*, a third figure watched. A man, dressed in an expensive, well-tailored suit, studied the hard silence of the major intently. He stood like an angel of death, waiting, watching impassively.

As light flickered upon his face for a moment, I noticed a glow upon him, an aura of sorts that was sending a message. Maybe he was an angel of light, or maybe he was no angel at all. Maybe he was just a man. The lights flicked as though a surge of power was haunting them, asking them to foreshadow the inevitable. Familiarity ran through my brain. *Had I seen this man before? Who was this stalker? Was he another reporter?* No. As the light flicked once more, this time like a mirror inside my eyes, it dawned on me. He was of the Imperial Royal Family.

Why was *he* here? At a military execution.

But before I could pursue that thought, the Kempeitai Colonel barked again in a clipped military voice. "Give the order to fire, Major!" The harsh growl of the Colonel's voice jolted the major from his thoughts. The Colonel shouted again. Louder. "Kasai! That was an order!"

What happened next was a surprise, but the end result was not unexpected.

The major slowly shook his head and peered at the ground.

He could not give such an order. These were men from his unit. They were once his brothers, comrades that he had trusted and respected at one time. Now they were convicted traitors sentenced to death, at his hand. His eyes turned to the Colonel, pleading release from his untenable position.

The Colonel sneered as he reluctantly nodded his consent.

The major's eyes returned forward in a hypnotic stare as he fell to his knees, opened his uniform blouse and slowly removed a tantō from his belt. He positioned the point of the small sword against his lower belly. After a few brief moments of meditation, and under the impatient scowling eyes of the Kempeitai Colonel, the major thrust the tantō into his abdomen. It was as though time had frozen for only the major. His body stiffened, but his hands held steady, his grip tight with strength and honor. The world moved around him as the blood began to pour like the shower of rain that fell from above him.

I averted my eyes for I knew what was to follow.

Seppuku!

I heard several grunts of muffled pain and when I looked up again, the major had fallen over, his face in the entrails of his own bloody intestines. His wide eyes staring at me, empty, hollow.

As my heart pounded louder in my ears and my vision started to blur, my stomach turned and bile started to rise into my throat.

As I tried to control my body, my turmoil was awoken by that word again.

"*Kasai!*"

A moment later, the volley of rifle shots echoed one after another in my ears as though they were being fired seconds apart. But in reality, it all happened within less than a split second; the five officers lay slumped against the brick wall, now broken and splattered with the souls of these men. The blood and gore of their lifeless bodies was the only sight left to behold.

I was mesmerized by the vision of their deaths, and as I tried to awake from the nightmare I'd witnessed, another sound awakened me from the coma of gunfire.

Laughter.

It was a hideous, malicious sound that roared from the belly of a gutless man. I looked to the Colonel who was standing beside the Army Lieutenant, smiling. The Lieutenant had his sword out and dipped.

He had given the order to fire.

As the smoke and smell of gunpowder dissipated, the other reporters and I were ordered to do the same. There was no more use for us. We had witnessed what they wanted us to see, and we were no longer relevant to them. As we were hastily ushered out through the courtyard, I glanced over to where the Colonel and Lieutenant were standing. They were speaking to the member of the Royal Family. The reporter inside of me couldn't help but lag behind as much as I'd dare. I'm not sure if it was by chance or by fate, but I was able to catch a snippet of their conversation.

It was a snippet that I often wish I could remove from my memory.

"The Emperor is in our hands now," said the Kempeitai Colonel, the scar on his half-closed eye making him look like he winked. The smile on the face of this mad man grew wide as he gloated over his kill.

Conspiracy

In the spring of 1937, my paper sent me to the United States to write a story on the treatment of Japanese-Americans. Being a Japanese-American myself, though not a naturalized one, I was doubly interested in covering the story. On top of that, it gave me a chance to visit my family who I hadn't seen for over a decade.

When I agreed to go, I must admit that it was partially for selfish reasons. Sure, I was interested in the story, but in many ways, going to America was a bit of a retreat; an escape from the turmoil that hung like low clouds over every street in Japan. I never thought the trip would be life changing. I had been to America before. It was nothing new or exciting. But on this visit, I met a young American boy, Connor Williams, and that meeting would foreshadow the challenges that both of us would eventually have to struggle with.

But I get ahead of myself. It's important that you know my background and the social environment of the time that I, and more importantly Connor, had been immersed in.

I was born in Japan, and when I was just a toddler, my parents immigrated to the USA. It didn't take long before we became Japanese-American truck farmers in the San Fernando Valley. Luckily for me, we were not yet at war with my ancestors. Conversely, my heritage subjected me to the anti-Japanese prejudice that ran rampant at the time. Because of such bigotry, I felt out of place, and I decided that I would find better prospects—and acceptance—in my paternal country. So I left for Japan soon after graduating from journalism school at UCLA.

The 1920s and '30s weren't good times for the Japanese in America. Discriminatory laws passed during the early 1900s denied the Japanese the right to become citizens, to own land, or even to marry outside of their race. They could not buy homes in certain areas and were barred from jobs in many industries. Some could only send their children to segregated schools, and in 1924, immigration from Japan was halted altogether.

It all spiraled downward from there.

Vicious rumors of the worst kind were spread about those of Japanese descent. It was said that *Japs* were responsible for crime and poverty. They were filthy—an ironic charge considering the Japanese obsession with cleanliness—and they spread disease.

As I arrived in San Diego, I wondered if the situation had gotten better or worse since I left. I was a journalist after all with an instinct and ability to pick up on things. That intuition was a major part of what had led me to the point where I was today. My intuition now feared that the situation hadn't gotten better.

I decided to surprise an old college chum of mine, Akihito Fujiyama, who was now a Commander and fighter pilot in the Imperial Japanese Navy. Fujiyama was a war hero in World War One. He won his honors at the Siege of Tsingtao when the Japanese Navy seized the German naval base there. In September of 1914, in the very first air-sea battle in history, four aircraft launched by a Japanese seaplane carrier attacked German naval warships. Fujiyama flew one of those aircraft and subsequently earned his honors.

Fujiyama was currently attached to the Military Mission in San Diego and was the person largely responsible for finding me a job at my newspaper. He lived with his wife, Miyoko, and their sons. Hiryo was fourteen, and Yoshi was thirteen. Fujiyama acted as military attaché to the U.S. Navy.

"Yoshihara Koga! What a surprise," Fujiyama exclaimed, slapping me on the back.

I gave a huff and bent over slightly from his friendly slap, pretending that I was seriously wounded by his strength. I am slight of build compared to Fujiyama and not quite the athletic type. I guess you might say that I was a typical-looking Japanese man—pale skin, dark brown eyes, and short, jet-black hair.

Fujiyama, on the other hand, had a well-toned body that filled out the sweat suit he wore. It was an unusual frame compared to most Japanese men. His square head was cropped by a short buzz of indigo-black hair, cut high and tight, in typical military fashion. His steely, probing eyes were distinctive of a fighter pilot, completing a picture of exactly what a competent warrior should look like.

"What brings you back to the States? Don't tell me you're tired of Japan already?"

"Nice to see you, too, Akihito." I cringed in pretentious pain, shaking off the greeting slap he gave me.

"Well, come in. I'll pour us some sake," Fujiyama offered as he led us into the living room.

I looked around his spacious house, a large, two-story tract home, and remarked, "Very nice living arrangements. Much bigger than the average house in Japan."

"Rank has its privileges," Fujiyama grinned.

"So where's your lovely wife, Miyoko?"

"At the Post Exchange. Shopping, of course," he said over his shoulder as he left for the kitchen.

I surveyed the living room for a place to sit and chose an ample sofa among the chairs, end tables and lamps in the room, all in the latest Western fashion. No futons or tatami here. Fujiyama was certainly enjoying the trappings of an American lifestyle.

My host returned and sat by me. He poured us both a round of sake into little white ceramic cups from a small, frosted bottle that was sitting in a dish of hot water. The water was used to warm the sake to the perfect temperature. He took a sip of his sake and said, "So. Tell me, my friend, what brings you to the States?"

"I'm doing a piece on the treatment of Japanese-Americans."

My eyes were wide as I awaited his response. I can't say that I was surprised at the amount of time that it took him to answer me.

Fujiyama chose his words carefully. "Not much better than when you left, unfortunately. And I'm afraid it's going to get much worse."

"That's why I wanted to speak with you." I nodded at him and pretended to enjoy the sake. "As you know, my parents live here in California, and I was wondering about the risk to them." I chanced to say, "You're in the military. What are the chances of Japan going to war with America?"

"That's a rather direct question. And from a reporter no less," Fujiyama exclaimed. "I am military, and anything I say could be misconstrued, or worse."

"This is off the record." I sipped again and kept my face relaxed. "A conversation amongst old friends."

He was silent again for a few moments. I could tell he was mulling over the right way to parse his words while pretending to trust me completely but subconsciously trusting no one completely. Japan happened to be in political turmoil after all, even if neither of us were willing to admit it openly.

"We both know the militarists are pressuring the Emperor to go to war and providing him a long list of reasons that we don't have to detail here," he said. "Suffice to say, the militarists, in particular the Army, along with the war faction in the cabinet, are telling the Emperor that the U.S. is strangling Japan with their political and economic sanctions."

"But surely, these disagreements can be settled through negotiations," I piped in. "The ones going on now in Washington D.C. Correct?"

Fujiyama stared into his sake cup as though my knowledge of the negotiations was uninformed. "From what I hear, they are not going well." He looked at his watch. "We should know more soon. Stick around. Kenta Hiyakawa of the Japanese Foreign Office has flown in from Washington. He is staying with us while he does work here in our San Diego Consulate."

"I know Hiyakawa. I interviewed him a couple of years ago. He doesn't sit well with the ultra-nationalists because as a moderate diplomat, he has the ear of the Emperor."

"Isn't he related to the Royal Family in some way?" Fujiyama interrupted.

"Yes, a distant relative and a thorn in the side of the militarists. Worse yet, he's married to an American woman." I winked at my friend. I had finished my sake while we talked.

Fujiyama quickly refilled both of our cups and took a hearty sip. "When I told Hiyakawa he was probably being watched, he just smiled and replied, 'Aren't we all?'"

I put down my sake and leaned towards Fujiyama. "You do know that you are on *the list*. People like you are of great interest to the Kempeitai, with your moderate views and all."

"And I doubt being born in Japan would carry much weight with them either," Fujiyama replied skeptically. "You grew up in America. Returning to Japan after these years only casts more suspicions on you."

I nodded my head and took another sip of my sake. "I understand that once your mission is finished here, you will return to Vice-Admiral Yamamoto's staff, correct?"

Fujiyama nodded. "They would not touch me or my family as long as Yamamoto is alive."

"And how long do you think that will be? He's already receiving death threats for being a leading advocate of peace and reason in the Imperial Navy." My speech was not as steady as it previously was. The sake had gone straight to my head, so I attempted to choose my words more carefully.

"Hai," Fujiyama replied. "The Navy has grim doubts of Japan winning a war with America and the colonial powers. I am worried that—"

Fujiyama was about to complete his thought when there was a knock at the front door. He excused himself and walked to the entryway. There were some cordial greetings in Japanese and then

Fujiyama escorted a petite, bespectacled middle-aged man into the living room. The small man ambled in as if he carried a heavy burden on his narrow shoulders.

"Hiyakawa-san," my host said. "I believe you know Yoshihara Koga."

I rose from my seat and bowed.

"It's good to see you again, Yoshihara," he said, bowing in return.

"Sit," Fujiyama invited. "Have some sake with us." Hiyakawa nodded and took a seat in a plush chair across from me.

"Yoshihara and I were speaking of the political situation between America and Japan. What is the latest news from Washington?"

Hiyakawa lowered his eyes. "Not getting any better, I'm afraid to admit. Since Japan has occupied Manchuria in '31 and walked out of the League of Nations in '33, there has been little venue for talks. And relations are continuing to be strained with the U.S. and the entire West for that matter. Shortly after President Roosevelt made his quarantine speech, labeling Japan as an aggressor, an embargo of oil and minerals was imposed. Especially oil, which the military needs to power their war machine."

"What of the political situation in Japan?" I asked. "Can the moderates in the Diet sway the Emperor towards peace?"

"Emperor Hirohito is a peaceful man," the little diplomat said softly. "However, he is no politician. And he is even less a military man. He is not a hero, but instead, he is a scientist who is happy studying marine biology." His eyes drooped in sorrow as he went on. "The country is being transformed to serve the militarists, led by the Army, in politics, culture, and education. With the militarists directing the government, any attempt at Imperial restraint could result in a coup. And after the February 26 Incident, I fear he will never face down the militarists again."

Even though Hiyakawa used the innocuous phrase *Incident*, we all knew what he really meant: an attempted military coup. I did not comment on his choice of words because I saw an opportunity to find out what the censorship of the Publications Monitoring Department of the Home Ministry would not allow the press to say.

And self-censorship was the rule of day. No one in Japan wanted to be accused of *dangerous thoughts* by the Tokkō, the Special Higher Police Force. The Tokkō, or civilian police, was one of two distinct police forces. The Kempeitai, or military police, was the other. The duties of the Tokkō police were not confined to just keeping public order. They kept strict control over anything or *anyone* opposed to the nationalistic agenda.

"Much is shrouded about the Incident," I said, "and in no uncertain terms was my paper allowed to look any further into it." I swirled the sake in my cup and watched it settle into a flat surface once again. "Young rebel officers charged into our offices and forced our employees to evacuate the building while yelling that the attack was 'divine retribution for being an un-Japanese newspaper,'" I mocked. "Then the rebels trashed the place, scattering type trays across the floor to prevent the newspaper from publishing any news about the military coup that was in progress."

I paused in thought, then looked to Hiyakawa and Fujiyama, both of their faces tense, their jaws set hard. "What we do know is that secret trials were held, but in actuality, we learned little of what really happened."

"And all done in the Emperor's name," Hiyakawa admitted sadly. He fidgeted in his seat and rubbed his hands together nervously.

"But who found the courage," Fujiyama added, "to order the coup to be subdued and command the Army Generals to put down the rebellion?"

"It was a direct order from the Imperial Commander-in-Chief," Hiyakawa responded. "The first of its kind in modern history." Hiyakawa stared into his sake for a moment before continuing. "I'm afraid that it is likely to be the last. He's too indebted to the military now."

I tried to remain neutral after Hikayawa's last sentence, but the sake had compromised my self-control, and I was visibly bothered.

Hiyakawa saw the effect his last remark had on me. "You know something?" he queried, furrowing his eyebrows.

I took another sip to give myself time to choose my words carefully. "Besides the young rebel officers," I began slowly, "what political support did the rebels have?"

"You mean from the political parties?" Hiyakawa replied evasively.

I shook my head and raised an eyebrow. "You know who I mean, Hiyakawa. The Royal Family."

Fujiyama sat up straight in his chair, glanced at me and then narrowed his eyes at Hiyakawa, who sat silent for several moments. I was not entirely sure if he was upset with me for answering, or eager to hear the response.

A heavy air of conspiracy hung over the room. We lived in a world where being a conspirator or knowing a conspirator meant certain death. So even when only referring to the elephant in the room, it could cause one to be buried underneath its massive footsteps.

Hiyakawa finally spoke. "Princes Mikasa, Higashikuni, and Takamatsu are against going to war and are trying to shield the Emperor from the militarists. But Prince Chichibu, Emperor Hirohito's brother, has repeatedly counseled the Emperor to implement direct imperial rule, even if that means suspending the constitution and creating a military dictatorship."

The little diplomat paused, wrinkling his nose and searching for the right words, fidgeting more than ever. "There are rumors, speculations, that Prince Chichibu was involved in the February Incident."

"It isn't speculation," I replied.

"How do you mean?" Fujiyama asked. Like a child excited to open a gift, he was on the edge of his seat.

"Prince Chichibu was at the execution of the remaining rebel officers," I replied. "I saw him there with my own eyes."

"What was he doing there?" asked Fujiyama, astonished.

"I don't know. But he was talking to a Kempeitai Colonel. That Colonel was there to make sure the execution was carried out. The major who was supposed to be in charge, refused to give the command to fire upon his brethren."

"Refused?" Fujiyama said. "What did he do?"

I was quiet for a moment as the memories of that fateful night played out in my head. "He committed Seppuku in front of our eyes for his disgrace. It is an image that still haunts my dreams."

As the impact of the sake grew stronger and the air in the room grew thicker, we sat in silence for what seemed like hours. Like a flicker of light at the end of a darkened tunnel, Hiyakawa spoke, breaking the quiet, but the definition of that flicker was unknown. Maybe it was a kind, hopeful ray of light at the end of the passageway, or maybe it was a lit fuse, ready to ignite a powder keg.

"Prince Chichibu and a Kempeitai Colonel? It doesn't bode well. Of the entire Royal Family, of all the Princes, Chichibu is pressuring the Emperor hard for war."

I agreed with a nod and another unnecessary slurp. "But not just pressuring. *Threatening.*"

"Threatening?" Hiyakawa's voice raised an octave.

"You said that the Emperor's order to his Generals would most probably be his last," I said. "I believe it was. I believe out of fear for his throne, he will now do the bidding of the militarists in the Army and Navy and the ultra-nationalists in the Diet."

"Why are you so sure?" asked Fujiyama. He had remained mostly silent throughout the initial conversation but suddenly had something more to say.

I'm not sure if the sake started to control my words, or if the truth had been bubbling inside of me too long, waiting for me to tell someone, but my secret finally exploded from my mouth. "I heard a troubling remark between the Kempeitai Colonel and Prince Chichibu." I swallowed the last drop of my sake. "The Kempeitai Colonel said, '*The Emperor is in our hands now.*'"

I waited for Hiyakawa's reaction, but just then, a young boy, no more than eleven years old, passed by the room. We all straightened ourselves and pretended to be engaged in a much less serious conversation than what was actually happening.

"Connor. Come here," Fujiyama said as he stood up and cleared his throat. "I want you to meet someone."

Connor reappeared and stepped into the room. Although he was an all-American boy, he appeared slightly frail and quite pitiful looking, with striking blue eyes and light sandy hair. He walked over to us, and stared up at me with indifferent eyes that were impossible to read.

"This is Yoshihara Koga, a reporter working for a Japanese newspaper. He's a good friend of mine. And this is Kenta Hiyakawa."

Connor nodded to us with a face offering zero affect.

"Connor lives with us, now," Fujiyama added, placing his arm around the young boy's shoulder.

"Yeah," Connor mumbled, pulling away. "Well, I gotta go."

"Hope to see you again," I said as I watched him exit the room.

When Connor was safely out of earshot, I asked, "What's his story? Why have you brought him into your home?"

Fujiyama sat down and finished the last of his sake. "Connor is a very troubled boy," Fujiyama replied, "and he needed our help."

"Tell us," I asked. I was relieved that the heaviness of the subject we had previously spoken about had dissipated, and a lighter air had filled the room.

Both Hiyakawa and I sat patiently as Fujiyama began to tell a tale of alienation, bitter prejudice, tragic death, and a boy's determination to beat the odds.

Connor

Fujiyama began to tell a story that took us back to an event that happened a few days before. The cloudless sky loomed blue above the sprawling middle school campus, and all appeared calm and quiet at the moment. The main building stood two stories tall, composed of stucco painted the color of cream. A playground was littered with an assortment of discarded balls and forgotten sweatshirts.

The school bell chimed, emitting a high-pitched screech across the grounds and into the residential neighborhood that surrounded the campus. The metal double-doors crashed opened and a flood of children came bounding out of the building, clutching backpacks and lunch pails, and chatting amongst themselves.

"Hey, Connor! Wait up." Hiryo, a pale-skinned, tall and slim tween of twelve, shouted, running toward Connor as the boy walked in the opposite direction of the schoolyard. Hiryo's slender face and pronounced wide eyes sat below a head of bushy, dark hair as he chased after the American boy. "Where you going?"

Hiryo's younger brother, Yoshi, trailed after his sibling, trying his best to keep up. Yoshi was a little pudgier than his *nissan*, his elder brother. Unlike his older brother, he sported an oval face and his hair was straight black, like his mother's. Yoshi was out of breath when he finally caught up with the two other boys. "Come on, we're late for the basketball game."

Connor turned and snapped at them both," Ain't goin'. Got stuff to do."

"But we thought..." Hiryo stammered.

Connor avoided eye contact, said nothing more, then hurried away without a glance behind him.

Yoshi shrugged, and as he walked back toward the bus, he seemed to have already forgotten Connor's curt behavior.

But not Hiryo. He appeared concerned by the American boy's strange demeanor. He watched as Connor turned the corner next to the Science Building and headed in the direction of the Navy base.

Neither boy noticed their father approach and give them a quizzical look. "Shouldn't you boys be at the basketball game?" Fujiyama asked them.

"Yes, Chichi," Yoshi replied. "But we were waiting for Connor."

"Where is he?" Fujiyama asked.

"He said he wasn't coming," Hiryo replied. "That he had things more important to do than the game."

"We need him, Chichi, for the game," Yoshi pleaded. "Can you talk to him?"

"I'll see what I can do. Where'd you see him last?"

"That's the weird part," Hiryo replied. "It looked like he was headed towards the base."

"OK. You two get on the bus. I'll see if I can find him."

At the bottom of a grassy knoll that sloped at a forty-five degree angle, Connor walked alongside the barbed wire fence line of the air base, searching for the small hole he had cut in the fence and had used on prior *acquisition* forays. The Navy air base was about a half-mile from school, and Connor knew all the shortcuts that avoided him being spotted by any of the neighbors.

The acquisitions, in this case, were airplane parts. And they were not just any airplane parts. They were valuable parts that he could sell to buyers, whose names he didn't know, and who didn't ask or care to know his.

Connor preferred it that way. The less they knew about him, the better.

One might wonder how or why this innocent-looking young boy was compelled to sell stolen airplane parts for money, but Connor had an overwhelming love that overpowered his judgment. Connor used the money from these transactions to give to Meiko Nemoto, his Japanese nanny, who was the only mother he had now.

Meiko used the money not for materialistic items, but to buy food that was so desperately needed. Being Japanese in California meant there was little opportunity for work and even less respect on the streets. The constant bigotry, prejudice, and hatred shown to Meiko and all Japanese-Americans fueled Connor's anger against those who mistreated the only person in the world who loved him—and Connor would do anything to protect her. In his mind the stealing, the act of breaking the law or accepted standards, was null if he was doing it for a deserving cause. He wasn't stealing so that he could buy lavish things or gamble. He was doing something noble, something *good*. Sometimes, committing an act that is absolutely unacceptable to the rest of society is a person's only answer to a problem that has no other solution.

Ever since Connor's mother died and his father made the decision to disappear like the mist that floats over a rice paddy, Meiko was the only person who cared for Connor. Day by day she scratched out a meager living for them both, living hand to mouth, breathing one moment to the next.

Sure, he could find work. But how much could a nine-year-old earn? Not enough to feed Meiko and himself. Besides, he knew everything about airplanes and had the ability to recognize the value of every single part. Airplanes were his obsession, his true passion. Instead of feeling sorry for himself and dwelling upon his plight of poverty, Connor left reality behind, burying himself inside magazines and books, consuming information about airplanes like others consume bread and water. Connor knew more about airplanes than most pilots, and he hoped to be able to fly them one day.

On this particular *acquisition*, he had his eyes on a Ryan ST military trainer that was under maintenance at the end of the airfield, knowing that its *Six Pack* would bring him a hefty dollar. A Six Pack, in this case, was not a six-pack of beer or a well-toned stomach, but the six primary flight instruments on a plane's dashboard, including the altimeter and turn coordinator, and the airspeed, attitude, vertical speed, and heading indicators.

Connor checked to make sure he wasn't being watched or followed, then passed through the hole in the fence, making his way to the end of the taxiway where his objective stood—the Ryan ST military trainer. He crept along the brown grass that surrounded the airfield, cocking his head left, then right, surveying the area for technicians, or for anyone that might prevent his covert operation. But the area appeared deserted as he finally arrived at the trainer.

Taking one final look around, Connor climbed the six-foot ladder into the open cockpit, and placed himself in the instructor's seat. He couldn't help but take a moment to imagine himself in control of the plane mid-flight.

In front of him sat all the glory of the instrument panel, beckoning him to proceed, teasing him with all its worth. He pulled a screwdriver and wrench from his jacket and proceeded to loosen each of the instruments from the control panel.

He had removed two of the six instruments when he heard a rumbling sound break the silence. Connor peered through the cockpit windshield and watched in sinking dread as a U.S. Army Jeep raced towards him, kicking up a cloud of brown dust behind the vehicle. Etched in white letters across the hood of the Jeep were the words, Military Police.

Connor felt his stomach drop, his heart machine-gunning in his chest. He considered jumping out of the trainer and taking flight on foot, but he knew there was no way he could outrun a Jeep.

Then a thought hit him.

The trainer.

He stared at the control panel, searching for the ignition switch, and quickly found it. His fingers trembled over the switch before igniting it. The trainer's engine barked, roaring to life. The engine's RPMs shook the entire cockpit, and Connor could feel the sheer power rumbling through his body.

He looked up and saw that the Jeep was nearly upon him—just twenty yards away. It was now or never. In a moment's time, all of Connor's reading and studying of airplanes shifted from theoretical to reality as he gunned the engine, and before he knew it, the trainer lurched forward. The powerful aircraft sputtered slowly at first, then quickly picked up speed.

Operating the plane became automatic as Connor manipulated the rudder and steered the trainer away from the onrushing Jeep, which by this time, had its siren blaring and its blue bubble gum machine-shaped light sending intermittent strobes of light, demanding to be obeyed. But Connor wasn't about to obey anything at this point. The line had been crossed.

Connor's smile turned to laughter, his chest filling with an arrogant air, as he opened the distance between him and the Jeep. Adrenaline rushed through his veins as the fuel ran through the engine of the aircraft. Their distance became larger and larger as the trainer picked up more and more speed, tearing down the taxiway.

Then it happened.

Connor held his breath as the trainer became light on its wheels—and within moments—the plane was airborne.

Flight!

Still no breath. He started to search through the cockpit, feverishly hoping to find the controls he needed to govern the plane before he finally exhaled.

Now his breaths grew closer together. They were fast, nervous breaths; an uncontrollable, involuntary need for more air to fill his lungs and feed oxygen to his brain. The trainer began weaving back and forth erratically in the air like a drunken bird, dipping up and down.

Although he was only ten feet off the ground, he was losing

control of the aircraft. He felt a mixture of emotion. Scared, invigorated, terrified, and enthused—all these feelings coursing through his entire body, causing him to finally feel alive.

He looked up from the control panel and watched in horror as the plane rushed straight towards a mammoth hangar.

Connor jammed on the rudder to turn the trainer away, narrowly missing the corner of the building by mere feet. The *whoosh* of the hanger soaring past the plane was magical in Connor's ears. But now he was crossing the taxiway and headed towards the main runway that was packed with departing aircraft.

He pushed his feet almost through the floor, smashing them against the rudder controls as the trainer made a 180-degree turn away from the runway. The plane rocked and settled, but was now headed towards three Military Police jeeps.

Connor had no choice. He had to ground the plane. He cut the engine. When he did, the trainer came down hard on its wheels, descending from its perch with a rattling thump, slamming Connor inside the cockpit. With a metallic groan, the trainer slowly came to an abrupt stop. The wheels squeaked and finally ceased revolving.

Connor tumbled out of the cockpit, landing on the hard concrete airstrip with his left foot first, twisting it under his weight.

He yelped in pain and collapsed onto the runway. Before he had time to analyze his agony or appreciate the fact that he had just flown an actual plane, Connor found himself surrounded by Military Police.

There was no way that this was going to turn out well.

Meiko

Meiko left the grocery store clutching a small bundle of food that she had carefully bought with the little money she had in her purse. She avoided eye contact with the other patrons as she hurried from the store, praying this trip would be uneventful. Even when they didn't stare, she felt like their eyes were eating into her, dissecting her, trying to decide if she was worthy of being an American.

She kept her eyes on the ground, watching her tiny feet and worn shoes as they glided briskly over the sidewalk down the street toward her apartment. She never looked up, not even once.

Meiko felt grateful that they lived close to the grocery store because she was afraid to be outside for too long. It wasn't paranoia, per se, but a subconscious admission of fear. There were, what the newspapers called *unfortunate incidents* over the last few weeks. These incidents had occurred with other Japanese men and women in the neighborhood. These instances were mostly harassments and bullying of anyone who looked Asian. If a person even liked to eat a fortune cookie now and again, they were a likely target. The absurdity of these ignorant actions left Meiko in a constant state of fearful awareness.

Hugging her cotton shawl tightly around her slim shoulders, eyes peeking under her sharply trimmed bangs, Meiko pushed back her medium-length charcoal colored hair, hair that was once rich and thick, full of life, and was now thinning and brittle from malnourishment. As her home came into view, she started to breathe with a sense of calm, comforted by the fact that she was just steps from safety.

But, unfortunately, Meiko's relief was premature.

She was almost at the staircase of her apartment when she heard a loud, threatening voice behind her.

"Hey! Jap!"

Meiko pressed on, her eyes straight ahead and her shoulders tight, staring at her destination, trying to ignore the voice as it repeated itself, even more vile this time.

"I said, *Jap!* You! Turn around!" This was followed by a chorus of sadistic laughter.

Meiko hastened her pace but she couldn't move quickly enough. An arm reached up from behind, ripping her shawl from her shoulders and sending the bag of food tumbling toward the ground. The paper bag thudded to the pavement, and a single apple rolled across the sidewalk and underneath the feet of her captors.

She turned to see three white teenage boys surrounding her.

"Whatcha got there, Nip?" the biggest of the three barked. Slurring and wobbling like he'd had a few too many drinks.

He kicked his feet through the exposed contents of her shopping bag. Like the other two boys, he wore a pair of ragged jeans and heavy brown shoes. A dingy blue work shirt with the name *Earl* above the pocket completed his shabby attire. He picked up the apple and took a bite out of it.

"Fish heads and rice, probably," the smallest of the three boys replied. He smirked as he scratched at a zit on his pasty, pimply face beneath a head of sparse red hair. When the zit popped, he wiped the repulsive yellow liquid on a Hawaiian shirt that was baggy and wrinkled.

"Please," Meiko pleaded. "Leave me be."

"These are *our* streets," the big thug growled as he chewed on the flesh of the apple. "And we don't like littering them up with Nips like you."

The third boy was wearing a black t-shirt that had some type of greasy food stain on it, like he worked in the kitchen of a diner, and perched atop his head, he wore a New York Yankee baseball cap. His eyes looked innocent and compassionate, but his need to feel included by his peers overtook the angel on his shoulder enough to compel him to give Meiko a hard shove.

Standing no more than five feet tall and slim of build, Meiko nearly lost her balance. She was a waif who fed all of her extra food to Connor and starved herself to provide for him. It wouldn't take much to knock her down. Not to mention the terror she felt left her legs shaking uncontrollably beneath her. She instinctively reached out and grabbed the smallest boy by the arm to keep herself from falling.

"Get your filthy hands off me, bitch!" he demanded, pushing her down into a muddy pothole.

Water splashed up around her head and sent specks of mud on her porcelain skin.

"See that?" the biggest boy growled. "She's a feisty one. She wants to fight back."

"No. No." Meiko pleaded, her voice squeaking pathetically. "Please leave me alone," she implored.

"*Please leave me alone,*" the third hooligan said in a mocking voice. "Should have stayed back in Japan, you dumb shit."

Meiko managed to struggle back to her feet, waving her hands in front of her face, but the boy shoved her to the ground again, harder this time. He stood over her, sucked up a mouthful of phlegm, and spit directly in her face.

The three boys pulled Meiko to her feet, then started to shove the little woman between them like a rag doll. Her arms flung in the air, and she lost all control of herself. The boys continued catching the poor woman as she lurched about, laughing, throwing her back at each other like it was a game.

Meiko was terrified. She only knew she had to get away. At the nearest opportunity, she tore herself away from the beasts and stumbled into the street, then, with eyes big as saucers, she screamed, "Yakudatsu! Yakudatsu!"

She turned around to find help, to run, but instead came face to face with an oncoming truck. The tires screeched, and the truck swerved, but there wasn't enough time. The sickening thump of flesh and bone connecting with one ton of steel filled the air. Meiko's body flew into the air like a stuffed toy thrown into a toy box and landed in front of the heavy wheels of the truck. Her arm slapped down on to the cold ground, right next to the bag of groceries and the apple core that her predators had consumed.

Reprieve

Neither of the barrel-chested MP sergeants uttered a word to Connor as they escorted the limping boy to a small but brightly lit room. The walls were windowless, and the low ceiling only added to the claustrophobic environment. It was wall-to-wall concrete, painted a dull shade of brown.

Without a word, the MPs unceremoniously plopped the kid into a cold, metal chair set in front of a small Formica table.

Connor grimaced as his injured foot twisted underneath him, but he tried to act tough.

Both men took their places in front of Connor, folding their arms to their chests. The only way to differentiate the two men was one wore a neatly trimmed brown mustache, whereas the other was cleanly shaved.

"We knew someone was stealing from us here on the base. Now we *have* you, punk," the clean-shaven MP sneered.

Although Connor knew he was in deep trouble and felt anxious about his predicament, he still managed to project an air of defiance.

The boy's insolent attitude didn't sit well with the other MP. The large man wrinkled his mustache up over his lip and growled, "We'll see how cool and calm you are, kid."

A moment later, an Air Force major in a Class A uniform strolled in and took a seat opposite Connor. The major didn't say a word at first, he only looked Connor over as though he was a spy or an assassin. It was obvious from the way the officer carefully analyzed the situation before he spoke that it meant one of two things: the major intended to tear Connor apart piece by piece, or help him. Connor hoped and prayed for the latter.

Connor returned the same scrutiny onto the major, looking him up and down as though he needed to decide something about him as well. He noticed that the senior officer had several types of service ribbons and hash marks on his sleeve, denoting years of service. His nametag read: BENSON.

After an unsettling span of dead silence, broken only by an offbeat rendition of reveille played by his fingertips on his metal chair, the major turned around and addressed the MPs. "Sergeants, I'll take it from here."

Both MPs saluted their senior officer and promptly filed out of the room.

The major continued to study Connor, his face unreadable. Finally, "How old are you, son?"

"Nine," Connor mumbled, refusing to look the man in the eye, gazing up at the ceiling instead.

"Nine years old, huh?" Benson pushed his face towards Connor. "You're a pretty seasoned criminal for only nine. A regular John Dillinger. You know you could have killed someone out there today? Even yourself."

Connor said nothing but felt a bit honored at being compared to an American gangster the likes of John Dillinger. He stared down at his hands clasped in front of him and listened to his stomach groan. He fully expected those hands be handcuffed but thought about how happy he was they weren't. Inside, he wanted to smile. Sure, he had been caught red-handed, but he had just flown a plane!

There was an introductory knock on the door, and the mustached MP sergeant came in. "Sir. There's a Jap outside. Said he saw the entire incident and wants to speak to someone in charge."

Major Benson gave Connor a look before standing up and stepping out into the corridor.

As the door closed behind the major, Connor strained to see who Benson was talking to, but couldn't make the man out.

Outside the interrogation room, Fujiyama extended his hand toward Major Benson. "Good afternoon, I'm Commander Fujiyama. I'm a Naval Air attaché here at the air base, and I would like to speak to you about the boy you have in custody."

The major raised an eyebrow, "Oh? You know this boy?"

"Indeed, I do. His name is Connor Williams. His mother is deceased, and his father abandoned him when he was a baby. Currently, he's being raised by his nanny. I know this information because my sons are good friends with him."

"And do you know the nanny, as well?"

"Yes. We attend the same Buddhist Temple in the city."

"Where is she now? I'd like to speak to her."

"I don't know where she is currently, but I'd like to take custody of the boy. Whatever legal attendance he needs to do, I will take responsibility for it. He deserves a chance."

The major was quiet for a moment as he considered the Commander's request. "This is highly irregular. You understand the situation, correct?"

"Connor has faced a tremendous amount of adversity in his young life. But I also happen to know that Connor is seeing a child counselor," Fujiyama responded. "I have his therapist's name. You can call him yourself and see if he approves of me bringing Connor home." Fujiyama pulled out a small notepad from his pocket and wrote the name, *Dr. David Shapiro*. He ripped off the page and handed it to the major.

Benson knitted his eyebrows together and nodded. "Well, if I can pass this off to a civilian, that would be one less pain in the ass to deal with." He jabbed his thumb over his shoulder toward the interrogation room. "Why don't you wait inside with the boy while I sort this out."

When Connor saw Fujiyama, the boy sighed a bit of relief, but remained silent.

"Connor," Fujiyama began, "I hope you know you're in a lot of trouble. What you did was reckless. Dangerous."

Connor nodded, staring down at his hands. He respected Fujiyama because he was a good father, and he didn't want to disappoint him. "Sorry," the boy managed.

Fujiyama shook his head. "You're lucky no one was hurt during your little stunt."

Connor nodded again.

Fujiyama sighed. "Well, I hope I was able to convince the major to have you released to me."

Connor's face brightened, and he broke into a smile.

"Hold on, now. There are some stipulations attached. If you don't do what I say and stay out of trouble, you will be headed directly for Juvenile Hall," Fujiyama warned. "Do we understand each other?"

Connor nodded once again. His heart pounded in his chest with relief and excitement. He always liked Fujiyama.

Fujiyama's demeanor shifted a bit as he scratched the short hairs on his head. "You actually *flew* that trainer?" He tried not to grin.

A broad smile crossed Connor's face. "Yeah. It was really super!"

Fujiyama held back that same grin when the interrogation door opened and in walked Major Benson.

"OK, Commander. I discussed the matter with Dr. Shapiro. He verified the boy's story and gave me his assessment. I can release Connor to you, but you have to bring him to the doctor as soon as possible for evaluation." He furrowed his brow. "Agreed?"

"Of course," Fujiyama replied.

"And any future legal action that is pursued against the boy is your responsibility from this point forward." Fujiyama glanced over at Connor who was nervous with anticipation and said, "Agreed."

"Fine," Benson said, then leveled his index finger towards

Connor's chest. "And I don't want to see you anywhere near my airfield again. 10-4?"

"Yes, sir. 10-4," Connor replied.

Dread

After a short cab ride back to town, Connor and Fujiyama approached the tiny studio apartment where Meiko and Connor lived. Connor's apartment was nestled down a narrow alley, deep within a rundown part of downtown San Diego. The neighborhood consisted of low-income housing, liquor stores, and countless bail bondsmen storefronts. Trash littered both sides of the street, and a handful of homeless men slept on the sidewalks.

As the cab pulled up next to the curb, Connor's heart sank at the sight of two San Diego policemen outside of the dilapidated building.

"You said I was being released," Connor cried. "They're here to take me to Juvenile Hall!"

"Settle down, Connor," Fujiyama replied, placing a reassuring hand on the boy's shoulder. "I didn't call the authorities. They must be here for another reason. Let's find out what this is about."

After paying their cab fare, Fujiyama approached the policemen. "Excuse me, officers. Is there a problem here?"

The policemen, one taller than the other, and the other of Spanish descent, surveyed Fujiyama before responding.

"We're looking for the next of kin of a…" the smaller officer said as he referred to his notebook "…a Meiko Nemoto." He tried to properly pronounce her name, but he butchered it anyway.

"Why? What happened?" asked Fujiyama.

"Are you next of kin?" the taller officer asked.

"No. This boy is. Meiko cares for him."

Connor broke away from Fujiyama's side and looked up at the tall police officer with his clear blue eyes. "Did something happen to her? Is she all right?"

"She was in an auto accident, son," the officer replied, then turned to Fujiyama. "She's at the County Hospital."

A Vow for Justice

Connor limped down the hospital corridor, trying his best to block out the assault on his senses that came from every direction. The distinct odor of illness, the wretched coughs from patients' rooms, the sight of men, women, and children in wheelchairs and propped behind walkers.

Fujiyama was right at the boy's heels. He considered asking Connor to slow down, to take it easy, but he followed in silence instead.

Connor finally arrived at the designated room and burst through the door. The young boy froze in his tracks at the sight before him.

Meiko didn't look good. Bandages covered untold cuts and lacerations on her face. Plastic tubes of colored liquid entered and exited her frail arms. A breathing mask covered what they could see of her face.

Connor didn't want to think about the condition of the rest of her body that lay buried under sheets and blankets. He hurried to the old woman's side and placed his hand in hers. "Meiko," he whispered, mustering everything inside of him to hold back the flood of tears that wanted to break at any moment.

She replied by squeezing his hand and attempting to smile.

Connor couldn't bottle up his grief. He pressed his head on their hands and began to sob.

Meiko looked up at Fujiyama and gave him a slight nod.

Fujiyama understood the woman's nonverbal wishes.

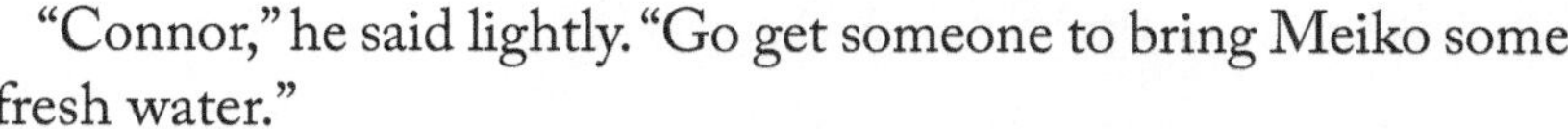

"Connor," he said lightly. "Go get someone to bring Meiko some fresh water."

Connor reluctantly agreed. Feelings of both anger and disgust screamed inside of his mind at the sight of this gentle, kind, cultured woman who had raised him. He had to either leave or he'd be forced to scream—the only way to release his frustration.

Who would do this? Why?

This woman, this beautiful woman, who sacrificed for him and loved him. She cared not of his transgressions but instead she loved him unconditionally.

When Connor left the room, Meiko slowly pulled the breathing mask from her face, wincing from pain in the process. She beckoned Fujiyama to come closer and, in a quivering whisper, said, "Your promise. You will keep your promise."

Fujiyama was quiet a moment, and then he bowed his head.

"Connor must never know," she rasped. Then raising her voice as much as she could, "Never-*ever*-know."

"I understand," Fujiyama replied. He squeezed her hand in affirmation as life slowly drained from her grip until it was no more.

Connor entered with a pitcher of water and immediately saw the mournful expression etched on Fujiyama's face. He dropped the glass pitcher, which shattered on the cold hospital floor in a hundred jagged pieces. As he approached Meiko's bedside, he could no longer control his anguish, and his body wretched from the devastating loss.

Inside of him, somewhere, Connor made a solemn vow to himself. His soul vowed to avenge her torture. He would not rest peacefully until someone paid the price for her death. It was a vow that he would keep.

A vow for justice.

A Home

"Connor out of bed yet?" asked Fujiyama, as he walked into the kitchen. It was half past six in the morning, the sun just peeking in through the window above the sink. "Almost, Chichi," Hiryo replied, sitting at the breakfast table with a mischievous grin on his face.

His younger brother, Yoshi, had the same grin.

"What are you two up to? What have you done?" their father asked.

Before they could respond, Connor entered the room. "Morning."

"You hungry, Connor?" asked Hiryo with a scheming smile.

"Yeah. Starving," Connor replied, rubbing his stomach.

"I'll get you some breakfast," Yoshi said.

Hiryo was content to let his little brother have the fun.

Connor sat patiently at the table, cocking an eye at Hiryo who was holding back a smile. Something was definitely up.

Yoshi returned with a plate of food. But to Connor, it didn't look like any breakfast food he knew. "What's this?" Connor said in disgust. On the plate were fish heads and what looked like rotting soybeans.

"Those are traditional Japanese delicacies. *Mmmm...*" Yoshi replied, rubbing his tummy and at the same time trying not to giggle.

The expression on Connor's face was too much for Hiryo. He burst out laughing.

"I'm not eating this!" Connor cried.

"No, you are not eating that," said a delicate Japanese woman, hair cut in the traditional manner, carrying a platter of eggs and bacon, biscuits, and assorted fruits. "But I have a mind to feed it to the two of you!" She waved the fish heads underneath Yoshi and Hiryo's noses. The two boys turned their heads and gagged.

The little round woman stood about five-foot nothing. She walked gracefully with small mincing steps, her legs traditionally bowed out due to constant squatting instead of sitting on the floor. The Japanese had an expression for it—*Daikon-ashi,* meaning *legs like a giant radish.*

Yoshi said, "We're just having fun."

The two boys looked over at their father, but Fujiyama was not at all amused.

"Very funny," Connor scoffed.

Miyoko Fujiyama patted Connor on the head and placed a plate of bacon and eggs in front of him. "Here Connor-san. This is what we eat in America. These boys of mine are just very silly in the mornings."

"Thank you, Mama-san," Connor replied with a smile. "Or should I say *Arigato.*"

"Dōitashimashite," she replied. "You know Japanese?"

"Some. My nanny, Meiko, taught me." His stomach sank even at the mention of her name.

"You need to have a good breakfast, Connor," Fujiyama said. "We go to see your counselor today." He turned to his two sons. "And you two *itazura* get off to school."

"Akihito. Have you forgotten what day this is?" his wife said in a soft voice. "It's Tango-no-Sekku Festival." She pointed out the small kitchen window to the front porch. There hung the Koinobori, the traditional carp-shaped windsocks on a long bamboo pole over the porch.

Connor and the boys stood up and ogled at the beautiful silk windsocks that hung on the pole below more multicolored streamers. The way the streamers snapped in the wind made the carp look like they were swimming. Just below the long multicolored ribbons streaming in the light wind was a black carp. The black carp represented the father. Below that was a red carp that represented the mother, and the last three carps represented the sons in position denoting their relative age.

Miyoko said, "The carp are in hope that you will grow up brave and strong like the koi and fight the river currents of life with ambition, strength, and willpower to swim upstream."

She pointed to one of the carp. "Connor-san. The blue koi stands for you. You are our son now." She completed her sentence with a short bow, reached behind her on the counter and placed a *mochi* rice cake wrapped in *kashiwa* leaves filled with red bean jam in his hand. This was indeed a special treat.

Connor felt a warm glow in his stomach, and a tear came to his eye. He was loved again, and this time he was finally home.

A Family

"**P**lease come in," Dr. Shapiro instructed Fujiyama. "Have a seat there in front of my desk. No need to be nervous, all is going to be well."

Fujiyama complied, leaving Connor to wait by himself outside of the closed door.

"I wanted to speak with you alone at first." The counselor cut to the chase. "I understand that Connor was in another predicament. And this one was very serious."

"Yes," Fujiyama replied. "Very serious, to say the least. I'm not entirely sure how the U.S. Navy is going to handle the matter."

"Perhaps we can work with the Navy to come to a mutually beneficial agreement."

Fujiyama could only nod, not entirely convinced that the Navy would be so sympathetic.

After a pause, Shapiro noted, "Connor is a very troubled boy. He has low self-esteem. He is alienated from his family, friends, and society at large—even from himself." Shapiro opened a file on his desk and scanned some documents. "But he has courage and inner strength like no young boy I've ever worked with before. He is a very determined youngster. Determined to survive with his Japanese nanny even amongst the bitter prejudice that is shown to her."

"Yes, I know the part about his family," Fujiyama replied. "But now, I'm sad to say that Meiko has passed away."

"Oh," Shapiro replied. "I didn't know that."

Not willing to get into details, Fujiyama said, "What will become of him now?"

The counselor looked up at the ceiling for inspiration and then finally answered, "Connor has to find something to ground himself to. Something that he can feel part of, a place to fit in." The counselor paused in thought. "We've tried a number of exercises but to no avail. And this latest incident…. Well, if he goes on like this, he will ultimately end up in Juvenile, and there will be nothing I can do or say to prevent that."

The two men were quiet for some time until Fujiyama spoke up. "I'd like to take custody of Connor. I'd like to have him live with my family on a permanent basis."

"Oh," Shapiro replied. He scratched his chin, thinking of the ramifications. "That might not be a bad idea. I minored in Asian Studies at the University. Self-esteem is viewed differently in the Japanese culture. More so than any other Asian culture. Am I correct in saying that an American's self-esteem comes from our accomplishments and who we are, while the Japanese derive their self-esteem from belonging to a group?"

Fujiyama nodded. "Yes. That is true. Relationships are nurtured and interdependence is very important in Japanese society. What others think is extremely important in our culture. The Japanese follow one set of values unlike Americans, who follow many different ones."

"Perhaps being in such an environment might bring Connor out of his shell. Remove some of his alienation. Give him the opportunity to connect to something," Shapiro speculated.

"Perhaps. At the very least, he will have adult supervision again now that Meiko is gone," Fujiyama added.

Shapiro stood up from behind his desk. "It's a good idea and worth a shot. You will have my support and full recommendation."

"Thank you. I appreciate all you've done, Doctor. I'll take Connor to his apartment and pick up his things." He arose and the two men shook hands to complete their agreement.

Luck Exists in the Leftovers

As I finished my fourth cup of sake, knowing I should have quit at two, Fujiyama ended his tale. "So you think exposing Connor to our culture will help?" I asked.

Fujiyama shrugged his shoulders. "Time will tell. But I must try—for his sake."

Fujiyama looked over to Hiyakawa, who stared down at his hands before offering his opinion on the matter. "You are taking on a great responsibility, Fujiyama-san. If the boy breaks the law again, it would reflect poorly on our people. He is in your charge. You will need much more than just good luck."

"Luck exists in the leftovers," Fujiyama countered.

Hiyakawa smiled and nodded. "There is luck in the last helping. Perhaps this is his *last*."

"And what about you, Yoshihara?" Fujiyama asked me. "How long will you be with us here in San Diego?"

"I leave tomorrow," I replied. "To complete my assignment I must go up the coast to San Francisco." I placed my hand on Fujiyama's shoulder and smiled. "You can fill me in on your luck with Connor when I return."

Militarists Take Command

In the late months of 1937, I returned to San Diego from my trip up and down the California coast. As the result of my research and interviews, I was disturbed by statements and rumors of the internment of Japanese-Americans if war should come between America and Japan. On a more personal note, I had the added concern for my family who were still living in the San Fernando Valley.

I had heard and personally recorded statements from the Asiatic Exclusion League, an anti-Japanese hate group in some of the areas I covered. Pamphlets of the vilest nature were distributed in towns and cities all over the state of California, deriding the *Japs*, instigating boycotts against Japanese businesses, and lobbying politicians who were sympathetic to their cause to pass anti-Japanese laws.

None of this bode well for Japanese-Americans.

Because of this, I decided it was necessary for me to spend some time with my family. While I was there, I urged my parents to consider moving back to Japan. My mother politely refused, but my father was vehement and became upset with my concern for their safety.

"After all," my father said, "we have nothing to fear. We are Americans. We have the same rights as everyone else."

We have nothing to fear. How those words would come back to haunt them.

I called and filed my story with my editor, and then asked him what, if any, news there was of importance back in Japan.

Sounding more American than I, my editor, Tomoko Sakura, saw himself as an ethical Samurai for truth, like his hero, Edward G. Robinson in the movie *Five Star Final*. He, too, was short and stubby, and had pronounced squinty eyes and a big mouth. A mouth that I told him the ultra-nationalists would shut permanently some day.

"Screw 'em, see," was always his response in his best imitation of Edward G.

But he wasn't stupid or incompetent by any means.

My newspaper shied away from anything *too* political. The *Tokyo Nichinichi Shimbun* was a 'Koshimbun'; a more plebeian, popular type of newspaper with a Western bent that contained local news, human-interest stories, celebrity scandals, and light fiction. Sakura walked a fine line with the paper. Enough to sell copies, but not enough to bring down the ire of the Publications Monitoring Department of the Home Ministry.

"While you were romping around America," Sakura growled on the other end of the line, "you missed a developing story here in Japan. A story that I want you to focus on right away."

"What is that?" I asked anxiously.

"The invasion of China, of course," he said impatiently. "Good human interest stories there." He paused a beat. "Don't they have newspapers in America?" he snarled.

"Of course. In fact, it's all over the papers here," I retorted.

The long distance phone line started to break up as my frenzied editor said something else. "Sakura, I can't hear you. Can you please repeat?"

The line cleared up a bit, and Sakura replied, "I said, you don't know this!"

"Know what?"

"Political parties are systematically being disbanded here." His words flowed faster and faster the more excited he became about telling me his news. "Democracy in Japan is as much as dead. The military is completely taking over our politics, and the entire nation is being mobilized to fight the war in China."

He paused to catch his breath. "The National Spiritual Mobilization Movement ordered representatives from seventy-four nationalist organizations to the Prime Minister's residence in October and were told that their organizations were now part of the Central League of the Spiritual Mobilization Movement under the joint supervision of the Ministry of Home Affairs and Ministry of Education. The purpose of the Movement is to rally the nation for a total war effort against China."

"That's not good," is all I could say. I didn't know how else to respond.

"But it gets worse," he continued. "The National General Mobilization Law was enacted. It called for an enormous increase in military spending, giving the Army almost absolute power."

It was happening. The military was now calling the shots in Japan, and I felt as if I had been hit square in the chest. "But what about the Diet? The Cabinet?" I countered. "Surely they are protesting this."

My editor laughed. "Good luck with that. They're afraid to stand up to the Military Affairs Bureau. Now, *there's* a pack of fascists. It's *gun-fuashizumu*, military fascism. That's what they want. Always interfering in politics, often by intimidation or worse." He scoffed as he finished this thought. "Welcome to the *New Order in East Asia*, my friend."

There was a lull of silence on the other end of the line, then he added in a somber voice, "Sad times. Dangerous times. I need you back here now."

"I'll leave first thing in the morning," I said and hung up. I stared at the phone, feeling an overwhelming sense of dread eat me up from the inside.

✷ ✷ ✷

I drove all night to San Diego and when I arrived, I called Fujiyama to say goodbye, and he immediately invited me to dinner.

When I appeared at his home less than an hour later, and told him of what I had heard and seen, he just shook his head. "I know the Asiatic Exclusion League. Connor's father, Vince, was a member. Meiko told me. She was their nanny."

"And how did he respond to Connor playing with your sons?"

"The problem never came up. Vince was long gone before I arrived." He raised one eyebrow. "Under suspicious circumstances, I might add. Shortly after, Connor's mother died, Vince abandoned his son."

"Suspicious?"

"The boy's mother's death was ruled an accident at home. Fell off the porch and broke her neck. But those in the Japanese community believed otherwise. They did not trust in the story. But we never knew for sure since his father skipped town."

"I see. By the way," I inquired, "is Hiyakawa still here in San Diego?"

Fujiyama shook his head. "He was recalled to Japan. Just before the China invasion."

"Do you know about the National General Mobilization Law that was enacted?"

"Yes. Hiyakawa told me. Bad news," he said shaking his head.

"Is the Navy in on this military takeover?"

"No. Yamamoto and the Navy are the voice of reason. They are against this China venture, but the Army is in control of everything now," he fretted.

"I myself have been ordered by my paper to return."

We fell into a moment of silence before I changed the subject. "So, what luck have you had with Connor?"

"My wife has been teaching him Japanese. He's getting quite adept at it. The boy has a good head for languages," he remarked, tapping his head with his forefinger. "Even taught him *O jigi shite*, how to bow properly. He's learned to bow deeply to older people and those senior to him, and only slightly to contemporaries and those junior to him." He chuckled. "Over the last month or so, he's been bowing every chance he gets."

"And..." I added.

"You really want the entire story?"

"Of course. I want to hear it all. I never thought of you as a sensitive child psychologist," I jested. "Doesn't mesh well with a warrior personality."

Fujiyama ignored the friendly dig. "Well, maybe it does. Maybe it does," he answered cryptically.

And so he began to tell me the story of Connor and his exposure to an aspect of Japanese culture I never thought would interest a young American boy. As it turned out, it was that very aspect that began his journey towards self-esteem, for better—*and* for worse.

The Honjo Masamune

One spring morning, as Connor hustled down the hallway so he wouldn't be late for school, he passed Fujiyama's study. Typical of any youngster, he couldn't resist the urge to peek through the office door that was unusually ajar. He peered around the room and couldn't help but notice how neat and organized the space was maintained. Nothing appeared that interesting or out of the ordinary—a desk, a pair of filing cabinets, a few chairs—but then something caught his eye on the other side of the room. A bright glint of sunshine reflected off of an object resting on a small table behind Fujiyama's desk.

Connor checked the hallway in both directions to see if any of the family was near. He hadn't specifically been told *not* to enter the room, but also hadn't been told that he *could*. The house appeared quiet, and he felt like he was alone for the moment. He didn't hesitate and quickly slipped into the study.

The object that glimmered in the shaft of sunlight was a long, highly polished and decorated metal cylinder that was uniquely colored black and red. The prize beckoned his curiosity. He stepped closer. The cylinder was almost four feet long and had a squared guard with a long grip that was wrapped in some kind of cloth that made a crisscross pattern across the surface.

Another step.

That was when Connor realized that he was looking at a long sword in its sheath sitting on a small, two-pronged pedestal.

Hung above the weapon was an oil painting depicting a Japanese warrior in combat in a ferocious stance, holding a long sword much like the one on the table. The ornate painting was entitled *Honjo Masamune*.

One last step.

Connor's curiosity got the best of him and he reached out, running his hand lightly over the sheath.

"Like it?" came a voice from behind him.

Connor pulled his hand back with a start and whipped around to see Fujiyama standing behind him.

"That's a katana, a Samurai sword," Fujiyama pointed to the Samurai warrior in the painting. "My family."

"*Your* family?" Connor said with eyes wide open. "You're a Samurai?"

"Not in the literal sense. But my family comes from a long line of Samurai." Fujiyama was amused by the boy's sheer awe. "Are you familiar with the Samurai?"

"A little," Connor replied, clearly impressed with Fujiyama's ancestry. "They were Japanese warriors."

"That's correct." Fujiyama moved to Connor's side and motioned toward the katana. "Would you like to see it?" Connor slowly nodded his head up and down, mesmerized by the idea of holding a sword that once sat in the palm of a real Samurai.

Fujiyama picked up the katana and withdrew the twenty-eight-inch sword from its sheath, revealing the perfectly polished and reflective steel.

It was love at first sight. Connor's eyes sparkled at the sight of it. "Can I hold it?"

Fujiyama complied and handed it to the boy. The first thing the boy noticed was the long graceful curve of the blade.

"Oh. It's bent," he said.

Fujiyama laughed. "It's not bent. Far from that. It's made that way."

"Really?"

"Would you like to know why the katana were designed in such a way?" his foster father asked.

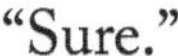

"Sure."

Fujiyama began to tell his tale while Connor admired the beautiful weapon clutched in his hands and imagined the story in his reflection.

"There once was a smith employed by the Emperor to make swords for his armies. The smith's name was Amakun Yasutsuna. But one day, after returning from battle, the Emperor and his warriors passed by Amakuni's forge and instead of the warm greetings he was used to, they coldly ignored him."

"Why?" asked Connor with piquing interest.

"Many centuries ago, the Mongols from China invaded Japan. Amakuni noticed that most of the samurai warrior's swords had been broken and badly damaged in the heat of battle. They could not penetrate the Mongol armor. After inspecting the damaged blades, he realized the reason. They were incorrectly forged." Fujiyama allowed these words to sink in before continuing. "Amakuni was devastated, embarrassed of his poor workmanship, and he vowed to forge the perfect sword in order to win back the Emperor's favor."

Connor pointed to the sword in oil painting. "Like that one?"

"Ones like it. That particular sword is the Honjo Masamune. It is a famous and powerful sword. It became the ceremonial sword of the ruling Tokugawa shoguns for two hundred and fifty years. There are many legends attached to the Honjo Masamune."

"So, how did what's his name make a sword that cut through armor?" Connor asked.

"Amakuni locked himself in his forge and prayed to the Shinto gods for inspiration. Legend says that in a dream one night, there came a glowing image of a slightly curved blade. The next morning, he knew what he had to do and created the sword that was revealed to him."

"I bet the Emperor was impressed!" said Connor, examining the curve in the sword once again.

"Not quite. In fact, the other smiths thought him quite mad and laughed at the strangely *bent* sword, as you called it."

"Then what happened?" Connor eyes were wide and his curiosity piqued.

"He ignored his detractors and continued to refine his forging technique until he felt that the blades were perfect. Then, finally, when the warriors returned from their first battle using their new weapons, not a single sword was broken."

"Payback's a bitch, huh?" Connor smiled.

Fujiyama couldn't help but laugh at the boy's honesty. "The Emperor was quite pleased and told Amakuni, 'You are an expert sword maker. None of the swords you made failed in battle.' And Amakuni became the Emperor's most trusted smith."

Connor slowly waved the sword side to side in the air.

"The katana was not the only weapon a Samurai held at his side," Fujiyama continued. "He also carried a much smaller sword, the wakizashi or tantō. The two weapons together are called the daisho. These swords represented the personal honor of the Samurai." He paused to get Connor's attention from the sword for a moment. "The katana is a Samurai's *soul*."

Connor was quiet for a moment, taking in what Fujiyama had said about a Samurai's sword. "Why the shorter sword?"

"The tantō was more suited for stabbing at close range, while the katana was used for piercing and slashing. The tantō was also used to decapitate the enemy on the battle field, and in seppuku—traditional, honorable suicide."

"Oh," Connor replied quietly. He examined the katana more closely. "And what are these two grooves in the blade?"

"Along with the blade, they're meant to make a whistling sound when the Samurai swings his sword. Three whistles from the grooves and from the blade signal to the warrior that the blade is perfectly angled for a good cut."

Fujiyama eyed the young boy. "Any other questions?"

"Yeah. What're those wavy lines on the bottom part of the blade?"

"Ah. Yes. In traditional Japanese sword making, the low carbon coal is folded several times by itself to purify it. Those wavy lines show that the sword has been purified of all contaminants that could make the katana weak. The waves in each sword are unique to the forger. Almost like a man's fingerprint."

Connor nodded as if he knew what Fujiyama was talking about.

"OK. Enough of the history lesson," Fujiyama said. "Off to school you go."

As Connor turned and made his way out of the office, Fujiyama cleared his throat. "Connor, one more thing."

Connor stopped and glanced back at his foster father.

"An open door is not always an invitation to enter a room."

Connor gazed down at his shoes before looking back to Fujiyama and nodding, "Yes, sir."

"Good." Fujiyama winked at the boy and smiled. "Now, don't be late."

Karma

"Hey, Jap lover," hissed a hostile voice from behind Connor, Yoshi, and Hiryo as they walked toward the naval base school. The antagonistic voice was accompanied by a clicking on the sidewalk.

Connor turned to see two teenage boys rapidly gaining on them, both clutching sawed off broomsticks in their hands, and tapping them on the concrete.

"Yeah, we're talking to you," growled a lanky, pale white boy with greasy brown hair that protruded from under a dirty knit cap. He was hitting the wooden broom handle on the pavement as he walked.

The second teenager, a squat, pudgy boy wearing thick-heeled boots, a black t-shirt, and a pair of denim overalls also clutched a similar broomstick. "Get your ass over here."

Connor knew these two boys. He had run-ins with them before. He chose to ignore their taunts and continued to walk faster with Yoshi and Hiryo.

The pudgy, squat boy played with the scraggly goatee on his chin as if deciding what to do. "What's the matter, Jap lover? You too good to talk to us or something?"

"We're not looking for trouble," Hiryo said.

The lanky teen joined his friend. "Hey, Connor, why don't you tell your rice eating friends to fuck off and go back to where they came from?"

"Screw you, Charlie! And screw Jack, too!" Connor yelled and continued walking away with his two Japanese brothers.

But the two teenage thugs had other plans. Jack, the pudgy teen, grabbed Connor by the arm, spun him painfully, then whacked him on the side of the head with his broomstick.

Connor teetered backwards, and a bloody gash on his forehead began to seep. He quickly regained his balance, swung back, hitting Jack square in the face.

Jack's lip cracked open and began to gush blood, a splatter of red rolling down his chin. Jack's eyes burned into Connor for a moment before a smile gave way. He licked the blood off of his lip and gave Connor's chest a hard shove.

Connor toppled backwards, landing square in the grasp of Charlie's wiry arms, who then proceeded to squeeze him hard.

With Connor immobilized, Jack walked up to Connor, and snarled at him. "Stupid Jap-lover." He thrust his fist into Connor's face, breaking the cartilage in his nose, then punched the helpless boy in the stomach, once, twice, three times.

Connor groaned and slumped to the ground, gasping for breath.

"Pick him up," barked Jack. "I'm not finished with the nip lover yet."

Connor felt Charlie yank him to his feet when he heard the bully scream out in pain and suddenly release him. Connor glanced up to see that Hiryo was standing in front of the goon, who was doubled over in agony. Hiryo had thrust a well-placed kick into Charlie's back.

Connor gasped for air when Jack rushed by him, cursing at Hiryo. The fat teen threw his solid bulk at the older brother with fists flying.

But Hiryo moved aside quickly and elbowed Jack in the chest, knocking the thug backwards.

Jack regained his balance and threw himself once again at Hiryo. The twelve-year-old boy took a quick step backwards, grabbed the flabby arm of the enraged teen, and flipped the older boy over his shoulder in a classic ju-jitsu move. Jack went flying, landing on his head with a loud crack to the pavement, and splitting open the skin on the side of his skull. Jack's body went limp immediately.

While Hiryo's back was turned, Charlie regained both his composure and his long wooden stick. He ran towards the young Japanese boy who had defeated his partner so easily.

He was almost upon Hiryo when Yoshi stepped between the thug and his older brother.

Charlie, surprised by the younger brother's sudden arrival, managed to raise his long broomstick over his head and swung with all his might.

Connor found himself frozen, still in amazement of Hiryo's defensive moves, and screamed out a warning to Yoshi.

But he was too late.

The broom handle came down with a *whoosh* and was about to make contact with Yoshi, when the young boy somehow ducked away from the blow and snatched the broom handle in midair. Yoshi allowed the momentum to relieve the thug of the stick, then crouched down low, swept his feet under Charlie's, forcing the tall teen to collapse under his own weight.

The thug was quick to recover and came at Yoshi once again.

Yoshi, with the broomstick now secure in his possession, stood back, positioned himself in the finest stance of a Samurai, and thrust the blunt tip at the tall teen, striking him straight in the stomach.

Charlie collapsed in a heap, moaning in pain, the air knocked out of his lungs.

Connor peered over to his two Japanese brothers and asked in awe, "Where'd you learn to *do* that?"

"In our martial arts class." A smile crossed Hiryo's face. "Better than smashing your fists into their faces, huh?"

"Damn, Yoshi. You looked just like that Samurai in the painting in your father's study." Connor touched his broken nose. "I want to learn that. All of that."

Loyalty and Honor

Over the next several months, Connor not only became proficient in speaking Japanese with Miyoko's help, but he also grew skilled in the judo moves he had seen his new Japanese brothers use on the thugs that assaulted them.

Fujiyama proved to be an excellent instructor. Connor had become so adept at various moves that he was able to win some matches with Hiryo, although most times it was a draw. On one particular day in the judo hall, Connor had gained so much confidence in himself that he adjusted his gi and walked over to Fujiyama, challenging him to a match.

"Hajime?" he teased.

Fujiyama just smiled and a put a hand on Connor's shoulder. "Later, son. Let's talk first."

Connor walked with great assurance alongside Fujiyama to a small bench in the rear of the judo hall. They both sat down and Fujiyama searched for the proper words to start. "Connor," he began, "the martial arts goal is to develop courage and fortitude."

Connor nodded. He agreed with that. "And honor, too."

"Yes, of course. Honor is part of the goal, but it is not the most important. Remember our talk months back about the sword of the Samurai? About the code they live by?"

Connor nodded.

"It's time you learned it as well."

Hiryo and Yoshi, noticing the serious discussion between their father and Connor, had walked over to eavesdrop. Spotting the two boys, Fujiyama asked, "Yoshi, what is the code of the Samurai?"

Without the slightest hesitation, Yoshi replied, "Justice, benevolence, veracity, politeness, and..."

"Loyalty and honor," Hiryo chimed in. "Loyalty and honor above all."

"Not necessarily," Fujiyama corrected. "Loyalty to family and friends is of high esteem, but honor can sometimes shift, leading to self-indulgence and needless self-sacrifice."

The three boys pondered Fujiyama's words for a moment.

Their father eyed the three boys before continuing. "As I told Connor, those who follow the martial arts develop courage and fortitude. These qualities do not have to do with only strong actions and the development of strong techniques. The martial arts emphasize the development of the *mind* in addition to the physical techniques." He leaned toward the boys. "In the martial arts, discipline of body *and* mind is of high importance."

He paused a moment to let this philosophy sink in. Then Fujiyama continued, "In other words, the martial arts are noted for placing significant emphasis on ethical development rather than merely on combat effectiveness. That is why so many Samurai practice Zen Buddhism."

"The religion?" questioned Connor. He knew something of Buddhism, and on some occasions he even attended the Buddhist temple with Meiko.

"Not the religion, Connor," Fujiyama replied. "It is a technique of meditation and contemplation. This type of mental discipline was popular with Samurai who understood the need to train and practice until their combat skills became like breathing—something they did naturally, automatically, without having to ever think about it." He eyed each boy individually. "Do you understand?" He could see them mulling over what had been said. "Well, in time you will." Fujiyama slapped his knee. "Now. How about some ice cream?"

The three boys nodded vigorously and beat Fujiyama to the front door.

In the Hands of the Gods

As Fujiyama finished his account of Connor, I realized he was a boy in transition. A boy that was slowly becoming more confident and feeling less alienated. I never dreamed my old friend was so much of a psychologist.

I politely said my goodbyes, gave my regards to his wife, and headed for the door.

"When will we see you again, Yoshihara?"

"That's in the hands of the gods," I cheerfully replied.

"But pray it's not the *war* gods," Fujiyama sadly replied.

Hiyakawa

My editor wasted no time putting me back to work once I returned to Tokyo. I was immediately picked up by a company car at the airport and whisked through a city that had drastically changed from the one I knew several months earlier.

It was December of 1937, and we were a country at war.

Jingoistic slogans had replaced deliberation and discussion. Martial arts music flowed from the radio in my car as I gazed out the windows to see uniformed soldiers patrolling the streets as though they had always been there. Handbills and posters praising the troops in China and urging support for the war at home lined the boulevards from nearly every window and light post. Some, with drawings of stoic Japanese soldiers, bluntly stated that it was one's duty to join the Army to protect the nation. Others praised the wounded in service to their country with sayings like '*Discipline is the lifeblood of the Army, wounds are the glory of the soldier*' and '*I will not let my comrades down who have already fallen.*'

Forty minutes later, I was standing in Sakura's office, and my editor had a surprise in store for me. "Here's your plane voucher. All of the other press have already left. I was lucky to get you on a military flight. You leave tonight."

"Tonight? To where?"

"Nanking. Our glorious Imperial Army has taken the city."

Sakura accented his statement with a scowl. "I was fortunate to get you on a flight on such short notice. When you land, the gods know where, you'll be convoyed to field headquarters to join the other media hounds." He shoved a thick manila envelope at me. "And take this."

Before I could ask what the envelope contained, my editor provided the answer.

"Reading material for your flight. These are news clippings of the stories we ran while you were in America. Read them carefully. They'll bring you up-to-date on the war."

"At least let me unpack. I just got off the damn plane."

Sakura ignored my plea and shuffled through stacks of papers and folders on his desk, looking for something, then shook his head as though he couldn't decipher one thought from another. "No time. Besides, you're *already* packed." He held up a half-smoked cigar and stuck it in the side of his wide mouth. "But before you go, I've requested an interview with that diplomat friend of yours. What's his name? You interviewed him awhile back."

"Hiyakawa?"

"Yes. That's the one." He reached for his lighter and lit the stub of his cigar, took a long puff, and exhaled the smoke above his head. "See if you can get some background on the political haggling in China that went on at the Palace. For starters, did the Emperor go along with this adventurism willingly or what?"

Sakura rummaged through his desk drawer, found a scrap of paper and handed it to me. "Here's Hiyakawa's home address. Get on it. You don't have a lot of time."

I sighed and grabbed my two pieces of luggage. I was about to leave when he added, "Take a cab. Not a company car. I don't want attention brought to you or the paper."

"Our new company policy?"

Sakura didn't appreciate the sarcasm. He took a seat behind his massive desk and proceeded to sort through his stacks.

I resigned myself to my fate and hastily left the building.

The heavy dark winter clouds that hung over my head turned into a downpour, cold and wet, matching my mood perfectly.

I cursed the fact that my raincoat was packed neatly away in my luggage. In December, Tokyo, being on the Pacific side of the country, got the rain. The western side got the snow. I guess I should be happy with that. I'd rather just be cold and damp than to have to slog my way through snow and slush.

I pulled the back of my jacket over my head to keep me dry and hid under an overhang. Something was off. I found myself looking around my surroundings, feeling like a man trapped in a foreign land. Did the nervous remark of Sakura make me paranoid? I shook my trepidation off. Work to do. Besides, what's to fear? I'm a reporter simply interviewing a government official, a friend.

I hailed a cab and proceeded directly to Hiyakawa's residence.

By the time I reached Hiyakawa's home, the rain had let up considerably, but the cold still chewed at me to the bone.

The cab dropped me off in front of an upscale Japanese house not at all like the common ones made with wood and paper, and with simple tiled roofs. Hiyakawa's home was made of brick and stone, and looked more like a small mansion. It had two stories and was adorned with a sloping grey tiled roof. It was quite elegant and fitting for a diplomat of his high rank.

I stepped up to the entryway and, before knocking on the front door, removed my shoes and placed them under a small bench.

I announced myself politely and waited, trying to shake off the uneasy feelings that were trying to creep into my mind.

A few moments later, a tall, elegant Caucasian American woman with short auburn hair appeared at the door. "May I help you?" I sensed a troubled tone in her voice, and her eyes had a suspicious mask to them.

"I'm here to see his Excellency Kenta Hiyakawa. My name is Yoshihara Koga. I'm with the *Tokyo Nichinichi Shimbun* and am here to interview his Excellency."

"We don't have to be so formal," a voice declared from behind the American woman. Then Hiyakawa stepped forward and grasped my hand in his. "This is *uchi no kanai desu*, the wife of my house, Barbara."

"Nice to meet you," I replied.

"Come, Barbara. Let's show our guest in." I was led down the hall to what was called the *foreign room*. It was mostly an extension to a home reserved for receiving foreign guests. The foreign room was used little except as a comfortable repository for items of foreign culture that a family may have acquired over the years. A piano and western-style tables, chairs, and sofas adorned the room.

I felt a bit embarrassed, wearing my rumpled, well-traveled suit. Compared to the blue and white pattern yukata housecoat worn by Barbara, and a red and black kimono sported by my host, I felt like one of those Depression Era, out-of-work vagrants that I'd seen so many times in the U.S.

I was struck by the kimono worn by Hiyakawa. It gave him an air of natural nobility, and there was something like a dark tiger in his looks that clashed with his typical air of a gentle and quiet man.

As I walked in the foreign room, an enticing aroma found its way from the innards of the house. In addition, I noticed the heat. The Japanese generally favored overheating their buildings, but on this occasion, I didn't mind since it felt good to warm my cold bones.

"Here, have a seat," my host offered. He pointed to a cushioned chair next to a simple sofa.

I complied while Barbara excused herself and exited the room.

Hiyakawa cut right to the chase. "I'm guessing you want to ask me about China."

"Yes. My paper would like to know the politics behind the curtain of the war. After all, you are part of the Emperor's inner circle," I replied. "A relative, correct?"

"A distant cousin." He nodded with a reminiscent smile.

"The Emperor and I grew up together."

"So, the rumors of you having the Emperor's ear are correct?"

"To some extent," my host replied. "I have been an assistant to several Ministries over the years. I would keep the Emperor directly informed on certain occasions."

At that moment, Barbara re-entered the room with a silver

platter of warm, green tea. She offered a cup to her husband and then to me. Finally, she seated herself on the couch to join the conversation.

I wrapped my cold hands around the cup and savored the warm glow. "What can you tell me about this war with China?"

Hiyakawa stared into his tea as he normally did while preparing his thoughts. Lost in the emerald brew for a moment, he finally took a breath, and spoke without looking up. "China has the distinction now of becoming part of our *East Asian Economic Prosperity Sphere*. Or roughly translated, a part of a continuation of the British Empire, but with a change of rulers."

He finally looked up at me solemnly. "You are aware of what happened in September of 1931?"

I nodded. "The Kwantung Army invaded Manchuria and began the occupation of Northeast China." I frowned at the memory. "A state was formed, and the last Emperor of the Qing dynasty in China was installed as a figurehead. But all real power was held by the Kwantung Army."

"And I'm afraid China will become the military and economic base for the Japanese invasion of the entire Asian mainland," Hiyakawa interjected.

I could see that Barbara was twisting in her seat. She obviously wanted to say something.

A Japanese woman would have remained quiet, but Barbara was not Japanese. So she spoke and spoke bluntly. "The Western powers have been feeding off of China for generations," she stated. "Now it's Japan's turn. The cheap labor and vast resources of China could not be ignored. It was too tempting of a target for the militarists here in the government. So the Army invaded China under the pretense of another engineered confrontation called the Manchurian Incident at the Marco Polo Bridge near Peking." Barbara's lips were pressed white as she continued. "The Army initiated an exchange of shots as an excuse to invade China."

"We don't know that for sure, Barbara," Hiyakawa counseled.

"*I* do. I know that it's true. I heard an Army officer at that last diplomatic shindig brag about it." She wrinkled her nose, obviously annoyed with the situation.

Hiyakawa looked at me with pleading eyes. "My wife is an American and was not raised to have...to put it delicately...the *dutiful* nature of a Japanese wife."

Barbara nodded in agreement before reclining in her seat, forcing herself to control her emotions in deference to her husband. She wanted to speak her mind, but she was also a wife that respected her husband, which had nothing to do with either culture.

I also knew what Hiyakawa meant. Japanese wives were subservient to their husbands, and Barbara's strong, unsolicited and opinionated nature was very *un*-Japanese. The rigidness and formality of the Japanese way of life was a burden to her. She was confined to a society of women. Her marriage to Hiyakawa must have raised a lot of eyebrows in Japan.

Hiyakawa continued. "What was said," looking over at his wife, "is conjecture, so please don't mention it in your interview."

I agreed. I could hear the anxiety, or possibly fear, in his voice. I quickly changed the subject. "But what of the Emperor? Surely he knew what the Army was attempting to do."

Hiyakawa paused in thought for a long moment, assuring that he spoke without error. "You must understand, Yoshihara, what is happening here in Japan, beyond what is reported in our so-called press." He swirled the tea in his cup. "Hirohito is bound by the *Emperor organ* theory."

"And what's that exactly?"

"In his court, the Emperor is only one, though the most supreme, of many organs of the State. Decisions on policy are made by working through the Imperial court. As it stands, this allows him to exert considerable imperial influence behind the scenes at court. But it's influence, *not* power." He stared into his tea. "The web of power of the Chrysanthemum Throne is a mystery, even to itself."

"I don't understand," I replied. "It sounds like he's a referee, and not an Emperor."

"Yes, you're correct. He acts as a referee between the cabinet, military, and other branches of government. His chief influence comes from asking the imperial question, the *gokamon*, during these discussions, in hopes that the policies he would ultimately be called upon to ratify reflect his personal desires. But his indirect imperial questions and occasional mysterious silences could be, and often are, interpreted as signifying his approval of the policies leading to war."

Hiyakawa looked to his wife for a moment, then bowed his head sadly. "Unfortunately, nothing in the Emperor's upbringing encourages him to take the initiative politically. Even worse, the Emperor is thought of by the people as being fully in control of national policy, and the militarists are seizing this belief to create an emperor-centered nationalism. The people do not know or understand the grim reality of the situation."

He took a long sip of his tea before continuing. "We moderates in the government tried to pressure the Emperor not to invade China. We did everything in our power, but the militarists are in control now. And with them currently directing the government, any attempt at Imperial restraint could lead to a coup."

"Yes. The remark by the Kempeitai Colonel at the execution," I said, adjusting myself in my seat.

Hiyakawa nodded.

At this point Barbara couldn't control herself any longer and jumped in again. "The threat is real. The Army led by Sadao Araki and his right wing followers want a return to the traditional Shogunate, a contemporary Military Shogunate, where the Emperor is once more merely a figurehead." She placed the cup of tea that was in her hand on the low table in front of her and thrust her hands forward for emphasis. "They want real power to be held by someone, whoever that might be, like a Hitler or Mussolini."

Hiyakawa lowered his voice and said gently, "Hai. Our history is filled with incidents where emperors were ignored or even killed by political regimes. On the other hand, traditionalists in the Navy defend the Emperor and the constitutional monarchy that he represents."

He paused a moment to reflect. "Hirohito, given his intensive indoctrination while growing up and his ever-cautious advisers, is anxious to preserve the dynasty. That, I'm afraid, is his primary objective, *not* to avert war."

I was about to ask Hiyakawa another question when he suddenly turned to his wife and asked gently, "Barbara, would you go next door and ask the Tanaka's for some of those delicious sweet rice cakes we had at their home last night? I want Yoshihara to try some."

I found Hiyakawa's request to be rather odd since Barbara clearly wanted to stay and contribute to the conversation. But she grudgingly nodded and left the room.

After Barbara was safely out of earshot, I asked Hiyakawa a slightly more personal question. "Has it been quite a challenge to be Japanese and have an American wife?"

"It has not been easy. Barbara's family was not pleased with her decision. It was even worse when she said she would be returning to Japan with me." He looked up at a picture hanging on the wall of the two of them. "There had been a certain amount of, let's call it *ostracizing,* that came from both sides." He chuckled. "In Japanese diplomatic circles, she is known as *Hiyakawa's folly.*"

"And her outspokenness doesn't help matters," I added with a grin. "However, she is quite beautiful."

"Hai. That she is. But that certainly hasn't prevented her from being extremely critical in private *and* public of the current state of affairs." He was quiet a moment, listening to make sure that Barbara had not returned to the room. "And this brings me to the reason for creating Barbara's little errand." He smiled. "Though you will enjoy the treats." He poured himself another cup of tea and offered more to me. I declined.

Hiyakawa leaned toward me and lowered his voice. "Information on military and even political matters coming into the Emperor is being deliberately withheld, or distorted."

"What?" I was shocked. "How?"

My host swirled the tea in his cup. "The militarists are trying to keep the Emperor in the dark, and I believe it's only going to get worse."

I didn't say a word because I didn't want to take the chance that anything I might say would prevent him from telling me more.

He continued. "After our meeting months back at Fujiyama's home, I asked him to see if he could find out who our Kempeitai Colonel friend was. The one at the execution. Anyway, I asked him to take a serious risk."

He took a gulp of tea. "After all, military matters are run through the military, the chain of command and all that. For him to give information directly to someone as high as me in the government, and bypassing the standard military command structure if it was found out, well, it would not be good for Fujiyama."

I agreed. "So what did he say?"

"He said he would."

"And..."

Hiyakawa glanced around the room as if the walls had eyes and ears, and I knew how he felt. "That Colonel's name is Haru Sato and he is on the Supreme Military Council that sits in Army/Navy Imperial Headquarters."

I whistled through my teeth. "He works at the Imperial Headquarters?"

"Hai." An air of anxiety came over my host. "And he was not alone. Sato was at the meeting with the Emperor with Prince Chichibu."

"Wasn't he the one hounding the Emperor? The very same who repeatedly counseled the Emperor to implement *direct imperial rule*, even if that meant suspending the constitution?"

"Correct."

I paused for a beat and then it hit me. "The military police arm of the Army is in cahoots with a member of the Royal Family."

"But it gets worse."

"How can anything be worse?"

"Princes Higashikuni and Takamatsu were at the war meeting. They, along with the others and myself, tried to persuade the Emperor against invading China. Those efforts did not sit well with Sato and Chichibu. And to make matters even more complicated, the Emperor thanked me for my wise counsel and appointed me Assistant to the Lord Keeper of the Privy Seal of Japan."

"Marquis Kōichi Kido?"

"Hai."

"That must have really gotten under Chichibu's skin," I reflected.

"Hai. And what he said to me after the meeting made me uneasy. His exact words were, 'Hiyakawa, we hope to gain your full cooperation in matters like these in the future and to preserve the Dynasty.'"

"A poorly veiled threat," I noted.

"But that was not all. Sato was beside him, and I heard him say under his breath to Chichibu as they turned away, 'And if not, we have our ways.'"

"You heard him say *that*?"

"I was meant to." He shook his head. "That is why I didn't want Barbara to hear this. If she knew I was being threatened—well, with her attitude towards what she called the *bullying militarists*, I am afraid of what she would say or do. I fear for her safety."

"And not yours?"

"They wouldn't dare harm me now that I work with Marquis Kido." His statement sounded more hopeful than factual.

"Why not send Barbara home to the States?"

"She would never go." He sounded exasperated. "She would never leave me."

We sat quietly for the longest moment, and Hiyakawa was the first to speak. "Please keep this discussion out of your interview. For my safety, for the safety of my family, and for Fujiyama's as well."

"What interview?" I held up my hands helplessly. "I'll tell my editor my cab got a flat and by the time it was fixed, I had to catch my flight."

Hiyakawa smiled broadly for the first time in the entire conversation. "Domo, my friend. You have my gratitude. So tell me, where are they sending you?"

"Nanking. Though I have one request before I leave," I added.

"What's that?"

"Whatever you find out from Fujiyama in the future, please let me know? I'll keep it confidential."

"Hai. I know you will."

At that point, Barbara returned with the rice cakes. She handed each of us one on an elegant dessert dish. "I hope I didn't miss anything," but by the tone of her voice, she sensed otherwise.

I wrapped my cake in a napkin and said, "Domo, Barbara. I'll take it with me to my plane. And no, you missed nothing at all." I stood up, gave my host my best bow, and he showed me to the door.

"Sayonara o daiji ni. Take care of yourself and be careful in China," Hiyakawa implored me.

"I will." Or at least I would try.

Nanking

I cursed Sakura the entire flight to Nanking. I was tired, hungry, and longed for the comfort of my own home, and the accommodations on the military plane didn't help with any of that. I was cramped between soldiers who were packed on either side of me. To add to the discomfort, the seats were constructed of hard metal with no cushions, and the plane was dark and unheated. I fumbled through the pages of background materials that Sakura gave me with fingers that felt nearly frozen.

The manila envelope contained news clippings and opinion pieces from my newspaper, and reading the material helped take my mind off the uncomfortable accommodations. As I read the reports, I gathered a solid understanding of the war and how it came to fruition. It all started with what was called the Marco Polo Bridge Incident. In June of 1937, in the vicinity of the western end of the Marco Polo Bridge, Japanese troops, in a training exercise, baited the Chinese into thinking an attack was underway. The Chinese troops fired a few ineffectual shots, and this led to a brief exchange of fire.

And just like that, the war was on.

By the end of 1937, Japan was engaged in a full-scale conflict with China. My editor would often scoff quietly under his breath that for diplomatic reasons, we didn't want to refer to it as the China *War*. Instead it was referred to as the China *Incident*. This was followed by the Battle of Beijing and Tianjin at the end of July, and the Battle of Shanghai in August, when the city was leveled by our air force and naval bombardment.

On December 13th, our troops entered Nanking. What I didn't know at that time, but was to find out later, was that this became the start of a horrifying campaign by the Imperial Army. They were participating in the targeted bombing of civilians, murder, torture, human experiments, rape, and even the use of chemical and biological weapons.

As we approached Nanking, the low clouds of the new morning dissipated, and I could see that it was a city devastated by war. Vast swaths of city blocks were swept away, and the buildings that were still standing were hollow hulks of what they once were.

We flew past the city and began to slowly lose altitude. Several minutes later, we approached a military airfield just north of the city. Almost immediately, my seat dropped out from under me.

With wide eyes, I looked over at a private sitting next to me. He just smiled and said, "Sudden drops in altitude prior to landing are a standard maneuver in a war zone." He pointed down between his legs. "Light arms fire from the ground."

After several more minutes of anxious anticipation, wondering when my seat was going to drop out again, and along with a teeth-rattling landing, the plane came to a jerking halt on the dirt airfield.

I was quickly ushered from my seat to the exit door, when an Army truck pulled up in a cloud of dust.

"You," barked a sergeant from the cab of the truck. "Come with us." He motioned for me to climb into the back of the truck with the other troops exiting the plane. "You must be a journalist," he snarled. He obviously did not have any respect for me or for my line of work.

I nodded. "I am. Where will you be taking me?"

The sergeant didn't bother responding. Instead, he just pointed to the back of the vehicle and lit a cigarette. I climbed into the back of the truck with the other troops, and we were soon headed into Nanking in a small convoy.

The city looked even worse up close. In the air the devastation was widespread and unspecific, but on the ground it was ruinous, and not just from the desolation of the fighting.

As we drove deeper into city, I was both shocked and sickened by the scene unfolding before my eyes. Three soldier stood on top of a pile of rubble, waving their rifles in the air shouting, "Banzai! Banzai!" Then they jumped down from the rubble, stepping over corpses like so much garbage haphazardly strewn in what was left of the streets. I forced myself, even as my gut turned, to look at the clothing if the bloated bodies round me, and I could see that they were not just those of Chinese soldiers, but innocent civilians as well.

To my left, shots rang out, loud enough to echo over the shouts of *Banzai!* coming from somewhere above me. I turned to see a few soldiers on my truck hideously laughing, firing at some Chinese who were running away from the convoy. More shots rang out from the small line of trucks ahead of us. One soldier took a bead on a group of children running in panic from the trucks. He picked them off like insignificant prey, like moving targets in a carnival game. They dropped one by one, shot after shot.

I struggled to hold down what little I ate on the plane as laughter and dancing on the smell of death erupted up and down the small convoy.

I lowered my eyes and stared at my feet. The soldier next to me grunted and elbowed me. As I looked up, he gave me a detestable sneer. I said nothing.

The jovial banter of the troops continued as I looked away from the dead and fleeing civilians. Instead, I focused my gaze towards the collapsed buildings that donned posters on their gunshot walls, posters that boasted slogans justifying our invasion. The propaganda made it clear that resistance was useless and gave a stark warning to those who considered rebellion. Any of the population cooperating with Nationalist or the Communist forces would be dealt with harshly and without question.

My brief respite from this nightmare was cut short by the snap of advancing gunfire followed by deafening explosions. The levity of the soldiers in the truck ceased, and a quiet hum of muffled prayers settled amidst the silence.

Before I was able to consider the severity of our situation, an ear piercing blast exploded behind me and to my right. Another shell made a direct hit on the truck in front of us. Shards of metal and chunks of dark earth enveloped our vehicle. I felt something rip through the truck and land beside me. As the dust settled, I stared over at what remained of a bloody human body—the very same soldier who had sneered at me.

As I repelled in horror, I found myself being pushed out of the truck and onto the ground.

I heard the urgent cries of soldiers commanding me to "Get down! Get down!" as I was shoved forward onto my face by some unseen hand. I had a mouthful of dirt, eyes stinging from smoke. I could see nothing, and all I could hear was hell breaking loose. More explosions resounded and then the sound of machine gun fire erupted around me.

I have never been more terrified.

I stumbled to my feet, desperate to seek shelter wherever I could but found nothing but chaos. Soldiers with blood spurting from gaping wounds where legs and arms once hung were sobbing and screaming in pain on all sides of me.

I started to scramble under our truck when I spotted an alternate safe spot. I crawled as fast I could through the stinging smoke into a bomb crater that had filled with stagnant, filthy water. The knees and elbows of my clothes were torn and the rest of me was soaked to the bone. The smell of cordite filled my nostrils.

More shells exploded around me, and as I peered over the edge of the crater, a young soldier who looked to be barely seventeen collapsed on top of me. One side of his face had been blown off. He gurgled something unintelligible through what was left of his bloody mouth, then his entire body jerked and twisted before going limp.

I prayed like I'd never prayed before. I prayed to the Christian God, the Shinto gods, and to the Buddha himself.

I fully expected a Chinese soldier to peer over the bomb crater and finish me off, but then a miracle happened. The fighting appeared to move away from me. The volley of gunfire, the explosion of shells, the screaming of soldiers, all of it slowly shifting to another location. I thanked whichever god had answered my pleas as I crawled out of the crater and away from the noise of combat as fast as I could.

I found my way down an avenue, away from the din of conflict, and passed more dead bodies. Civilians, soldiers, Chinese men, women, and children. My eyes bore witness to horrors I never expected to see. The long avenue was littered with filth, discarded Chinese uniforms, rifles, pistols, machine guns, field pieces, knives, and knapsacks.

As I stumbled over rubble into another street, I saw a tank gunner slaughter more than one hundred Chinese soldiers near a large bomb crater. Then from behind the tank, an Army bulldozer sputtered smoke and came to life. It advanced on the bodies, plowing the pile of undulating, lifeless forms into the crater to level the street for vehicles and tanks to pass.

My stomach wretched as I watched the tanks roll over the bodies like they were waves in the ocean. A combat newsman filming the event added to the macabre scene.

I averted my eyes, looked up and saw another ghastly sight. Indiscernible figures hung from lampposts, and near them, grotesque heads hung from trees, the result of brutal beheadings. I turned and ran from the scene only to confront three women who were naked from the waist down lying over some rubble, their legs spread wide, a testament to the violent rape they endured.

A thought raced through my mind. *I've entered the seven gates of hell.*

A small child sat crying at the feet of one of the women that had been raped and murdered. I felt the undeniable urge to go and pick up the child and give the innocent boy some comfort, but he was immediately swarmed by men, women and children, fleeing from an armored personnel carrier that fired its machine gun as it rumbled down the other end of street.

I caught my reflection in what was left of a shattered window. My clothes were ripped and torn, and I looked more like one of the refugees than a Japanese journalist.

I sought safety inside a demolished building off the street, only to see a group of Japanese soldiers looting stores. They had commandeered a cart and were piling on whatever they could find of food, small livestock, and personal valuables.

A few soldiers threw a Chinese soldier into a bomb crater and lit him on fire. They cheered until one looked up at me. I quickly dodged back into the protective hollows of the building.

I had to find a way out of this nightmare.

I stumbled my way down one unnamed street after another. For how long, I don't remember. It may have been hours or just a matter of minutes. Finally, I came to district that seemed to be relatively unscathed by the fighting. I made my way along the outside wall of what looked like an administrative building until I found a small entryway.

A clatter of panicked voices suddenly erupted from behind me. A group of desperate refugees rushed at the entryway, climbing over each other and banging on the door. I was pushed aside and saw the reason for their terror. A Japanese tank was bearing down on us. The turret spun in our direction and opened fire.

The portal above the civilians exploded into a thousand pieces, showering the Chinese huddled in the doorway with rock and debris.

I scrambled to the safety of another entryway when an arm grabbed me by the scruff of my shirt and yanked me through an open door.

The arm offered two surprises. First it wore a black, white, and red Nazi armband. The second, it belonged to someone I hadn't seen since college. "Russell?" I said in disbelief. "Russell Brady?"

"Yoshihara?" the arm replied. "What the hell are you doing here?"

"I could ask you the same question," I sputtered with astonishment. "And what the hell is that swastika doing on your arm?"

"Later," he said staring at the tank coming down the street. "Follow me." Being the college football player I once knew, he easily pulled me by the arm through the small portal and into a courtyard where I was met with yet another surprise.

A Nazi flag flew high on a flagpole over the main building and a much larger Nazi flag covered most of the courtyard. Beneath it, a group of frightened Chinese refugees huddled together on the hard cobblestones.

"What is all this?" I asked.

"A sanctuary," Russell replied. "Come. I want you to meet someone."

An Old Friend

I found myself sitting and drinking coffee in a small office in a building that looked like one of the foreign embassies. Brady sat behind a carved Chinese maple and walnut desk that seemed to clash with the other western appointments in the office. It may sound odd that I noticed such a thing, but I was a journalist first and foremost, and now that my life was no longer in danger, it was my job to find a story, and I was taking mental notes with every breath.

I leaned back in my cushioned chair and looked at my hulk of a friend who was squeezed into a tailored business suit. He was quite a different picture from the beer guzzling jock I once knew.

"So what are you doing here in China?" I asked. "Last I heard, you were voted All-American. I assumed you would go on and play professional football."

"Naw," Brady said with a scowl. "I considered it, but the life span of a football player is rather short and only the top draft picks make real money. So I earned an MBA and became an entrepreneur instead. Started an export business here in China. Silk and all that." He grinned slightly. "Bad timing, no?"

"That's an understatement."

"Yeah. It was going extremely well. At the time, I was shipping tons of the stuff to the Kwantung Army in Manchuria—oh, I forgot. *Manchukuo* to you guys." He raised an eyebrow and watched my expression.

I put on my best poker face.

"Anyway, I assumed it was part of the Japanese attempt at reconstructing the country," he remarked in a poorly guised satirical manner. He took a sip of his coffee. "And what about you? Why exactly are you here in this hell-hole?"

"I work for a Japanese newspaper. On assignment." I leaned forward in my chair and asked intently, "What is going on here? What kind of war is Japan fighting?"

"You've been on the streets," he noted.

I nodded. "Unfortunately."

"Things are bad. Very bad." He paused. "To answer your question, what's happening to Nanking is no longer a war, buddy. It's vengeance."

"*Vengeance?*" I was shocked.

"I don't know what your paper is telling your people, but I can bet it's far from the truth." He pulled a silver cigarette case from his inside coat pocket, opened it, packed a cigarette on it, and offered me one.

I declined.

"Suit yourself." He pulled an ornate lighter from his other pocket and lit a fag. "Let me fill you in on what's really happening."

"The battle for Shanghai was a shock to the Japanese Army," he began. "Instead of an expected quick victory, the battle dragged on for months. After their embarrassing conquest, the Army advanced on Nanking with heightened aggression. It was no surprise that this unbridled aggression would manifest itself in the atrocities that were carried out in Nanking."

He took a drag on his cigarette. "The Imperial Japanese military taught the Samurai code of Bushido." He looked at as if I knew what he was talking about. "But apparently, what they taught was a perverted form of it. To the Japanese military, Bushido meant dedicating their lives to the Emperor. Defeat was considered shameful, and surrender was dishonorable. Those that surrendered were worthy only of contempt and were considered weak, whether they were male, female, old, young, or even children."

He continued. "But that was only half of it. Another contribution to this unbridled aggression was the make-up of the troops themselves. Much of the Japanese frontline troops was comprised of poor farmers, criminals, and low wage industrial workers. They had lived rough lives of hard work and minimal reward. A culture of brutality was reinforced in the military as part of their training.

Soldiers were routinely beaten and punitive exercises for all were the order of the day for the actions of one member. Even officers were not immune. A colonel displeased with one of his officers would strike him. He in turn, would strike an officer lower than him. The violence had a never-ending trickle effect."

"The aim of this indoctrination and brutality," Brady emphasized, "is to produce fanatics who would sacrifice their lives without hesitation for the Emperor." He stopped and thought a moment. "The Jap soldier follows orders, ignores personal feelings, and treats those beneath them with the same contempt they experienced themselves in training."

He waited again to see what affect his diatribe had on me, but I said nothing. I was taking it all in and silently processing the information. More importantly, I knew how to keep a straight face.

Brady stood and went to the office window, staring out over the stricken city of Nanking. "Jap soldiers are behaving like wild beasts of prey. They call the Chinese *chancorro*, sub-human, and killing the Chinese has no greater significance than killing vermin."

He stopped, turned to me and continued on. "And it won't stop there. If the Japs believed the Chinese are vermin, then it's a short leap to the belief that anyone who is not Japanese is vermin."

I sat numb, incredulous, for a few moments until Brady spoke again. "Vermin. That's what the Japs believe. They marched through the city like a barbarian horde, smashing windows and doors and taking whatever they pleased. The sons of Nippon, often under the approval of their officers, entered nearly every building, taking anything they wanted. They even made the Chinese carry their loot. If the Chinese soldiers surrendered, the Japs killed them along with any refugees they discovered. Those people were tied in batches of fifty and led off to be executed."

Brady's voice hardened. "The Japs executed POWs and civilians at will and violated women by the thousands, while burning and looting the city. Many were killed where they stood, and the streets were littered with dead. Often they were left there for days. Tanks, trucks and troop transports ground over the remains of men, women, dogs, and horses. Resist Japan and these horrors would fall upon you."

My old college chum returned to his desk, then leaned forward and spoke empathically, "Nanking wasn't invaded, my friend. It was *raped*."

I didn't want to believe that my country would degenerate to that level. But I had seen much of what he said with my own eyes.

"You seem to know a lot about Japan. Especially the military." I narrowed my eyes at him. "You don't sound like a silk merchant to me. What are you *really* doing here in China?"

"Let's say I do a little government work on the side. *My government.*"

Just then, there was a knock on the door. "Enter," Brady snapped.

A wiry, balding, middle-aged man with round wire rim eyeglasses entered. Like Brady, he wore a business suit with a Nazi armband.

"Ah, Mr. Rabe," Brady said as he stood up. "I want you to meet a very old friend of mine. Yoshihara Koga. He's a reporter for a Tokyo newspaper. Yoshihara, this is John Rabe. He's the Director of the German Siemens AG China Corporation."

"Nice to meet you," Rabe said, extending his hand. "So you are here reporting on the Nanking invasion?"

I nodded. "Nice to meet you, as well."

"And I certainly hope that you choose to report the facts." Brady answered before I was able to respond. "I was just giving Yoshihara some background on what is happening here."

"I see." Rabe raised an eyebrow a bit, found a chair next to me and sat down. "And what do you see happening here?"

"Nothing good," I replied. "Nothing good at all."

My remark seemed to soften up Rabe's obvious distaste of my presence.

"If I may," I asked, "what are you doing here? And why the Nazi flags above the building and over the courtyard?"

"For protection. Protection from the Japanese. Protection for my Chinese workers and refugees." He stood and walked toward the window that overlooked the Nazi flag canopy. "When the Japanese invaded, fighter planes and bombers attacked the city. They bombed part of my factory and strafed my employees. The only thing I could think of was to show them that we were allies. So I hoisted our flag and sheltered the Chinese under another."

"And that stopped them?" I asked incredulously.

"For the moment," Rabe reflected. "We dug foxholes in the backyard to shelter several hundred Chinese refugees. But Japanese troops tried to climb the walls in order to get at them and to try to rape the women." He paused for a long time and an unsettling hush came over the room. Then he turned and finally looked back at me. "The Japanese had pistols and bayonets, and all I had was my swastika armband. Pray God it worked. We have created a Nanking Safety Zone for Westerners and the refugees who could get in."

At that moment of reflection, his jaw tightened and his eyes rimmed red. "They raped girls, very young girls. Just children. Grabbed young babies from their mothers and bayoneted the infants from behind and paraded them around for their fellow soldiers to see. Those they captured were tortured, burned, and even buried alive. Decapitated, bayoneted and shot en masse."

The agony in his voice was palatable. He was a soul in pain, unable to comprehend the viciousness of what one human being could do to another.

I was stunned into silence.

That silence was abruptly broken when Rabe said to me, "You look terrible. I'll have one of my people find you some clothes and something for you to eat." And with that, he exited the room.

"That man's a hero," Brady said. "But I'm willing to bet that what he's done here will be forgotten to history." He stood and patted me on the shoulder. "And what about you?"

"I need to find the Army field headquarters. Any way of getting me there?"

"Not by the streets. But there is a way. Most of the Western contingent is leaving the city. Tonight we make our way to the docks and board an American gunboat. It will take us safely away from the city down the Yangtze."

"A gunboat?"

"The USS Panay. A flat-bottomed craft built in Shanghai specifically for river duty along the Yangtze River. It and fellow sister ships are responsible for patrolling the river to protect American lives and property in China."

He scratched the stubble on his chin. "Anyway, the Captain should have a good idea of where you want to go."

USS Panay

That night a line of businessmen and diplomats quietly left the compound and made their way to the nearest dock to wait for the American gunboat.

It was a short wait.

As the assembly stood there on the dock with our meager belongings, we heard the sound of the ship's horn announce its arrival just minutes away. The water battered against the dock, second by second, like the ticking of a clock. Or perhaps more appropriately, a time bomb. The boat finally arrived after a few tense minutes. Though it was not an elegant ship, the *Panay*, painted all in white, proved to be a beautiful godsend to the awaiting entourage.

As the *Panay* docked and we boarded, I noticed some activity on the far shore. A troop of Imperial Army soldiers had lined up a hundred ragged Chinese soldiers on the dike at the opposite bank of the river. Without warning, an execution squad opened fire on them with machine guns blasting from armored personnel carriers behind the prisoners.

There was an audible gasp from our small crowd as we hurried to board the *Panay*. I looked back to see a number of Japanese armed with pistols stroll nonchalantly around the crumpled bodies, pumping bullets into any that still moved. Sailors on a Japanese naval warship that was anchored off the dike viewed the gruesome scene with unbridled enjoyment, cheering, "Banzai."

I was physically ill. I'd had enough of this. What had Brady called it? Yes. A *rape*. This sickening spectacle called an invasion.

I could not believe that the time-honored courteousness of the Japanese people and our sense of chivalry had sunk so low that Japanese soldiers had been reduced to a group of rabid madmen. I couldn't wait to get to the field headquarters and plead for a flight back to Japan.

As we steamed down the river, I stood by the rail of the ship, viewing the red-orange sunset blend with the fires of Nanking over muffled explosions. It truly was a city in agony.

I was deep in troubled thoughts when a whirling sound caught my attention. I looked around and saw a man holding a movie camera by his side filming the devastation on shore. The man finally noticed my observation of his activities.

"Hi. Norman Alley." He extended his free hand.

"Yoshihara Koga. I'm with the *Tokyo Nichinichi Shimbun* newspaper."

"A newsman, huh?" He flashed me a warm smile. "I'm with *Universal News*."

I pointed to his camera. "That's an odd way to film something."

He laughed. "You would think so, but a year ago when I was filming a Jap Zero strafing the area, a soldier mistook my camera for a weapon, and he turned his gun on me. Nearly got my head shot off." He patted the camera and laughed. "Now I film from the side. My credo is, *Go to hell if you must, but bring back pictures of it.*"

"There you are," a voice said from behind me. Brady approached and acknowledged my new acquaintance. "Spoke with the Captain. He says there's an Imperial Army field headquarters about an hour down river. I convinced him to drop you off there."

"Thanks," I replied, taking another look out over the destruction of what was once a thriving city.

Brady took note. "I bet your paper, or any paper in Japan for that matter, won't print what really happened here."

He was correct, of course. Sure, the Western media outlets will report the barbaric behavior of the Japanese, but the military will adamantly deny it, and the Japanese people will never read of it.

We were silent for the longest time until Brady piped up, "But there *is* something that you could investigate and report. If you dare."

I looked at him, puzzled. "What would that be?"

Brady looked around to make sure Alley had left to film on the other side of the boat. "What I'm going to tell you, I really can't prove, but a Chinese Shanghai banker related it to me before the Japs killed him."

I wondered if he was trying to provoke me by continuously using the derogatory term, *Jap*. I decided to ignore his attempts.

Brady reached into his jacket and pulled out a pack of Lucky Strikes and offered me one.

"No thanks. So what did he tell you?"

Brady lit up and took a long drag. "When the Japs invaded Shanghai, their soldiers did their usual looting, but a special unit had other plans."

"Special unit?"

He looked out over the water and lowered his voice. "A group of covered trucks pulled up to the Central Bank of Shanghai and stripped the bank of its gold bullion. The banker believed the Chinese banks were not the only ones. He heard that some European banks were robbed, too."

"Did this special unit have a name?" I asked.

"The banker didn't know for sure. Only that he overheard the words *Unit 731* mentioned."

"Did he say who was in charge of this special unit?"

Brady nodded. "He overheard a Manchukuo Army Captain refer to a Colonel Sato."

I raised an eyebrow.

Brady noticed. "That name familiar to you?"

"Yes. *Haru* Sato. A Colonel in the Kempeitai."

"Secret Army Military Police?"

I nodded.

"Well, that's interesting. If so..." He stopped and looked up over our heads. "Looks like we have company."

I gazed skyward and saw six Japanese twin-engine bombers in V-formation approaching the gunboat.

"Probably just scoping us out," I noted, sounding more hopeful than assured.

"Yeah," Brady replied. "They've got to know this is an American ship. How can they miss the large American flags that are lashed horizontally across the upper deck awnings, not to mention the gigantic Stars and Stripes displayed from the gaff."

At that moment, the *Panay* loudspeaker shouted orders to man defense stations and close watertight doors and hatches.

"Just a precaution," Brady noted, trying to comfort me, but it sounded as if he was trying to comfort himself as well.

We watched as the bombers broke formation and the six planes strung out in a line ahead of the gunboat. Then, almost immediately, three of the leading planes rapidly lost altitude, dropping into a power dive.

"That's not good," I shouted and pulled back from the railing, taking Brady with me.

Suddenly, the three planes released a string of bombs. The first bomb hit just above the pilothouse and tore it apart, sending shredded steel and glass flying.

"Fire! Fire!" I heard the command from someone above us, and the sporadic sound of machine gun fire came from all sides of the gunboat.

But the attempt at self-defense was futile.

The machine guns arranged on the decks of the *Panay* were aimed towards shore to defend against where Chinese river pirates would normally operate. But the ship's guns could not be elevated enough to take on the bombers. They were never designed for bringing down belligerent aircraft. Worse yet, the three-inch gun had been hit and was immobilized.

I chanced another glance skyward and saw six single-engine

dive-bombers swoop in, unleashing their machine guns and dropping their bombs.

Explosions rocked the ship, knocking Brady and me off our feet. I screamed toward Brady, and when I looked over at him, his body, riddled by machine gun fire, twisted and bloody, lay perfectly still on the deck next to me.

"No, no, no!" I screamed as I reached for Brady to check to see if he was still alive. That was when the deck of the ship radically tilted towards the bow. I tried to maintain my balance, but to no avail, and I slid down deck and tumbled into the gray, icy waters below.

I sunk deep below the surface of choppy waves. The water swirled slowly around me, and a dead body of a refugee floated past, the man's eyes stared into my soul. Explosions rained in muffled sounds above the water, and the gunfire lit my way back towards the air.

As I broke the surface, I desperately attempted to control my panic, spitting out river water and gasping for oxygen. I bobbed atop the turbulence, and saw two motorized sampans on the water that were swamped with passengers who abandoned the ship.

I began to swim towards the sampans against the strong current when suddenly one of the dive-bombers roared from above and released a bomb near one of the boats.

Fortunately, it fell short, and as the water rose up in waves around the sampan, I felt a moment of relief. That moment was short-lived as another plane dove behind the first and raked the boat with a barrage of machine gun fire.

I stopped struggling against the current and instead let the waves sweep my exhausted body downstream. After a few minutes, I was able to maneuver myself towards the tall bamboo on shore and regain my footing in the thick mud.

Several Japanese planes circled above me like vultures, so I planted my face into the muddy water and tried to flatten my body as much as I could amongst the reeds. The foliage provided the cover I desperately needed, and the planes soon flew away.

I pulled myself up from the sucking mud and stumbled towards solid ground, prostrating myself on the welcoming dry earth.

I lay there for I don't know how long, when I heard the distinctive sound of a rifle bolt being pulled back. I looked up and found myself staring into the muzzle of an infantry rifle aimed at my head by a young, nervous Japanese soldier. By his uniform, I could see that he was a private. He looked no more than sixteen. He pointed to the sinking *Panay* in the distance.

"I am a Japanese journalist," I stuttered, but he kept glancing nervously at the *Panay*.

Just then, a Manchukuo Captain walked up beside the young private. "Who is this?" he snarled.

"He came from the American gunboat," the private replied.

The Captain, who looked strangely familiar, barked, "Shoot him."

The young soldier took aim, and just as he was about to fire I recalled where I had seen the officer before. "Wait! You know me, Captain!"

The officer placed his hand on the private's shoulder to stay him.

"You're the officer who gave the order to fire at the execution of the February 26th Incident traitors," I shouted. The memories of that night came flooding back. "You were a Lieutenant then. I'm Yoshihara Koga. I was one of the reporter's present that night."

The Captain raised an eyebrow, considered my words, then said, "Bring him."

The young private ordered me to get up and sit by the road as I watched the Captain drive off in an armored car. As we waited, I disrobed as much as I dared out of the dirty wet clothes and listened to the young private confess how enamored he was of the Manchurian officer, Captain Hidaka Takahashi, and the present competition he was involved in.

To my horror, I was soon to find out exactly what kind of contest it was.

Twenty minutes later, an Army truck pulled up, and I was unceremoniously tossed into the back. The private climbed in beside me.

After a short ride, we arrived at the outskirts of the city, and in an area that was relatively intact. I stepped out of the truck with my young guard in tow and was faced with a gruesome sight.

Dozens of severed heads that were impaled on small stakes stared back at me—each face frozen in terror.

Suddenly, behind me, I heard the urgent cries of *Banzai*. I turned and saw Captain Hidaka Takahashi towering over a Chinese soldier that knelt before him. The lean, muscular Takahashi had his samurai sword positioned at the ready, raised over his head, as a group of Japanese soldiers sat nearby, guzzled sake, and watched on in amusement.

Takahashi's eyes burned into his victim, and his sword came swooping down, easily detaching the soldier's head from his body. Blood spurted up like a morbid crimson fountain from the soldier's neck, and his trunk slumped forward in a heap.

But the ghastliness didn't end there. Takahashi picked up the severed head, looked into its eyes, smiled and impaled it on a stake with the other heads.

"One hundred," he declared. "I win!"

A second officer, who stood nearby and held a bloody sword, threw his weapon down in disgust.

The young private nudged me. "See. I knew Takahashi would win the contest," he said smugly.

Takahashi walked off laughing, proudly accepting the congratulations of the gathered troops.

"Come," the private instructed.

As he led me toward a group of tents, I saw Takahashi had stopped to speak with a high-ranking Kempeitai officer. I looked closer and realized who it was—Colonel Haru Sato. The two officers were observing Japanese soldiers who loaded heavy boxes and canvas bags onto a convoy of Army trucks.

I walked towards the feverish activity, but was pushed away from the scene by the young private. Just then, one of the soldiers that was loading a truck, dropped a box to the ground. It broke open and out spilled several gold bars—gold bars engraved with the words *Bank of Nanking*.

The soldier was immediately pistol-whipped to the ground by Takahashi. "*Baka da yo!*" Takahashi screamed. "Stupid idiot!"

Brady was right. This was the systematic looting of conquered territory; looting with the sanctioned approval and involvement of high-ranking officers.

But that wasn't all. My biggest surprise came a few minutes later.

I was directed to a tent that was far removed from the loading scene and ordered to stay there until called for. Two guards were stationed outside the tent to make sure I complied.

I was about to sit down on one of the crates when I heard the sound of a sedan pull up across from my tent.

Odd, I thought. I took a chance and looked out.

It was a black town car, civilian by the look of it, with dark tinted windows, and as I watched, the driver jumped out of the vehicle and opened the rear door. Out stepped a tall, regal looking man, dressed in a business suit. I found it quite unusual for such a man to be in a combat zone.

I squinted my eyes to get a better look and I realized who it was. It was the man who hid under the eaves of the courtyard where the execution of the Army traitors had taken place. It was Prince Chichibu!

I wondered briefly if he was here to protect the reputation of the Royal Family and the Emperor, and to cease the looting. Sadly, that was not the case. He wasted no time greeting the Captain and Colonel, then started to direct the operation.

I noticed an Army sergeant walking towards me, so I quickly retreated back into my tent.

"Come with me," he ordered when he entered.

"Where?"

"To join the other journalists."

Stolen Gold

The next day, I filed my report with my newspaper. Almost immediately, I received a phone call from Sakura at the press pool in Nanking.

"I read your report," he said.

"I hope it was adequate—"

"It's bullshit," he cut me off sharply. "Don't you think we know from the Western news sources what happened?"

"And would you have printed that if I had reported it?" I replied angrily.

"Of course not." He took a deep sigh. "The Army was delighted with the news of their glorious victory reported by our newspaper."

I said nothing.

Again, he took a deep sigh. "It's time to get you home. I'll arrange..."

"Don't bother. I want to stay here in China for a while."

"Oh? Why is that?"

"I want to chase down something here. Something that is a very important story. The looting of Shanghai and Nanking."

"Yes, yes. We know all about that. Rampaging soldiers looting... eh, I mean scavenging..."

"No," I interrupted. "It's more than that. I saw a convoy of trucks being loaded with gold from the National Bank of Nanking." I paused a beat for effect. "Looting that is approved and directed by a member of the Royal Family."

"Who?" If my editor could have jumped through the phone, he would have.

"I'd rather not say until I find more proof. I don't want the newspaper or you to get into trouble. Let me take it on myself."

"Hai. How can I help?"

"Do what's necessary to make me an official war correspondent. That way I can snoop around with the military wherever they go."

"Done deal. I'll get right on it. And Yoshihara, be careful."

A New Brother and Sister

Over the next couple of years, I traveled the country with the Army filing reports on the Sino-Japanese war, as it was being called at the time. In between filling my duties as a war correspondent, I would ask around discreetly if any soldier or Chinese native had heard of Unit 731 or any government sanctioned gold-looting that might be going on in the country.

While I was in China, other events were transpiring for Fujiyama's family, including young Connor. It turns out that Fujiyama had formally adopted the American boy. To the delight of Connor, he even gave him flying lessons with Hiryo in attendance. Fujiyama felt it would help the boy's self-esteem and confidence.

In the spring of 1938, Fujiyama was ordered back to Japan to join Yamamoto's staff. But when he arrived, his world had changed, and Japan was not the place he knew a few short years before. For Connor, too, his transition to his new country would include disappointment, but ultimately lead to an unexpected transformation.

"That's Mt. Fuji!" Connor exclaimed. He pointed out the window of the Pan Am Clipper toward the snow covered, dormant volcano. "Just like the picture we have back home in San Diego."

"And there's Tokyo," Hiryo said, pointing to the sprawling city below and jumping up from his seat. He rushed to the window, climbing over Yoshi.

"Hey!" his younger brother yelled. "Get off me," as Yoshi's face was smashed underneath Connor's elbow.

The plane was losing altitude rapidly, and through the light wispy clouds, the sprawling cosmopolitan city materialized before them.

"Are we getting off the plane in Tokyo?" asked Connor.

"Yes," Fujiyama replied. "Then we'll ride the Tsubame train to our home in Hiroshima."

"Can we visit Tokyo for a while?" Hiryo asked.

Fujiyama shook his head. "No. We have to go straight home." He paused a beat. "I tell you what. On my first leave, I'll take you all to Tokyo. I'll show you the Mitsukoshi Department Store on the Ginza and the Yasukuni Shinto Shrine. The Mitsukoshi is even bigger than the department stores in America."

The three boys seemed satisfied with the compromise, and settled in their seats with their faces pressed to the window.

It took the train almost eight hours to reach Hiroshima from Tokyo. Connor observed through his window as the train approached a monotony of small villages that were dwarfed by a chain of mountains in the background. Every so often, a picturesque, white wooden castle would tower on the horizon.

It was dusk when they arrived at Fujiyama's home. Connor had seen pictures of traditional Japanese homes before, and this one seemed to be no exception. It was a one-story flat roof building made of wood, and had a terrace constructed on the top. In the front yard stood a large persimmon tree that produced delicious sweet fruit in the fall. A short bamboo fence with white rose bushes climbing around it led to a backyard that opened up onto a stone covered patio. On the spacious patio, there was a small rock pool with large Japanese carp swimming leisurely under trickling water.

Connor followed the family toward the inside of the home. They walked along a path of flat round stones through a gate made of two wooden doors and a straw roof. They removed their shoes in the *genkan* and slipped on light slippers. Inside, all was surprisingly modest and restrained. The rooms were divided by sliding doors called *shoji* that were made of rice paper squares glued on a wood lattice that allowed soft sprigs of light to pass through. In the main living area, the floor was covered with tatami mats that had both square and circular cloth cushions gathered around a short flat table. In the corner, what looked like a cabinet with doors that swung open, stood a *butsudan*, a Buddhist altar, common to many Japanese homes.

As Connor took a seat at the table, surrounded by all this tradition, a picture flashed in his mind of how the Japanese slept—lying flat on their back with a small block to lay their heads on.

I'm gonna miss my bed back in the States, Connor thought.

Anticipating Connor's discomfort, Fujiyama said, "You'll sleep with my youngest son, Kenji. He smiled. "You'll get along just fine."

Miyoko quietly piped in, "He and my daughter should be back from my sister's home in Tokyo tonight. I'll get dinner ready. We are going to celebrate our family reunion."

Fujiyama clapped his hands, "OK. Let's unpack. And Connor, let's put your gear in Kenji's room."

Connor followed Fujiyama down a hall to where the bedrooms were located, stopped at one, slid open the door, and prompted Connor to enter.

Connor stepped inside, and his face lit up with surprised delight.

Instead of traditional Japanese bedding, there were two small mattress beds. Although that came as a total relief, the beds weren't what truly amazed Connor. Two of the walls were covered with posters of Hollywood movies and actors. The likes of Gary Cooper, Errol Flynn, Tyrone Power, Jimmy Stewart, and Charlie Chaplin welcomed him into his new bedroom.

Another wall had pictures of Glenn Miller and various American jazz performers. On the ceiling, there were posters of the New York Yankees and the movie *Gone with the Wind*.

The whole room reminded Connor of his room in America. It felt as if he was coming home.

"As you can see, Kenji is enamored with the West, especially

America." Fujiyama laughed at the boy's broad grin. "We've tried to make a Japanese out of him, but to no avail." He directed Connor to place his gear on the bed nearest him. "When Kenji heard you were coming, he could hardly contain himself. You two should get along quite nicely."

After Fujiyama left to let Connor unpack, the boy pulled his clothing from his suitcase and started to dream about what this new life was going to be like and how he never thought he would get to visit such a beautiful place.

He was halfway through stowing his gear when he heard the elated sounds of a family reunion echoing through the straw and paper walls. Connor finished unpacking as quickly as he could, excited to be a part of the celebration. As he began to leave his new room, he quickly turned the corner to run smack into a small Japanese boy that was no more than nine years old.

The Japanese boy had straight black hair, parted on the side, and wore American Wrangler blue jeans that were two sizes too big. He must have found the jeans somewhere in Japan and decided that he had to have them, no matter the size or fit. Besides the jeans, he sported a well-worn, white T-shirt with a black and white photo of a Ford Model-T on it.

Connor thought it was unusual attire for a Japanese boy, but he quickly discovered so, too, was the kid's *unusual* manner of speech.

"Hey Joe, whaddaya know?" Kenji said, reaching out his arm and grabbing Connor by the hand.

"What's steamin', demon?" Kenji gentle eyes were enlarged behind thick-lens glasses.

Connor laughed. "Where did you pick up that lingo?"

"From American movies, Joe," Kenji answered proudly. He reached into his pocket. "Check this out!" he said breathlessly. "A Babe Ruth baseball card. I carry it with me wherever I go."

Just then, a petite figure appeared behind the young boy. To Connor, she was the picture of pure loveliness. A young girl, just shy of five feet with long, black hair that hung over dark eyes that danced on high cheekbones made of light amber skin, glowing like creamy butter.

"Is my little brother bothering you?" Suki asked playfully.

He should have answered or commented on something, but Connor could only stare with his mouth open at this alluring female. Suki was almost Connor's height, and though he knew she was almost a woman, she looked younger than her real age, which Connor guessed was a little older than himself.

After his dumbfounding silence, Connor finally found his voice. "Umm... no, he's not bothering me. We were just getting acquainted."

Suki just looked at him, and Connor tried to steady his breath as he began to drown in the pools that filled her dark eyes.

"Come. Mama-san said dinner is ready," her gentle voice danced down the hall as she walked away.

Connor finally exhaled and followed Suki and Kenji down the hallway to a small dining area. The rest of the family sat around a low table on small cushions, and waited for them to take a seat. Connor found his place, sat down, and tucked his legs under the cushion following the traditional Japanese custom.

The menu for the average Japanese family was a large portion of short-grained rice, vegetables, and fish. Chicken was available frequently, but beef and pork were considered a luxury. Because of Fujiyama's rank and access to military stores, the family was able to dine on such luxuries more often than the general household.

As Connor dove into his rice bowl filled with grilled Ahi, Fujiyama spoke up, pointing to a woman about the age of Miyoko. "This is Miyoko's sister, Mai, our children's aunt. She has been watching over Suki and Kenji while I was on assignment in America."

The little woman, dressed in a yukata with a yellow butterfly obi on the back, bowed her head slightly. Her long, dark hair passed over her eyes, and she gave a reserved smile. "Nice to meet you," she said softly.

Mai meant *elegance* in Japanese, and she was every bit of that and then some. Connor bowed his head in return.

"School starts on Monday," Fujiyama stated. "Miyoko will call and register Hiryo, Yoshi, and you, Connor."

A definite mood of gloom passed over all the children at the mention of *school.*

Fujiyama took note of the looks of disappointment. "Hiryo, why don't you and your brothers and sister take Connor and show him Hiroshima tomorrow?"

Suki softly interrupted. "I can't go. Hidaka is coming here tomorrow. He's on leave from China."

Fujiyama was visibly irritated, but held his tongue, and an air of disquiet filled the room.

Connor wondered at Fujiyama's obvious displeasure, and who was this Hidaka?

Fujiyama turned to his oldest son. "You're old enough, Hiryo. Why don't you take responsibility for the others."

Hiryo's eyes brightened at the vote of his father's confidence. "We leave at eight in the morning," he decreed.

"Hiryo," his father coaxed. "You're leading a sightseeing tour, not a platoon."

Everyone at the table laughed, but Hiryo took his father's teasing in stride.

Hiroshima

The next morning, Hiryo led Yoshi, Kenji, and Connor on a tour of the city. Hiroshima was situated on a beautiful delta filled with towering trees and surrounded by the sea, rivers, and rolling mountains, as though there was something priceless to be guarded.

Kenji jabbered away, peppering Connor with a thousand questions about America. In a way, Connor wasn't annoyed since it gave him a chance to talk about his old home, the very home that he found himself beginning to miss. Since he hadn't expected to miss America, it came as a quite a surprise to him. But Kenji's unbridled curiosity and genuine admiration of Connor gave the American boy a sense of pride.

As they explored the city by foot, Hiryo explained to Connor that Hiroshima was known as an academic metropolis with numerous institutions of higher learning. Although interested in this knowledge, Connor couldn't help but notice all the soldiers and sailors that seemed to be everywhere, and he asked Hiryo about their presence.

Hiryo shrugged his shoulders, not knowing exactly how to respond to the question. What Hiryo did *not* know, was that the city had become the Imperial headquarters for the China war, and now had the distinction of being a military city.

The group of children passed by hundreds of different posters that read, *Waste is the enemy* and *Doing without until victory*, and seemed to follow them wherever they turned.

As they walked, Hiryo explained what he had learned about the city through numerous grammar school field trips. He pointed out the elegant Hiroshima castle and the domed building of the Hiroshima Prefectural Commercial Exhibition Hall.

They walked through the famous Shintenchi, nibbling on many delicious snacks. The famous shopping district was a spectacle of dozens of vendors and restaurants crammed with shoppers. But the outing was highlighted by the opportunity to eat wheat buns from a man on a bike with a megaphone who was hawking, "Hot wheat buns!"

They strode through the Hondori, with its attractive lily-of-the-valley lanterns lining the streets, and past men wearing the national uniform. This outfit was a dull, khaki affair, with puttees wrapped around the trousers, along with a field cap similar to the ones worn by the military troops.

As Connor turned a corner, Hiryo quickly stopped him. "Not that way," he instructed. "That leads to the Yoshiwara."

"What's that?" asked Connor.

"The brothel district," Yoshi giggled.

Connor pointed to an ornate red gate to his left. "And what's that?"

"A torii," Hiryo replied. "A Shinto shrine. There is at least one in every city in Japan. Shinto believes in many gods and spirits. We go to Shinto shrines to pray to the gods for blessings and happiness, and on special occasions, we wear fancy kimonos, put money in the donation box, and pull the rope that rings the bell calling the spirits." He elbowed Connor. "Want to give it a try?"

Connor quietly declined. He wasn't in the mood to meet any spirits. All of the cultural changes were enough to overwhelm him already—the food, clothing, architecture, and the people themselves. The last thing he needed was some ominous cloud of spirit-filled prophecy hanging over his head.

The sun began its descent, and the entourage felt exhausted from all their site-seeing and turned to go home. As they came upon their house, they encountered a long procession of people carrying lanterns.

"What's that?" asked Connor.

Hiryo answered quickly, excited to be the source of knowledge once again. "That's the Obon Festival. It's an important celebration for the dead, and paying respect to our ancestors. The burning of incense and the lanterns help the souls find their way back to the living. Once the souls enter the lantern, it is lit, and the souls are carried back to their homes inside of the lantern."

"Oh," was all Connor could manage to say. This was a lot to take in.

After passing the lanterns and heading up the path into their little palace of peace, the group of makeshift tourists found Suki at the dinner table. And she was not sitting alone. A tall, lean Japanese officer sat with her; and a bit too closely, if you were to ask Connor.

Connor looked around for Fujiyama and Miyoko, but they were nowhere to be seen.

"Connor-san," Suki said. "This is Captain Hidaka Takahashi, my boyfriend." The young woman smiled as Hiryo and Yoshi gave their respects and left for their rooms. "Hidaka-san, this is Connor. He is our adopted brother."

Takahashi did not smile or change his expression, and something about his detachment made the hairs on the back of Connor's neck rise. The boy felt an emotionless, cold cruelty emanate from this man. Instinctively, Connor knew that he was not to be trusted and someone that needed to be watched very closely. Or was he having a tinge of jealousy?

What was sweet Suki doing with a man like this? Connor wondered.

"Hidaka is on leave from China." Suki pointed to Takahashi's pressed uniform, adorned with various battle ribbons. "He has won many medals," she said, sounding as if she was expected to show off Hidaka's awards.

Connor just nodded, and without skipping a beat he asked, "Where's the rest of the family?"

"My mother and Kenji are shopping for dinner, and my father is packing for his trip tomorrow to Tokyo."

Connor caught a hint of impatience in her voice and appeared to be somewhat uncomfortable. It was almost as if she wanted Takahashi's visit to end sooner than later.

She turned to Takahashi and smiled. "My father is on Vice-Admiral Yamamoto's staff."

Takahashi's made a small, subtle scowl. Suki didn't catch his response, but Connor did.

One more reason not to like this man, Connor thought again.

At that moment, Fujiyama interrupted Connor's thoughts and entered the room.

Suki visibly stiffened as Fujiyama and Takahashi shared the same room together. Even Connor could feel the tension hover over the two men like a toxic cloud.

"So, did you have a nice tour of Hiroshima, Connor?" Fujiyama asked, ignoring Takahashi at first.

"Umm, yeah. Very interesting."

Fujiyama nodded then turned to Takahashi, jaw tense, and stated coolly, "Suki will see you out."

At that, Suki rose, and she and Takahashi bowed to Fujiyama.

A few moments later, after Suki had led Takahashi from the house, she went straight to her room without confronting her father.

Connor sensed that whatever the family dynamics were at play, it was not his business to inquire, so he quietly excused himself and went to his room to listen to some of Kenji's American records.

Yamamoto

The cherry blossoms were in full, exquisite bloom in Tokyo on this particular day in 1938. Fujiyama was eager to report to his new post on Vice-Admiral Isoroku Yamamoto's staff. He took a moment to watch the blossoms as the petals fell away like snow, reminding him how beautiful, yet short, life could be.

Fujiyama found the atmosphere in the Imperial Naval Headquarters building was much different than when he had left to go on assignment to America. The building was on a war footing, and that was reflected by numerous checkpoints that were secured by armed Imperial Marines.

Fujiyama, dressed in full naval uniform, approached the first checkpoint, presented his orders and ID, and declared formally, "Commander Akihito Fujiyama reporting to Admiral Yamamoto."

The young marine gave his superior officer a crisp salute, looked over the documents, then nodded and motioned for Fujiyama to pass.

Several minutes later, Fujiyama was standing in front of Yamamoto's aide, a young ensign. Fujiyama repeated what he said to the young marine at the checkpoint and handed his orders to the aide, who took a moment to read them thoroughly.

"The Admiral is expecting you, sir," and he motioned for Fujiyama to enter Yamamoto's office.

Upon entering, Yamamoto said cordially, "Commander. Come in." Fujiyama saluted as Yamamoto came around his desk.

Yamamoto ignored the salute and extended his hand instead. Fujiyama shook it eagerly.

"So, how are you? You look fine. America treated you well, I take it?"

"Yes. It was quite an experience."

"Please. Sit down. Let's talk," the Admiral said, motioning to one of the office chairs.

Rather than sit behind his desk, Yamamoto took a seat next to Fujiyama. "So. Tell me about your impression of America and its Navy."

"As ordered, I submitted regular reports, sir." Fujiyama replied.

"Those were just facts," Yamamoto dismissed the formality. "Just numbers. I want your personal impressions." He pulled his eyebrows together. "What do you think about the Americans?"

Fujiyama collected his thoughts before replying. "The Americans are perceived to be decadent and soft. We see their movies and read their newspapers and believe they are nothing but gangsters and playboys."

Yamamoto raised one eyebrow. "Right. Go on."

"But that's an unfortunate misperception. I saw a tremendous amount of discipline in their Navy and honor among their airmen. It would be a drastic mistake to think Americans as a whole will not fight for what they believe in."

Yamamoto was silent for several moments, processing this insight. "I agree. Americans are a proud and just people. My time at Harvard as a student helped me understand them more than I ever thought I knew."

Fujiyama smiled. "Ah. I believe poker assisted in your education of America, sir."

"You remembered our conversations." Yamamoto grinned and straightened the pleat in his uniform pants. "Yes. I loved poker. I would stay up all night playing the game at Harvard and then as a naval attaché in Washington, and the monies I won I used to travel the country to learn more of America."

He paused a moment, and his voice became grim. "I believe if we went to war, America would be a most formidable enemy. The Army hotheads should realize that."

Fujiyama nodded in agreement. "And what about you, sir? You are an outspoken advocate of peace, and as a result you are a target of the ultra-nationalists as a member of the Treaty Faction. What about the rumored threats to your life?"

Yamamoto laughed. "I'm not so easy to kill." He grew more serious and lowered his voice in thought. "I survived the purge of the Treaty Faction officers by the Fleet Faction. I can survive whatever else those warmongers do. The Fleet Faction and the Imperial Japanese Army had their chance, but they could not exert enough influence in the government to have me removed from the Navy."

"Because you are a favorite of the Emperor," Fujiyama noted.

The admiral laughed again. "And because the Fleet Faction needs me for my technical abilities and knowledge of naval tactics." He paused and once again grew more solemn. "As with you, I serve the Emperor and my country first, and will follow whatever orders are given me."

"Hai," Fujiyama responded. There was a reflective pause, after which he asked, "Sir, how did Japan come to this?"

"To begin with," Yamamoto replied, "in the years you were away, the Army pushed to gain control of the government and the country." He hesitated a moment. "But you must be aware of this."

Fujiyama nodded. "And the Emperor has tried to keep the militarists in check."

"Hai. He used moderate ministers and Admiral Yonai as Naval Minister, and myself as Naval Vice-Minister. As Vice-Minister of the Navy, I worked hard to counter the Army's agenda. I realized that if the situation went unchecked, it would lead to war, and ultimately, our country's ruin. Both Yonai and I refused to compromise our position and have remained critical of the Army, the right wing politicians, and even the hawkish Fleet Faction in our Navy itself."

"And the moderate faction in the government?"

Yamamoto shook his head. "They did not succeed. Then things went from bad to worse." He leaned forward in his chair. "Have you heard of the Tripartite Pact?"

"Hai. But to be frank, politics is not my strong suit."

The two were silent a moment and then Yamamoto sighed. "The radicals in the government want Japan to join with Nazi Germany and fascist Italy in a self-defense pact. Admiral Yonai and I have raised strong opposition to this pact. We believe it is not in Japan's best self-interest to move closer to those two countries. What we received in turn was a steady stream of hate mail and death threats from the nationalists."

The Vice-Admiral slowly shook his head. "Our entire country is being transformed to serve the military. The State is being transformed to serve the Army and the Emperor. The military has brought back the symbolic katana swords for officers as the martial embodiment of these beliefs. The Nambu pistol is carried as a badge of rank and has become the katana's contemporary equivalent."

"And the martial arts schools, as well?"

"*Especially* the martial arts schools. Martial arts are now included in school curriculums. The Samurai Code is now the Bushido Code, the way of the warrior, and any martial arts school that refused to teach the bushido interpretation of the Samurai were closed. Worse yet, the militarists have permeated their version of Bushido down from the Samurai social class, where it originated to the population. It takes the best parts of the Samurai Code, transforming it into a corrupt moral standard for the entire nation. Now the code is turned from one of personal honor and loyalty, to one that advocates blind sacrifice and allegiance to the Emperor."

Fujiyama was silent for a moment. The thought of these transformations were terrifying to him. "I can see now, sir, why you are so vehemently against the militarists."

Yamamoto smiled and patted his junior officer on the leg, and then changed the subject. "I suppose you might want to know what your duties are here."

Fujiyama nodded.

"You'll have an official position on my Intelligence Staff, but will spend much of your time in War Planning under my Chief of Staff, Rear Admiral Matome Ugaki. I think that you two will get along quite well."

"I would be very happy to work with any officer here under your command, sir,"

"Oi. My aide will set you up and find you quarters in the city. As a senior officer, I think we can find you more comfortable quarters than the barracks."

Fujiyama stood and saluted Yamamoto. "Domo arigato, sir. I'll do my duty."

"As will we all," Yamamoto said pensively. "As will we all."

Disappointment

"Really?" Fujiyama replied to the voice at the other end of the phone. "Have you told Connor?"

"No," Miyoko answered.

"Is he at home?"

"Hai. Will you be returning home from Tokyo soon?" She had hoped that her husband would be the one to break the sad news to Connor.

Fujiyama let out a sigh. "No. Let me speak to him." As he waited to talk to his American son, Fujiyama grew frustrated with all his country's complications.

A few moments later, Connor was on the line.

"I'm afraid that I have some bad news, Connor. Miyoko told me that when she tried to register you boys for school, you were denied entrance."

"What? But why?" Connor nearly shouted.

"Because... you are not Japanese."

There was a long pause on the end of the line and then Connor spoke. The disappointment in his voice was strongly evident. "But you adopted me. I'm part of your family."

"I know. I'm sorry, Connor. A lot has changed while we were in America." He sighed. "Japan has changed. Give me some time. Let me see what I can do. I'll look for a non-Japanese school that you can attend."

There was a short period of silence at the other end of the line.

"Whatever," Connor replied halfheartedly.

"In the meantime, I need you to help Miyoko and Suki around the house," Fujiyama stated. "I don't know when I'll be leaving Tokyo. I may be away for quite a while. Can you help take care of them while I'm away?"

"Yeah, sure," Connor replied, then abruptly hung up.

Indoctrination

Over the following weeks, while Fujiyama desperately tried to find a school for Connor, Hiryo and Yoshi were introduced to, or should I say indoctrinated in, the Japanese Imperial education system.

The two boys would soon learn three cultural beliefs.

First, Japan was the center of the world with the Emperor a divine being through the ancestral decent of Amaterasu Omikami, the Goddess of the Sun. Second, the *kami*, Japan's pantheon of gods, had Japan under their special protection. This meant the Japanese were superior to all others. And third, all of these attributes were fundamental to the Imperial Way and gave Japan a divine mission to bring all nations under one roof, so that all of humanity could share the advantage of being ruled by Japan.

All school children in Japan at that time had their hair cropped very short, nearly shaven, and wore the required school uniform. The attire had short, upright collars around their necks with golden buttons down the front. They were light gray in color during the summer, and black the remainder of the year. A military style cap topped the uniform.

Their new school experience was vastly different than the air-base school the boys attended in America. Their new school was plastered with slogans and posters, and songs continually played at recess and lunch extolling the Emperor and the military. There was even a mandatory movie shown every month in the auditorium that reinforced the country's new doctrine.

As the term progressed, so did the advertising. Anti-British and anti-American slogans appeared in every classroom.

Grammar school children were instructed to go to assembly spots in their neighborhood where they would march to school in military-like formation. Yoshi and Hiryo, being in secondary school, wore military style leggings while walking to school and saluted any military officers they pass.

The secondary school the boys attended had retired Army officers and non-commissioned militants on the faculty who taught the subject of military training. Most of the training consisted of marching and the handling of a Model 38 Infantry Rifle—the same rifle the military used. The students were also lectured on military history and various strategies.

Both Hiryo and Yoshi were eager for the end of the term to arrive when they would be sent to the shooting range to practice with real bullets.

Though it was done in all seriousness and in strict compliance with Army regulations, the boys, as boys are, eagerly absorbed all of this as great fun.

On their first day of school, the two boys, now in the same grade due to being close in age, noticed that there was a shrine-like fixture on the wall. It had two wooden doors that opened to display two oval-shaped portraits of both the Emperor and the Empress. The head teacher ordered the class to do *Saikeriei*, or Deepest Bow, when the doors were opened. The students would hang their heads very low until the teacher told them to raise them.

After the students paid their silent respects, the principal came into the classroom and stood erect in front of a small table where an oblong box stood in the middle. The principal would proceed to bow low before the box before opening it and withdrawing a neatly folded piece of rice paper. The parchment paper was so long that he had to raise his arms high above his head to fully unfold it. The two boys came to know this long document as the Imperial Prescript on Education written by Emperor Meiji.

The Imperial Prescript was read at the opening of school and on special occasions. It emphasized the necessity of obedience. The principal's voice was to be heard as if it was that of the Emperor's voice, and while the doors were open, the students were supposed to imagine that the Emperor and Empress were actually present.

The Prescript contents were not lost on Hiryo and Yoshi.

This adoration and reverence for the Emperor was repeatedly instilled into the minds of the young students. Every morning, Hiryo and Yoshi and their fellow students would leave their belongings in the classroom and hurry to the playground. Once there, each class lined up in a neat military fashion and each homeroom teacher would stand in front of the assembly.

The principal would stand on top of a three-foot platform, face the students, and bark orders to the teachers. At his command, the teachers and students bowed to each other with a shout of *ohayo gozaimasu*, good morning. Then the entire formation faced east, towards the Palace, and everyone bowed deeply.

Occasionally, the principal would update the students of the latest victory of the Army in China, or a significant diplomatic move made by the government.

One morning, troops from the newly formed 39th Infantry Division left the south gate of their compound and marched to the Hiroshima train station. Along with many of the people of Hiroshima, Hiryo, Yoshi and their fellow students lined the sidewalks to see them off.

Some of the spectators were seeing off brothers, fathers, or sons. The crowd yelled "Banzai! Banzai!" and waved small Rising Sun flags. The first column of troops was led to the station by a mounted officer, followed by buglers and a local school brass band.

Soon, Yoshi and Hiryo would need little coaxing when it came to speaking highly of Japan's military strength and the people's nobility. They were being trained well.

One day, at the end of summer, Yoshi and Hiryo prepared for a night march as part of their martial training at school. Since the starting point was not at the school but twenty kilometers away, the boys had to leave home dressed in full battle gear that they had brought home.

When Miyoko saw them come marching into the kitchen looking like soldiers complete with rifles, she was appalled.

"What is this? Are those *real* guns? You could *kill* someone!"

The boys tried to explain to her that it was only a school night march and that it would be fun. Formations, uniforms, rifles—they were normalcy to the boys at this point.

Their explanation did not placate Miyoko, who saw her young children growing up into potential soldiers. Tears filled her eyes, and she left the kitchen.

Connor, noticing Miyoko's condition as she quickly passed him in the hallway, wondered what happened. But when he saw Hiryo and Yoshi dressed in their uniforms and clutching weapons, he realized what had made his adopted mother so upset.

"Connor!" Hiryo exclaimed. "Come here. Let me show you this rifle!"

Connor shook his head, confused by what his brothers were becoming. "No thanks." And neither Hiryo nor Yoshi noticed as Connor turned and walked out of the kitchen, down the hallway, and out of the house itself.

Left Out

On a brisk autumn day, Hiryo bounced into the house waving a pamphlet with a picture of a red banner and white circle inside it on the cover.

He ran up to his fourteen-year-old brother Yoshi and shouted enthusiastically, "We all have to join!"

"Join what?" asked Kenji, as he chewed on some rice crackers.

"The *Dai-Nippon Seinento*. The Great Japan Youth Party. Look here." He pointed to the pamphlet.

Yoshi and Kenji gathered around the older teenager to take a look.

"See?" Hiryo noted. "They teach basic survival skills, first aid, cultural lessons, traditions, and basic weapons training. They even have uniforms!"

Yoshi's eyes lit up. "Who can join?"

"Any Japanese boy," Hiryo replied.

"I'll join," Yoshi said without missing a beat. He looked at Kenji, who was studying the handout.

"No. Not me," Kenji said quietly. "Not interested." He shoved another cracker in his cheek.

Hiryo shook his head. "Kenji, you're Japanese, not an American. You will have to decide to be a real Japanese one day."

The comment from his brother stung Kenji, and the young boy stormed past Connor as he entered the kitchen.

"What's going on?" Connor asked. "What's Kenji so upset about?"

"We're joining the Great Japan Youth Party for Japanese boys," Hiryo replied. "Kenji is Japanese, but he refuses to join."

"I guess that leaves me out," Connor noted. This confirmed what he'd been feeling recently. He felt like a *mukokuseki*, without nationality, a stranger in his adopted land. He didn't fit in back in America, and now he didn't fit in while in Japan. Maybe he really was a mukokuseki. Maybe he would never fit in.

Hiryo and Yoshi saw the look of devastation on Connor's face, lowered their eyes and silently wished that they didn't make the statement. They said nothing, and an awkward silence filled the room.

"I'll go and cheer Kenji up," Connor said, breaking the lull. As he went looking for his youngest brother, he was met by Miyoko entering the house.

"Connor-san," she said happily. "I have good news. We found a school for you. Akihito already registered you. He called me today from Tokyo."

"What kind of school?" he asked.

"It's a school for British nationals living in Hiroshima, but they have American children attending as well." she smiled. "You start tomorrow."

Three Classes of Enemies

The months in Tokyo flew by for Fujiyama, and in August of 1939, he was preparing to make a much-needed visit to his home in Hiroshima. That morning, while working on a report for the Chief of Staff with Admiral Matome Ugaki, Vice-Admiral Yamamoto poked his head in the open door of Fujiyama's office.

Yamamoto was gracious enough to provide a spacious office overlooking the Emperor's Palace for Fujiyama, along with a big desk to work from. Looking out from his window, Fujiyama could see the oddly constructed building that stood by the Imperial Palace. After it was built, the Metropolitan Police Board building had to have its tower removed because it stood several feet above the Palace. No building in Tokyo was to look over the Palace.

"You can finish that report later," Yamamoto said. "Walk with me. Let's talk."

Fujiyama nodded and followed Yamamoto down the hall.

"How do you like working for Ugaki?" the Admiral asked as they walked.

"He's a good man. Very dedicated," Fujiyama replied. "To both Japan and you." He paused a beat. "He's very meticulous. Always scribbling down notes in a small book."

Yamamoto laughed. "That's his diary. He wants to chronicle his personal experiences, opinions, and impressions of the war." Yamamoto waited and then smiled. "I think he's titled it the *Wastebasket of War.*"

Yamamoto changed the subject. "I am told you know Kenta Hiyakawa," Yamamoto began, shifting his briefcase from one hand to the other. "The Assistant to the Lord Keeper of the Privy Seal."

"Yes. He is a friend of mine. Why do you ask?"

"The Tripartite Pact Treaty is being discussed, or should I say, argued over, at the Palace. Prince Chichibu is visiting Hirohito three times a week, pressing him to join. Yonai and I, and the moderates in the Cabinet, including Hiyakawa, are arguing against it. We believe that if we join the Pact, it will bring us closer to war with the United States."

Yamamoto appeared tired and seemed to have lost some weight since Fujiyama began his post. "If that happens, we will be fighting a two front war in Asia and in the Pacific. A two front war with limited resources, I should add. Even Tojo has expressed doubts. He believes we could fight the Americans to a stalemate. I'm not so sure."

Fujiyama was silent. He knew Yamamoto was correct.

"So," the Admiral continued, eying Fujiyama and trying to predict his response, "with the signing of the Pact, we will be left with three classes of enemies. True enemies, neutral enemies, and friendly enemies—The Axis making up the last one. We'll have no true allies."

"You are getting more personal threats I assume," Fujiyama noted.

"Yes. And so is your friend Hiyakawa."

"They wouldn't dare touch the office of the Lord Keeper of the Privy Seal," Fujiyama exclaimed. Not only was the thought outrageous to him, but he also feared for his friend's safety.

"Don't underestimate the radicals in the Army and the government, Fujiyama." Yamamoto seemed to know more than he was saying and that made Fujiyama even more nervous.

"But that's not the worst of it." Yamamoto pulled a cigarette case from his uniform pocket, chose one, and lit it. He blew a puff of smoke into the air. "The Army is now firmly in control of the government. Yonai and I have been dismissed."

"*Dismissed!?*"

"Hai. Yonai will no longer be Minister of the Navy, nor I Vice-Minister."

Fujiyama shook his head in disbelief. "Unbelievable! When is this going to happen?"

"Soon. I thought you should hear it from me personally."

While Fujiyama digested this distressing news, the two men approached the building's exit.

"I'm going to the Palace," Yamamoto said, "to support Hiyakawa and the others. Maybe we still have a chance to keep the dogs of war at bay."

"Good luck, sir," Fujiyama replied and turned to return to his office.

He didn't get far.

Off to the right were two burly Japanese men, one short and other one tall, both dressed in business suits. Both men approached Yamamoto with great purpose, but the Admiral was oblivious to their advance. As they neared Yamamoto, the tall man reached into his suit jacket to pull something from it.

Fujiyama, keyed on the threats to the Admiral, bolted towards the man and bowled him and his partner across the hallway, and into one of the marine guards.

Yamamoto reacted to the disturbance behind him. "*No!*" He dashed towards Fujiyama, who wrestled the tall man while two marine guards tried to restrain him.

"Fujiyama," Yamamoto barked. "It's okay. These men are here to guard me."

The tall man picked himself up, cursed in Japanese, showed Fujiyama the wallet he had been retrieving from his pocket, and straightened his suit.

"*Guarding* you?" asked Fujiyama, befuddled, as the marine soldiers withdrew.

"The Navy has sent military police, the *Tokei-Tai*, Naval Secret Police to guard me," Yamamoto admitted. He looked at the two men standing off to the left, and lowered his voice. "Hai. An attempt to keep an eye on me."

Dismissal

Later that afternoon, after the staff meeting, Yamamoto was told to report to Admiral Yonai's office.

"So this is it," Fujiyama noted. "The official dismissal?"

"Most probably. I'd like you to join the meeting with me."

"Of course."

The two men boarded a staff car and soon found themselves in Admiral Yonai's office. Sitting across from the Minister's desk, Yonai shook his head at Yamamoto. "Our services to the Emperor in this capacity end tomorrow. The Army has won, my dear friend."

Yonai gently pulled a formal document from his desk and handed it to Yamamoto. "A final act for a friend."

Yamamoto started to read the document, his forehead creasing before stopping and staring back at the Admiral. "You are making me Commander-in-Chief of the Combined Fleet?"

Fujiyama could hardly hold his enthusiasm at bay, but out of respect, he knew he had to remain silent.

Yonai nodded. "That is the only way I know how to protect you from the radicals in the Army. It is only a matter of time before the very same men that guard you receive orders to assassinate you. If you remain ashore, I'm certain you will be killed before the year is out."

Yamamoto gave Yonai a tepid, "Domo."

Seeing Yamamoto's reluctance, Yonai said, "I know you are hesitant to give up the political fight, but there is little more either of us can do to avoid the steady movement towards war with Britain and the United States."

Yamamoto nodded. "I'd be grateful to be back at sea."

Yonai continued, "Your work at the ministry has made the fleet's naval air force the most powerful in the world. Now, my friend, you will have to take that power and prepare the Navy for war. A war we've opposed for so long."

Yamamoto stood, followed by Fujiyama. "We have much to do."

Outside the Admiral's office, Yamamoto stopped and faced Fujiyama. "I hope you understand what this means." He thought carefully about his next words. "I don't want war, but the only way to win a war with the United States is a quick defeat of their fleet."

Fujiyama understood this very well.

"I'll use the battleship Nagato in Hiroshima Bay as my command headquarters. I want you to finish up the preliminary planning here in Tokyo, and then join me there."

Fujiyama nodded. He had mixed emotions. At least he would be closer to his family. But it was also a family he knew would soon be living in a war zone.

Justice Served

While Fujiyama dealt with the various politics in Tokyo, Connor was settling into his new school. The first few months were uneventful, but as time wore on, international tensions and the foreign nationals that were affected by them began to directly affect Connor.

He was becoming uneasy with his status at the school. There was talk by the students, mostly British and Americans, of Germany and the threat to their respective countries.

One early September afternoon, Connor came upon something unsettling in the courtyard at school. He overheard two of the schoolboys heatedly talking about something. Connor knew these two teens in passing, but neither were more than acquaintances to him. One was a pasty, stout Brit named Archie, whose parents taught at the school. The other was a tall, buff American named Russell, noted for his blustery rhetoric and unbridled mouth.

When they mentioned Japan, Connor walked over to hear more.

"It's war now," Archie declared. "Hitler will be sorry he ever invaded Poland. And what about America? Will they join now in defeating Germany and, if necessary, fight Japan?"

"Fight Japan?" Connor piped up.

The two boys turned their attention to Connor. "Yes," Russell said defiantly. "My father told me that Japan will form an alliance with Germany and Italy."

"The Tripartite Pact," Archie jumped in.

"Right," Russell replied. "That means we go to war with the Japs."

When Connor frowned at the derogatory remark, both boys took notice.

"What's the matter," asked Russell. "Wouldn't you kill Japs?"

"No," was all Connor said.

"What? Are you a Jap lover or something?" asked Russell, clenching his fists. "You hate Americans?"

"No. I don't hate Americans. I hate *bullies*," he said, staring directly at Russell. "Americans killed Mieko, my nanny. She got no justice."

"He *is* a Jap lover!" Archie shouted.

Connor's body stiffened, sensing that he might be forced to defend himself at any moment. Connor swore justice for those who killed Mieko. If this American bully was to be the recipient of that justice, he would have to do what he had to do.

Russell stared down at Connor, then reached forward to grab his shirt. But that was when Connor instinctively reacted. He grasped Russell's shoulders, fell back on the ground, and tossed the surprised American over the top of him. Connor quickly stood up and assumed a karate defensive posture.

Russell pulled himself off the ground, his face blossoming crimson. "*You ass-hole,*" he screamed and came at Connor with fists flying.

Connor parried his blows and hit the American teen in the chest, sending Russell flying backwards. Unfortunately, Connor's attention was focused on Russell and not the Brit. Archie, who was older and heavier than Connor, had maneuvered behind him and grabbed him in a tight bear hug.

Connor struggled to get free and was just about to get away, when Russell lunged at Connor and started punching him in the stomach. Connor collapsed in Archie's arms, the air knocked out of him and gasping for breath. Russell delivered a final brutal blow across Connor's face.

Russell stared down at Connor and spit on him. "He even fights like a Jap."

The two boys kicked some dirt over Connor, covering his face and neck, then laughed and walked away.

After a few minutes, finally catching his breath, Connor managed to struggle to his feet. He wiped the blood from his swollen lips, brushed himself off, and stumbled from the school campus. Confused, angry, and embarrassed, he headed home. Just like everything else in his life, Connor was being persecuted for being different.

Just outside the school, he saw a commotion to his right. A small group of Japanese students from a neighboring People's School, older than Connor, and dressed in gray military-style school uniforms, were beating a red-faced man to the ground. It was *Red Man*, a teacher at Connor's school, and Archie's father. He got the nickname due to his perpetual red-sunburnt face.

The man's clothes were ripped and torn and covered in dirt, and the teacher's body fared no better.

Connor had heard from Miyoko that Westerners were being harassed and even beaten in the city. She was concerned for Connor's safety, and always instructed him to be careful while walking around.

But this was the first time he saw such an incident.

When the students saw Connor, they stopped beating the American teacher, and focused their attention on him. They waited to see what Connor would do. If he would fight to protect a fellow American.

Connor, at first, had the urge to help the American, but thoughts of Meiko came flooding back. So he merely stared back at the group of boys with a blank, unemotional gaze.

Justice, he thought. He turned his back and walked away.

A Favor

In the spring of 1940, I returned to Tokyo. My efforts at locating Unit 731 and any leads to official looting of gold in China were a complete and utter bust.

Tokyo was experiencing a rare snowstorm with three inches of snow covering the streets. I slugged my way through the cold and bitter wind to my newspaper offices, where I was brought up to date by my editor on the political happenings in the country during my absence.

Sakura told me the news about Admirals Yamamoto and Yonai, and how the Army ousted them from their respective positions. Knowing that Fujiyama was on Yamamoto's staff, I decided to look him up. Since my own investigation of Unit 731 with the Army in China produced nothing, I thought perhaps the Navy might know something.

When I arrived at Imperial Naval Headquarters, I was surprised to see Fujiyama packing up his office. "Leaving?" I asked as I walked through his office door.

"Yoshihara, where have you been hiding yourself?" he said beaming, dropping a handful of maps to come over to shake my hand.

"Don't you read the newspapers? My dispatches from China?" I responded. "I've had my hands full acting as a war correspondent."

"To tell you the truth," Fujiyama replied, "I've been too busy here. Haven't even had the time to visit my own family back home." He looked me over. "War correspondent, huh? Seen any action?"

Fujiyama asked, picking up a box of documents and emptying them into a large trunk.

"Some." I answered. Then, correcting myself, I admitted the honest truth. "Lots. Too much." I stared at the floor, trying to shake the vivid images that flooded my brain.

Fujiyama gave me a knowing look. "War can change a man."

"So, what is all this?" I asked, pointing to the trunks full of his office supplies.

"Yamamoto has set up headquarters for the Imperial Combined Fleet in Hiroshima. I'm joining him there in a few weeks."

I was quiet for moment and Fujiyama knew I had something on my mind. "Okay. So what do you want to know?" he smiled.

"Can't hide anything from you, my old friend," I said. "Have you heard of something called Unit 731?"

Fujiyama arched his eyebrows and shook his head. "No. Why? Is it important?"

"I thought the Navy might know something. Can't get anywhere with the Army." I opened my hands in defeat. "No matter. But if you hear anything about it, please let me know."

"Sure." He lowered his voice and grinned, unable to resist the temptation that went along with whatever this Unit 731 might be. "As long as it's not a military secret." He pulled a detailed map of the Central Pacific off the wall, rolled it up, and placed it on his desk. "I'll finish this later. I'm having lunch with Hiyakawa. Being in Tokyo these past months, we get together every so often. Why don't you join us?"

I nodded, and we set out in a staff car to go to the *Gajo-en*, a popular restaurant in Tokyo that was famous for its size and the astonishing display of art that adorned its walls. The famous restaurant is so sizable, that it could accommodate a thousand guests in its ballroom. So large, in fact, the building reminded me of a Tibetan monastery.

As we traveled, the driver had the radio tuned to a station playing *The Patriotic March*.

"Turn that down," Fujiyama ordered curtly.

"Can't go anywhere these days without that music blaring or seeing street propaganda." He sighed. "Can't even find a decent symphonic venue anymore. Replaced by brass band and military music. Western classical music is being banned except for Wagner because he is Hitler's favorite."

Several minutes later, we arrived at the restaurant and entered the *Gajo-en* through an artificial grotto of bigger and better massive rocks. The proprietor wanted to make the place bigger and better than any other institution in all of Japan. There must have been almost a mile of corridors covered in massive art pieces, including enormous goggling statues of geishas, gigantic cows, lobsters, and prawns.

Fujiyama critiqued the art as we walked. "I think it's necessary to see the *Gajo-en* firsthand in order to realize the depths to which our art can sink."

When we arrived at the dining area, Hiyakawa was already seated. I stood by the table, bowed, and took a seat. "Nice to see you again your Excellency." I said. "You're looking well."

"I might say the same for you." He noticed my weathered face and dark rings under my eyes. "You haven't been working in an office very much, have you?"

I smiled at his observation. "No. I've been on assignment in China for a couple of years. Covering the war."

Hiyakawa frowned. "Hai. A dirty war. At least that's what my friend here tells me." He motioned to Fujiyama. "So, where to next?"

"My paper is sending me to Manchuria, or as the government calls it, Manchukuo. To report on the Japanese businesses that have been established there."

"Ah. The Manchurian lifeline," he responded.

"That's what my editor called it as well," I said.

A waitress appeared and took our order of sushi and sashimi. I was happy with the choice of cuisine since some restaurants went into a more *non*-traditional fare like bees and bullfrogs. I never could bring myself to try the latter that were normally kept in a pool beneath a counter. They were the size of a small lap dog and did everything but bark.

When the waitress left I asked Hiyakawa, "Will the Emperor sign the Treaty?"

Hiyakawa was silent for a moment, and then glanced towards a thin, lanky man in his mid-forties, wearing a dark button down suit, and sitting alone at a table. He had a nasty scar half-closing his left eye and ran to the bottom of his cheek. On his lapel was an insignia of a small chrysanthemum. He had small, disturbing eyes that stared at the three men.

Fujiyama and I followed his gaze. I recognized him immediately. "Kempeitai," I whispered.

"Probably," Fujiyama nodded. "Or Tokko, the State Police."

Hiyakawa sighed. "Doesn't matter. Their eyes and ears are everywhere these days." He looked back at me. "To answer your question, the Emperor is under immense pressure to sign the Tripartite Treaty. He's being pressed from all sides. Prince Chichibu, the radicals in the government, and the Army. I don't know how long he can holdout." He turned his attention to Fujiyama. "And what is the Navy's view?"

"Right now, this is the Army's war, but the generals are trying to draw the Navy into it. Yamamoto and I, along with the other conservative elements, are resisting it. As for the Tripartite Pact, joining Rome and Berlin will most certainly bring us closer to war with the United States."

The mood turned somber, and I decided to divert the conversation as our food came, accompanied with a pot of hot green tea, miso soup, and rice. "So, how's the family, Commander?"

"As far as I know, they're well." Fujiyama replied, picking out a piece of sashimi. "I'm told the children are doing well in school. Connor is enrolled in a British school there, and Miyoko and Suki volunteer at an Army hospital in Kobe a couple of times a week."

"Have you spoken with your older boys yet?" asked Hiyakawa curiously. "About their experience at school?"

"No. Not much. They don't like to stay on the phone with their parents for long. You know teenagers," he laughed. "Always in a hurry to go somewhere or do something. Why do you ask?"

He leaned closer to the Commander. "The current moral education is not what we would traditionally call moral. A child is taught from infancy that its primary duty is not to its parents, but to the State itself, and to be done with as the State deems fit."

He sat back in his seat. "The entire emphasis is on the cult of Emperor worship, and loyalty to him is the most important value of the nation, second only to the importance of ancient military virtues. Children are marched to school and spend half their time being indoctrinated on loyalty to the Emperor and obedience. I find it frightening to see children saluting crowded streets of soldiers instead of playing or laughing."

"So, you're saying I should see how all of this has affected my children in few short months since they've been in school?" Fujiyama replied, his voice sounding defensive.

"I'm just saying you should be aware of what's happening and act accordingly with your children. That's all," Hiyakawa replied.

As we finished our meal, the three of us sat in an uncomfortable silence, the tension tangible.

After we finished and paid for our meal, I said, "It was nice seeing the both of you again. My plane leaves tonight." I paused seeing the troubled look on my friends' faces. "I hope my editor didn't put me on one of those god-awful military planes again."

We all shared a laugh, the friction finally lifting somewhat.

"Stay safe," Fujiyama said.

"And keep up the good fight," I said to Hiyakawa. I made eye contact with both of them. "And watch your backs." I glanced at the scar-faced man, who had continued to observe us during our entire meal.

I exited the restaurant and basked in the warmth of the spring day. I found myself content in the knowledge that Fujiyama would soon to be basking in the harmony of his family. I was also pleased that my next assignment would have nothing to do with war. Sadly, I would ultimately be wrong on both counts.

Swordsmanship

Hiryo and Yoshi were at home practicing swordsmanship with bamboo poles when Connor came through the door. The boys had to take an hour of judo and kendo, sword fencing, every week, and were instructed to practice their technique at home. The bamboo poles, called Shinai, were made from bamboo slits, and bound together with leather cords to form a rounded surface.

The two boys immediately noticed Connor's bruises and his dour mood.

"What happened to you?" asked Yoshi.

"Got into a fight at school," Connor mumbled and went into the kitchen for a damp cloth.

The boys followed, and Hiryo tried ribbing Connor to lift his spirits. "And what does the other guy's face look like?"

"I got my licks in," Connor replied, grinning.

"Who did it?" asked Yoshi. "The Brits or Americans?"

"Both." Connor pressed a damp cloth against the bruise on his head. "They were talking about fighting Japan. I told them I wouldn't fight Japan if war came and, well, you know."

"I hope we do go to war with the Americans," Hiryo sneered. "We can beat them *and* the British." He regretted it as soon as the words came out of his mouth, but they had been ingrained in his head.

Pushing their bravado aside, Connor looked at the long sticks in the two boys' hands. "What are you doing with those bamboo poles?"

"Part of our training at school," Hiryo replied. "School and our

Youth Party are teaching us the traditional values of our nation and the symbols of our superiority."

"Watch," Hiryo said as he took a combat stance and positioned his bamboo sword in front of him.

Yoshi imitated his brother's combat stance as well.

Over the next few minutes, the two boys displayed the art of swordsmanship they had learned over the last few months.

To Connor, they looked and acted like the Samurai he had seen in motion pictures popular in movie houses at the time. As he continued to watch his brothers move with grace and deliberation, he knew this was something he wanted to learn.

Once the short demonstration was over, Hiryo said, "We have to go. Have a Youth Party meeting this afternoon. See ya later."

The two boys rushed off to dress in their Youth Party uniforms.

Connor sighed, feeling a combined sense of alienation and loneliness, and continued to clean his injuries with the damp cloth.

Recruitment

"Our chapter leader told us we were having a special guest today," Yoshi said.

"I heard. Very special," Hiryo agreed.

The boys had joined several dozen other boys, both younger and older, in a large meeting hall at the local university. The hall hummed with excited voices when a slender, middle-aged man approached the podium. Behind him stood a large, red flag with a white circle in the center, the bold symbol of the Great Japan Youth Party.

Immediately, all talking ceased as the boys' full attention focused on their chapter leader. The man had the stern expression of a drill sergeant that exhibited little tolerance or compassion. He wore a light brown uniform with an armband of red with a white circle in the center.

After a moment of silence, he ordered his audience to attention.

"Today, I have the honor of presenting to you our founder, the esteemed Colonel Kingoro Hashimoto."

A startled, collective gasp arose from the audience as a middle-aged man clad in a brownish-grey uniform wearing a military cap and Party armband, approached the podium.

The chapter leader bowed deeply as did all the boys in the hall.

Hashimoto looked over the sea of eager faces and surveyed his latest catch. Hashimoto modeled the Party after the Hitler Youth of Nazi Germany, even to the extent of using a light brown color for member's uniforms and the adoption of a red banner with a white circle in the center as the party flag.

The objective of the party was to teach Japanese youth basic survival skills, first aid, life skills, cultural lessons, traditions, and basic weapons training. However, Hashimoto's primary intent was to create an idealistic young cadre of supporters ready for induction into the Japanese military.

"Be seated." Hashimoto said in a gravelly voice.

After the boys complied, he began his message.

"There is a foreign conspiracy bottling up our people, *your families*, to the point of starvation, with their embargoes and political maneuverings. A foreign empire is vital to Japan, and our enemies will not deny us that. We must strive to purify our land, our minds, and our souls against the decadent democracies that seek to poison our culture with foreign ideas."

His eyes burned into the young initiates. "Our inspiration comes not from the decadent cultures of the West. Our inspiration for living comes from our ancient myths of the Japanese and our devotion to the Emperor." His voice bellowed across the hall with passion and utter devotion. "Our emperor! A living god descended from the Sun Goddess, Amaterasu Omikami!"

The youth cheered as he let that last statement burn into their young minds.

"We must restore our racial and spiritual purity lost over the last fifty years. Look not to the West for answers, but instead, search inside yourselves and worship our sacred ancestors."

He took a deep breath. "We are close to war with the democracies. A war that will purify you, our nation, and ultimately the entire world. And if you should die in the process? The supreme sacrifice of your life is the purest of personal accomplishment for the Emperor."

He snapped to attention, and his piercing black eyes burned once again into the crowd of boys. "Become modern day Samurai! Die a noble death with honor intact!" He looked around the room and cried, "Who here will join me?"

A voice rose in the back, "I will!" Then another. "I will!" And another. "*I* will defend our country," dozens of voices echoed throughout the hall.

Hiryo could not contain himself. "My father is a fighter pilot! A war hero! I will fly Zeros against the enemy!"

Yoshi stood up and shouted, "I will join the Army!"

Hashimoto smiled. *Such devotion.* The aim of the Party had succeeded.

"Tomorrow is our rally," their leader said. "There will be over two thousand of us in the streets. Soon our membership will grow to *one hundred thousand* or more when others like you see our dedication to our country, its sacred values, and spiritual traditions."

Hiryo and Yoshi remembered the Imperial Rescript and beamed with pride. They reveled in the moment, embracing that they were going to be a part of something truly spectacular.

Youth Party Parade

The next morning, after Hiryo and Yoshi ate a quick breakfast, they dressed in their Party uniforms, wearing white knee high spats and military caps, and prepared to catch the train for the Youth Party parade in Tokyo.

They stood in front of the mirror, admiring their uniforms, when Hiryo looked to his brother. "Let's ask Kenji and Connor to come with us."

The boys returned to the breakfast table and asked Connor if he wanted to come, but the boy declined. It was no contest. Being with Suki was head and shoulders above attending a rally he knew little about. Besides, he enjoyed Suki's company—or was it something else. His feelings for her had evolved into more than a love of a sister. Suki was always friendly and affable, but as far as Connor could see, her affections ended there.

"Kenji, you *have* to come," Hiryo pleaded, not giving up on his little brother. "Come and see what it means to be Japanese."

Kenji looked at his sister, and she encouraged him with a silent nod to join his siblings. Eventually he shrugged, giving into his older brothers.

The three headed for the door when Miyoko caught up with them. "Boys, your father will be home this morning. Don't you want to be here to greet him?"

"Can't," shouted Hiryo over his shoulder as he hurried through the front door with his brothers in tow. "Gonna be late for the rally."

In the past, the boys would have never missed the homecoming of their father, but they were so infatuated with living up to the expectations of the Youth Party, that they momentarily forgot about the expectations of their father.

After a restless three-hour trip along the rails, the three boys arrived at the Tokyo train station. Never having been in Tokyo before, the boys were both enthralled and overwhelmed by the massive crowds. Within minutes, they were corralled with other boys attending the rally. Most of the boys were between thirteen and nineteen, and they hailed from cities all around Japan. They lined up and were led onto buses that would carry them to the parade.

"Look at that," Yoshi exclaimed, pointing out the window of their bus as they approached the city center.

Hiryo and Kenji stared out the window at the congregation that had grabbed Yoshi's attention. In the sprawling square there was a gathering like they'd never witnessed before. Hundreds and hundreds of boys stood dressed in the same brown uniforms they wore, proudly displaying the symbol of the Youth Party on their arms.

Just then, the bus stopped, and all the boys were ordered off. Ten minutes later, they were in parade formation and marching down a wide Tokyo boulevard that led past the Imperial Hotel located just south of the Imperial Palace grounds next to the Palace moat.

"Look at this. Isn't this spectacular?" Hiryo asked Kenji.

Kenji shrugged, not really thinking the parade was anything special. He walked the designated route with disinterest, and when the parade finished its course, he watched his two brothers chat enthusiastically with some other Youth Party boys. The group of boys felt like they were heroes of some sort; a part of something that would make them legendary.

When Kenji approached his brothers' group, some of the other boys eyed him with suspicion, unsure if he was one of them.

"Why isn't he in uniform?" one of the boys asked.

"He's our little brother," Yoshi said. "He's not interested in joining the Youth Party."

A big teen with strapping arms that Hiryo recognized from their neighborhood approached Kenji and leered down at him. "Why didn't you join the Party with your brothers? Are you Japanese or not?" He then turned to Hiryo. "What kind of family do you have, that your own brother is not a member of the Party?"

"We have a very *honorable* family," Hiryo snapped. "Our father was a war hero in the Great War, and he's a fighter pilot in the Navy."

"Then why does he harbor a coward like this?" the teen sneered, pointing at Kenji.

"That's enough about my family," Hiryo demanded. "My father's patriotism is beyond question."

Yoshi stepped in to defuse the tension. "It's just that our little brother has different ideas."

"Different ideas? Individuals serve the nation. They serve the Emperor," the big teen shouted. He stared over at Kenji, scrutinizing his Wrangler jeans and Model-T Ford t-shirt. "And what are these?" he said, poking his finger into Kenji's chest. "He wears the clothes of a decadent democracy."

Kenji slipped out his Babe Ruth baseball card from his pocket and stroked it, as he was apt to do. It was what Kenji did when he was nervous. But today it provided little comfort.

The big teen snatched the card from his hand. "To hell with decadent baseball. To hell with Babe Ruth," and he ripped the card in two.

Kenji watched the pieces flutter to the ground and began to cry.

"You're either with us or against us," the teen demanded.

Yoshi leaned toward Hiryo and whispered, "I think we better leave." Hiryo glared at the teen for a moment, then took Kenji by the arm, and the three brothers walked away under the hateful stares of the other boys.

Disapproval

The incident with Kenji was quickly forgotten by Hiryo and Yoshi, but it was embedded in Kenji's mind. They finally returned to their home and came bounding into the house with enthusiasm. Their father was there waiting for them, and wore a look of unease on his face.

"Chichi!" shouted Kenji and ran into his father's arms.

The older sons gathered around Fujiyama and hugged him as well. Within moments, they were chattering about the Party, the parade, and what they learned over the last several months.

The blatant propaganda the boys gushed made Fujiyama realize that Hiyakawa's warning was right. He might have lost his boys to the ultra-nationalists, and it took all his willpower not to react to the strong beliefs that had been brainwashed into their minds.

But it got worse.

"Colonel Hashimoto, leader of the Youth Party, arranged for me to register for naval air training next week. I'm going to be a fighter pilot just like you," Hiryo boasted.

Fujiyama responded with a blank stare. He had heard of Hashimoto, and nothing he had heard was good. Hashimoto had been temporarily forced into retirement from military service due to his involvement in the failed February 26 Incident—the attempted coup against the government.

"You are too young," Fujiyama countered. He did not want his young son to honor this man. It was going to be difficult to remain the good guy in Hiryo's eyes when there were things Fujiyama knew that he couldn't tell his aspiring son.

"I just turned seventeen," Hiryo responded. "I qualify."

Yoshi jumped in. "And when I turn seventeen in a few months, Colonel Hashimoto will help me register for the Army."

The two boys stared at their father, disappointed by his reluctance.

"Why are you not happy?" asked Yoshi. "We want to make you proud."

Miyoko watched as Fujiyama fought the urge to respond with strong disapproval, but her husband kept his counsel.

Fujiyama repeated, "I think you're both too young."

As Connor came into the room, Hiryo diverted his enthusiasm to his American brother. "Hey Connor, guess what?"

As Hiryo and Yoshi filled in Connor on their enlistment plans, the three boys left the room.

Fujiyama was silent, and Miyoko took her husband's hand in hers. He saw the deep concern on his wife's face as she confided, "I don't want my boys giving their lives for the Emperor. They are much too young."

Her eyes teared up as she told him the gruesome stories of wounded soldiers at the Kobe Army hospital where she and Suki volunteered. "When I arrive at the Kobe train station, I see group after group of wounded and crippled soldiers lined up on the platform. And strangers would go to them, bow low, and say, *Gokuro sama.*"

She grimaced at the memories. "There was one young soldier, no older than our sons, who had lost his legs from a landmine. And there were more, far too many more, with part of their faces shot off, arms gone, or their bodies horribly burned."

After a long pause she repeated sternly. "No. My sons are *not* ready to die for the Emperor."

Fujiyama held her face in his hands. They would not die so young. Not if he had anything to do with it.

Fujiyama wasted no time calling the Youth Party and speaking directly with Hashimoto.

After explaining his concern about his two boys' enlistment, Hashimoto calmly replied, "This is all in order, Commander. The Ministry of Education approves. They are of age, and they will be accepted."

When Fujiyama objected once again, Hashimoto was quick to cut him off, "Commander Fujiyama, you are a high-ranking officer in the Imperial Navy. You wouldn't want your position to be jeopardized by anti-nationalist views, would you?"

Fujiyama was silent for a moment. He knew a thinly guised threat when he heard one.

"Should I pass your objections onto the Ministry?" Hashimoto asked.

"No," Fujiyama replied. "That won't be necessary."

"Good. Your sons will make you proud serving their Emperor and their country. After all, it is their choice, not yours, to decide," he said coolly before hanging up.

Fujiyama slowly placed the receiver down and rubbed at his jaw.

Miyoko entered the room in anticipation, saw her husband's body posture, and quickly understood that her worse fears were realized.

Fujiyama turned to her and shook his head. "I tried. I tried," he said in a somber voice.

The two were silent for the longest time when Miyoko said, "You must speak to Connor-san. He is very sad. He feels he does not belong."

"Yes, I noticed his mood," Fujiyama replied. "I don't know quite what to do. I feel helpless."

Miyoko took his hand in hers. "You need to tell him the truth." She raised her eyes in an unspoken acknowledgment.

Fujiyama was startled. "How did you know?"

"Women talk," she nodded.

"No. I must keep my promise to Meiko. I made that promise in the hospital room in America. If I don't, it will only make matters worse now for Connor."

"I understand," she replied, stroking his hand. "Sometimes a promise is best unkept when it makes the world a better place. You must do whatever's best for Connor-san."

Nurikabe

C onnor sat on the edge of his bed and stared at all the American posters in his room. Instead of giving him comfort and a sense of nostalgia, he felt despondent and depressed.

Miyoko knocked on the door, then walked in with some sweet rice cakes and a cup of green tea. "Here, Connor-san," she said softly. "This will make you feel better." She patted his shoulder and kissed the top of his head.

Connor shook his head. "Mama-san?" He looked at her, holding back his emotions. "I feel so lost. In America, I'm too Japanese. In Japan, I'm too American. Everywhere I turn, my way is blocked."

"Nurikabe," she whispered.

"What?"

"Nurikabe," she repeated.

"What's Nurikabe?" Connor questioned.

"It's a character in Japanese folklore." Miyoko had told many *shushin*, Japanese moral stories, to Connor and her children in the past few months. She shared these stories with Connor especially because she wanted to expose him to the best qualities of Japanese culture.

"A Nurikabe," she continued in her gentle voice, "is a huge invisible wall that blocks a traveler's way on the road. If they move right, it moves right. If they move left, it moves left as well. There seems to be no way around it."

"What does it look like?"

"It is said that a Nurikabe manifests itself in visible form that looks like a huge stonewall with pairs of small arms and legs. When people are walking for long periods of time without reaching their destination, the delay is blamed on the Nurikabe. In a way, a Nurikabe is blocking your way to true happiness."

She held his hand. "You will find a way, Connor-san. You will because you are unique. You are special, and you will find your way through the Nurikabe someday."

"How?"

She squeezed his hand. "Hai. That is for you and only you to figure out. But never stop searching for your path. Your father is will be home soon. I think he has a surprise for you."

Miyoko turned to the door. "Here he is now."

"Hello, Chichi. Mama-san says you have a surprise for me."

"Come," Fujiyama said with a devious grin. "We're going to the airfield. I'll show you."

An few hours later, they arrived at a small hanger at the airfield where Fujiyama kept his private plane outside the city. It was a Tachikawa Ki-9 dual seat bi-plane trainer used by the Japanese Air Force. Fujiyama had been using it to train Connor.

"You've been taking me for flying lessons all these months," Connor said, raising an eyebrow. "What's the surprise?"

"You are going to solo today." Fujiyama smiled. "I will not be flying with you this time."

"Fly? On my own? You will not be sitting behind me?" Connor said nervously.

"Hai. I will watch you from the ground." He pointed to the small bi-plane. "Go ahead—*pilot*."

Connor rushed to the small plane and climbed into the cockpit, started it up, and taxied it onto the runway.

He surveyed the instrument panel and confirmed that the small plan was ready to take off. He revved the engine until the trainer strained against the brakes that were holding the airplane in place. Then he release the accelerator. *Whoosh!* The plane hurled down the tarmac spitting out runway dust behind it, and within half minute, he was airborne.

For once, I am in control of my own fate.

He flew around the airfield a few times then took up his approach for landing. The runway came closer and closer in his windshield as he slowly guided the little bi-plane home.

His hands were sweaty. He rubbed them together. *I've done this a dozen times before with Fujiyama sitting with me. Nothing is different this time.* Those thoughts calmed him as he guided the plane over the runway and then touched his wheels to the tarmac.

Home, he thought. Then yelled, "I did it!" as the plane taxied towards Fujiyama and the hanger.

He stopped and climbed out of the cockpit smiling from ear to ear.

"You're a real pilot now," Fujiyama said, slapping Connor on the back. "I'm proud of you."

Manchukuo

While Fujiyama wrestled with the worries and struggles of his family in the new Japan, and as Connor's alienation spiraled further, I made my way to Manchuria shortly after *O-shogatsu*, the beginning of the New Year.

You could go nowhere in occupied Manchuria, or Manchukuo as it's called today, without the knowledge and permission of the Kwantung Army. Sankuru, after handing me the briefcase full of background information on Manchukuo before my flight of 1940, made it clear to me and gave me strict instructions to report to the Kwantung peninsula where the Kwantung Army gets its name. This part of the country was nestled in a cove of the peninsula, almost as if it were its own place that was protected by the arm that reached out into the Yellow Sea.

The Kwantung Army first came into prominence in 1931 when it set about annexing Manchuria without troubling to obtain permission from Tokyo. It was at this point that the Kwantung Army began to acquire its overwhelming control of politics, and it was doubtful that the supreme command had any real influence over the Army. Its real power came from the use of Japan's semi-secret political societies like the Black Dragon Society and the Black Ocean Society.

It was feared whether in certain eventualities, the Kwantung Army would even be loyal to the Emperor. Being an army within the Army, some wondered that if Japan was forced to accept defeat, the Kwantung Army might refuse surrender orders from the government.

I paged through the background material and tried to absorb as much as I could so I would be able to make accurate reports back to my newspaper.

Now having the privilege of being included in the Greater East Asia Prosperity Sphere, Sakura's cover pages stated that Manchukuo served three purposes for Japan. First, the Japanese government set up Manchukuo as a puppet state, and the Kwantung Army was the armed forces of that new state. Second, Manchukuo was also the launching point for the invasion of China. Finally, and more importantly, Manchukuo was an important source of vast natural resources and raw materials much needed by Japan to advance its economic and political goals. The iron, coking coal, and salt were all held in the grip of the land itself, which had a value much higher than all the resources combined.

In March of 1933, the Kwantung Army declared the creation of the Manchukuo Empire to protect the interests of its population. It took as its formal leader the former Chinese Emperor Qing Henry Puyi, who had been deposed in 1911. Former Qing officials were placed in administrative posts adding legitimacy to the new State.

Germany was the exception. This declaration didn't fly with the international community, and especially the League of Nations. The disapproval led to boycotts and trade sanctions against Japan. Still, there was little that the League of Nations could do to force Japan to leave Manchuria, and so the new state of Manchukuo became a part of the growing Japanese Empire.

I landed in Kwantung, reported to Army Headquarters, and was in for a rude awakening.

"Mr. Koga," a tall, lean, malevolent looking young man, wearing the standard M1938 field uniform with high black leather boots, called out as I entered the headquarters building.

"It is very nice of you to remember me, Captain Takahashi." I then noticed the insignia of rank on his collar. "Or should I say major, now."

"Yes," Takahashi smiled, fingering his insignia of rank. "In recognition of my service in China." Then he added with a hint of menace, "I never forget a face."

He now wore some new additions to his uniform. A black chevron on his blouse, and a white armband on his left arm with the characters *ken* meaning law, and *hei* together meaning Law Soldier. There was also a small gold star–like emblem behind his rank insignia. I recognized it immediately.

Kempeitai.

I wondered what Takahashi had done to earn such a distinction. The Kempeitai were evil personified and had a reputation for a level of persecution that involved far more than that of the left-wing liberals. The unremitting persecution pervaded their sadistic ranks.

They were a law unto themselves, and I would soon discover that their bestial torture and inhuman acts would far surpass what the Imperial Japanese Army performed in China. There were even wild rumors surfacing that the Kempeitai were arresting those that they believed were even *thinking* something that was against the Empire. It didn't matter that no words had left their mouths or had been written by their hands. Those that were considered independent thinkers were taken prisoner because the Kempeitai felt compelled to observe their possible disloyal behavior.

I pointed to his Kempeitai emblem. "For meritorious service, too?"

Takahashi lost his smile. "And you are here for what reason?" The man found no humor in my sarcasm.

"To do a report on the Manchurian Lifeline for my newspaper. I'm told I would expect the cooperation of the Kwantung Army in this regard." I handed him my ID and authorization papers.

Moments like this always made me extremely uncomfortable. I knew that Japan was a police state now, and I also knew the powers that be were aware of my growing up in America. Still, up to this point, no one had questioned my loyalty as a Japanese citizen. What if Takahashi believed he was reading my own thoughts at this very moment?

Takahashi's smile returned. "Of course. I personally would be happy to show you what we have done here in Manchukuo, and the importance of it to our Empire."

More the better to watch me, I thought.

The word Empire flowed from his lips easily—*too* easily.

But I didn't reveal my distaste. I've seen the abject brutality of this man firsthand and his total disregard for human life, so I intended to be a civil guest, file my stories, and return home to Tokyo.

"I will show you an example of the successes we have had here in Manchukuo," he said proudly. "Come. We'll take my staff car."

A few minutes later, Takahashi and I were traveling out of the peninsula of the high mountains and low-lying plains, into a wide expanse of countryside. Although the weather was pleasant during our trip, this wasn't common of the area. Luckily, my tour was in the spring, and the transition from a brutally cold winter into a thick, humid summer, left March with a mediocre climate. But the aura in the air was dense nonetheless.

"Manchukuo is the lifeline of Japan," he proudly explained as we rode through the countryside that was dotted with small farms. "We see Manchukuo as a bulwark against European powers or any powerful country for that matter that can attack Japan. In addition, Manchukuo addresses the population pressure in our country and our need for food and natural resources. We envision large-scale emigration to the Asian continent as a viable option for farming communities."

A couple of hours later, we arrived at a remote farming village. I could only imagine this to be a model example of the type of community that Japan wanted to project for Manchukuo.

As we toured the village, Takahashi informed me of how the Japanese immigrants struggled to adapt to their new home. He painted a heroic pioneering picture that focused on the colonists' struggle against Chinese bandits, the burgeoning prosperity of the settlements, and their role in raising the cultural standards of the local people.

"These Japanese immigrants," he continued proudly, "fought off bandits, disease, and devastating natural disasters. But the thundering summer rains did not drown their dreams. Wives followed and so did home building, bumper crops, and a colonial baby boom. Prosperous fields of soybeans, rice, wheat, and kaoliang were produced, and the Manchus partook in the peaceful prosperity of the village."

All this, of course, was the party line and had been covered in the research material that Sankuru gave me to read on my flight. What wasn't in the formal material was his sarcastic remark written in the margin of the last page of his report—*Just one big happy family.*

Thirty minutes into our tour of the village, the young staff car driver hustled up to Takahashi and whispered in his ear.

"You have to excuse me," he said. "I have a call at the staff car." He motioned for me to continue looking around the village myself.

As I explored the settlement, all I saw were hard working residents with smiling faces going through their daily tasks. As I turned the corner by a corral of cattle, a large hand grabbed me on the shoulder.

Startled, I turned to face a stout elderly man dressed in priest's garb, with piercing eyes and a tussle of brown hair.

"So," he remarked sarcastically in a French accent. "You buying that propaganda?" He waved his hand around him, and then motioned to where Takahashi had left with his driver.

I avoided answering his question. "I'm sorry... Father...?" I replied instead.

"Father Marquette. I run the French Catholic mission here in *Manchuria.*" He deliberately emphasized the word. "I was sent by the Société des Missions Étrangères de Paris."

His steely blue eyes glared into mine. "And I repeat the question. Did you buy that Kempeitai Officer's propaganda?" I paused a moment, not knowing what this priest's agenda might be, so I was careful with my reply. "I took it with a grain of salt."

A deep laugh arose from Father Marquette's round belly. After his laugh faded away, his face grew serious. "And why are you here?"

"I'm a reporter. My name is Yoshihara Koga, and I'm doing a piece for my newspaper."

"Oui. Looking for facts, I hope."

I nodded my head.

"Then let me give you some." He looked around and added, "Someplace a little more private. Come to my quarters."

Father Marquette led me to a small, clay building on the outskirts of the village, constructed in a similar fashion as all the others. Fields of grazing sheep littered the green hillsides behind the village like a beautiful painting.

"Come in and sit." He guided me through the small entrance and into a room lit only by two small dirty windows that allowed just enough light in so that I could still see my surroundings. "Would you like some tea?"

I declined. "Takahashi will be looking for me. I'm afraid I can't stay long." I took a seat in a rustic wooden chair. "So what do you know?" I asked. "What's the story behind the story here?"

The priest lowered his bulk into the second chair with a frayed seat cushion and sighed wearily. "You are probably aware that the initial Japanese immigrants created self-defense compounds here under the direction of the Kwantung Army."

"Quieting any unrest. *Chian iji*," I added, reiterating the background information my editor gave me. "And facilitating sovereignty of a puppet state to Japan while merging this military role of the colonists into action on the ground."

"Correct. But the immigrants were expected to merge to this military role with racial harmony, as I'm sure Takahashi told you. But this notion was compromised early on by the first group of immigrants." His demeanor took on an offensive stance. "Instead of projecting the propaganda notion of racial and cultural harmony with the Manchurians, when they arrived, the Japanese immigrants marched through the streets in rank with the Army to intimidate the locals."

He sighed again and continued. "The settlers looted, swindled and raped the local Chinese. They didn't pioneer uncultivated land or raise the sheep for their wool." He motioned out the window at the picture perfect hillside and took a sip of his tea. "Aided by the heavy-handed methods of the Kwantung Army, the East Asian Development Company, and the Manchukuo government, the settlers simply stole the farms from the Chinese who were pressed into selling their property at rock-bottom prices. Either move out or work for the new Japanese owners as chattel."

He pressed his two weathered hands together. "Here, in this model *Potemkin village*, armed men were sent to settle a land dispute between the Chinese villagers and immigrants. Farmers were either bayoneted if they didn't comply with the Army's orders, or their cattle, dogs, and chickens were butchered."

The priest stared down at his clasped hands. "That's Takahashi's reality of Manchukuo. And Manchuria will be the stepping stone for Japan to become an imperial power like the British and the other European powers—to create a new heaven on earth."

At that moment, a Manchu peasant entered the priest's quarters. When he spotted me, he quickly turned and started to leave.

"Wait," Marquette urged. "Please, Huan. Stay. I want you to meet someone."

The young peasant, dressed in Chinese overalls and a heavy brown parka, eyed me suspiciously. He was not the picture of a happy, pleasant Manchu that was proud to be a citizen of Manchukuo.

"This is Yoshihara Koga," Marquette introduced me. "He's a reporter." He beckoned the peasant over to him, placing his massive hand on the small man's shoulder. "And this here is Huan Quang. His village is near here." He added satirically, "I was informing monsieur Kogo about the wonderful paradise we have here in Manchuria."

Quang just snorted his disapproval.

"What about the natural resources here? How have the Manchus been exploited in that regard?" I asked Marguette.

Quang answered for the priest. "Even more than the farmers."

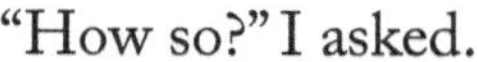

"How so?" I asked.

"Take the mining operation near Pingfang," Quang replied. "It is a large city just an hour or so from here. The mineworkers live in a compound at the mine. They have no comforting homes to go to, or families to celebrate the Banjin Festival with. In truth, they're simply slave laborers made up of Chinese prisoners of war and civilians."

That was not in Sakura's research material. I needed to know more. "I'd like to see that operation."

"Ask Takahashi," Father Marquette scoffed. "He'd be more than happy, *unashamedly*, in fact, to show it off to you."

I had one more burning question on my mind that I felt compelled to ask. "Father Marquette, have you ever heard of something called Unit 731?"

As I said those words, I notice Quang's entire body stiffen.

"You know something about it?" I asked the peasant.

He was about to reply when we heard a car rumbling down the street. I glanced out the window then back to Quang and Marquette. In a flash, Quang had disappeared out the back door of the dwelling.

"You should go as well," Marquette instructed.

I stood to leave, and extended my hand to the priest's. "Thank you for your time, Father. I would very much like to speak to Quang. I think he knows something about Unit 731. Do you know where I can find him?"

Marquette shook his head. "I don't know. He..." Marquette stopped himself and then repeated, "I don't know."

After I left the priest's home, I sought out Takahashi, whose staff car was parked down the street.

"Where were you?" he demanded.

"Got lost," I replied.

Takahashi gave me an unconvinced look but let my response pass when I asked, "I'd like to see an example of the natural resources acquired here. Are there any nearby?"

"Hai. There's one about an hour from here near Harbin, the largest city in Manchukuo."

I followed my tour guide back to the waiting car, and we set out on our way.

Family Reunion

An hour later, we approached the mining facility that stood many miles west of Pingfang. Takahashi pointed out the large compound of workers surrounding the mining operation. I wondered if the Manchus were volunteer workers or pressed labor.

Takahashi answered my question. "The Manchus are paid workers. It's part of our shared enculturation process." His voice had a ring of sarcasm to it. "But the Chinese prisoners of war and Chinese civilians, that's another matter. We sell their services to the mining company."

Slave labor by any other name, I thought.

We drove past the mine and stopped at a small quasi-Japanese style house outside of the workers' compound of thatched roofs and mud walls. "This is the Director's home. He lives here with his family."

We approached the entrance to the house and removed our shoes. Takahashi knocked on the door, and we waited.

A few moments later, a young, attractive Japanese girl, wearing a blue kimono with an ornate butterfly pattern, answered the door. She was no more than thirteen. "How may I help you, Officer?"

"Is your father at home?"

"Yes. Please come in," she replied.

She led us into a tasteful, well-appointed living area unlike what you would expect in a Manchurian home. "Please have a seat," the young teenager offered pleasantly. "I'll get Papa-san."

A few moments later, a middle-aged man with short-cropped black hair and a weathered face, wearing round, rimmed glasses and sporting a thin mustache, entered the room. "Oi. Welcome, Major Takahashi." Then he turned to stare at me. "Hello, Yoshihara."

"You know me? Have we met?" I asked, quite frankly puzzled.

"I've followed your news articles for many years. I'm Masao Koga," he half-smirked with a hint of antagonism as he let his name sink in. "I'm your older brother."

I stood speechless. A beat later, I finally found my voice, but it quivered feebly. "I... *we*... thought you were dead."

His mood turned dark. "I *am* dead—to our family."

I turned over in my mind the story my mother told me only once, in secret, and when my father was away from the house.

Masao was responsible for my mother and father leaving Japan with me many years ago. My father saw what was happening in Japan. The nationalist politics and military propaganda were becoming overwhelming. My father wanted no part of it for himself or his family. He was an outspoken opponent of what the militarists were doing to his country, and found himself to be constantly harassed by the police.

But when Masao, his oldest son, succumbed to the propaganda and joined the Black Ocean Society, an ultra-nationalist organization, my father made up his mind that I was not to be subjected to the growing indoctrination of the Japanese youth, and moved me far enough away so the propaganda could not pervert my ideals.

I wanted tell him that, but with Takahashi here, I kept my thoughts to myself.

"I don't know quite what to say. All this... is rather shocking."

Masao appeared to take some form of delight in my utter state of bewilderment. "I suppose we have much to catch up on."

"Hai. Are you the director here at the mine?" I asked.

Masao nodded. "A reward for my service."

I could guess what that service may have entailed. The Black

Ocean Society had been founded by Hiraoka Kotaro in the late 1800s. Kotaro was a wealthy ex-samurai and mine owner, with, coincidently enough, mining interests in Manchuria. I assumed Masao's reward was running this mine.

I sensed Takahashi smirking beside me. The man found the air of tension between my brother and I quite amusing.

Masao looked at Takahashi, and his mood turned somewhat affable. "But enough of that. We are just sitting down to dinner. Please join us."

He led us into the dining room that was traditionally Japanese endowed with a low table with soft cushions on the floor surrounding it. Seated at the table was a woman about Masao's age, who was dressed in a traditional Japanese robe, the young teenager daughter I met at the door, and a little girl in a bright yellow kimono, no more than eight years old.

Masao started the introductions. "This is my wife Mayumi, my daughter Keiko, and my youngest, Karin. We already know Major Takahashi, of course."

I nodded and bowed to Masao's family, though I was still quite taken back by the unexpected reunion with my older brother. Not only that, but now I was being introduced to my nieces for the very first time. "I'm Yoshihara Koga," I stammered. I looked at the two children and smiled awkwardly. "I am your uncle... and I'm honored to meet you."

Mayumi bowed her head in return, but her face was impossible to read. "What brings you to our village, Yoshihara-san?"

I attempted to regain my composure the best I could. "I'm a reporter with the *Tokyo Nichinichi Shimbun*. I'm doing a story here on Manchukuo, and I'd like to learn more about the mining operation here."

"We'll talk business after dinner," Masao replied gruffly as a young female Manchu entered the room. She wore a traditional single pigtail, and at the end of her hair, a red cord wrapped around the tip. The young woman's bangs were cut short and straight across, and a small, metal bead was fastened on the tip of the pigtail. She carried a tray of miso soup, octopus, and cucumber salad.

"Lunch is served, *brother*," Masao declared in a tone that seemed to mock our relationship.

The young Manchu approached our table and instantly froze. She began to shake, causing the bowls to clink together like the rattling teeth of a cartoon character. Her dark brown eyes were wide in distress as she stared at the Kempeitai insignia on Takahashi's uniform.

A moment later another sound joined the clinking of the bowls. It was the sound of trickling liquid. I glanced down at the young Manchu's feet to witness a pool of yellow spreading across the floor.

The terrified woman had lost control of her bladder.

"Li!" Masao snapped. "Leave immediately." He then turned to his guests. "I am so sorry. She hasn't been feeling well." But Li didn't look sick to me. In fact, she looked in the prime of health.

Masao's wife ushered the young Manchu out of the room, and returned with the soup and salad as another servant cleaned up the urine. Mayumi served us and urged us to eat, hoping that we could forget the incident.

"Li is our nanny and housekeeper. My children adore her," Masao said looking into his soup and more to himself than us.

We all let the matter rest, but the amount of terror in the young woman's eyes haunted me for the entire meal. Sure, the sight of a Kempeitai can provoke fear in most people, even the Japanese, but to experience such a reaction from the Manchu girl who was supposed to be living peacefully and happily in this oasis that had been provided her? It honestly did not make sense to me.

After dinner, Masao invited us into the living area for sake. His wife, Mayumi, served the three of us and then left with the children.

I tried to put the surprise of my resurrected brother out of my mind for the moment, and focus on the reason I was there. "Are the Manchus happy working in the mine?"

"Oh, yes." Masao replied. "They are well cared for here. If and when they are unable to complete their trying work in the mine, they are sent to the Epidemic Prevention and Water Purification Department to work there instead. The duties are far less laborious at that facility."

I thought that was an odd name for a medical clinic, but I didn't question it. So, I dared asked what I really wanted to know. "Then, no forced labor?"

Masao answered without the slightest bit of hesitation. "We purchase their services from the Kwantung Army." He replied as if the exploitation of these human beings was a normal everyday business transaction.

"Can I see the mining operation?"

Masao looked over at the Kempeitai. "Oi. Of course. I'll be leaving for the mine soon, and I'd be thrilled to share my success here with *family*," he smirked with a twinge of arrogance.

I turned to Takahashi for his reaction. Or was it consent? "Is that permitted?"

"Hai," he said gruffly. "I'm due at headquarters. Perhaps Masao can put his brother up for the night. A long overdue family reunion?" He smiled.

Takahashi arose from his seat, and without so much of a nod or a sayonara, he abruptly left for his staff car.

The Mine

As we traveled to the mine the next morning in his personal vehicle, Masao took it upon himself to lecture me. "Mining is expensive. Not like the other businesses here in Manchukuo. The challenge is simple. Maximize profit in order to pay the bills, and get a good return on investment. ROI."

The idea of him using slave labor never seemed to enter into his explanation, but I wasn't prepared to press the point. I had to remember I was a guest of Takahashi and the Kwantung Army, and I surely did not want to remain there as one of their *happy citizens*.

An hour later, Masao and I arrived at the sprawling mining operation. I noticed a high perimeter fence around the mine, manned and armed by Kwantung soldiers.

Seeing Masao, the guards passed us through the main gate without delay and toward a large mine entrance that was dug into the side of one of the low-rising hills. In front and to the sides of the entrance, were massive piles of dirt and debris, the result of the constant and invasive tunneling.

Masao led me towards the mine entrance, handed me a steel hard hat, and pointed to an elevator shaft in front of us. "This elevator takes the miners down almost a mile into the pit where it connects with several miles of tunnels."

At that moment, a middle-aged Japanese man strolled past us. Masao noticed and motioned for him to join us. "This is Kaji

Yamamura. He is my supervisor here. Kaji, this is Yoshihara Koga. A newsman."

"Nice to meet you," Yamamura replied.

"You as well. Can I ask, what do you mine here?"

"Coal, mainly," the mining supervisor replied.

"Would you like to go down and take a look for yourself?" Masao said.

I hesitated.

"Oi. Don't worry, brother." He placed his arm around me. "It's safe," he laughed.

As we approached the elevator, I heard yelling and screaming to my left. A Japanese foreman was beating a Chinese miner with a pick handle. The poor, little man was groveling on the ground with hands held above him in the futile attempt to ward off the blows. Once the assault was over, two guards dragged the unconscious—or dead—miner away.

I stared at Masao, whose face showed zero affect. The incident didn't make an impression on him in the least. "It saddens me to see that, but sometimes it must be done to..." he searched for the right words, "...to stay on a tight schedule." He said this without a hint of empathy in his voice.

On the other hand, Yamamura averted his glance, and I could see the disgust in his eyes.

Masao pulled me away from the entrance to allow the guards to pass by with the bloodied miner.

However brutal and senseless the miner's beating happened to be, the distraction proved to save our lives.

As I stood there, staring with horrified dismay at the limp and disfigured body of the miner, I felt a heavy, abrupt rumbling beneath our feet that slowly subsided after a few seconds.

A moment of calm, then an explosion.

To my left, towering flames burst out of the mine entrance, instantly incinerating the two guards and the miner. The fireball ripped passed my face, singeing my skin and day old beard. I was tossed off my feet when another explosion erupted below, and the ground under our feet tilted downward.

The earth opened up below my feet, and I felt a hand yank me by the neck and pull me away. I landed face down, just feet from the gaping abyss.

When I looked up, I saw Yamamura standing over me. I could tell by the look in his eyes that he was utterly alarmed, and he appeared to be speaking to me, although I couldn't understand a single word as my ears were ringing like church bells.

Dozens of guards and miners scrambling around in a state of panic. The ringing in my ears slowly ebbed to a dull buzz. I could hear the guards shouting orders to seal the mine and cut off the ventilation in order to smother the fire. My stomach tightened with the realization that there would be no attempt in rescuing the miners trapped below.

It required every fiber of my will not to run toward the opening to try and save at least one man.

I had no idea how many miners might be trapped in the unchecked inferno, and as the guards rushed to close off the hole, I imagined the helpless workers waiting, wondering when they would be saved. I knew that their hope would drain as quickly as the oxygen disappeared from their tomb.

Their final gasps would confirm their darkest fears. They were not necessary. They were not needed. They were expendable and nothing more than collateral damage in a war they didn't even know about it. One by one, each man would die, forgotten in the belly of the pit.

Yamamura grabbed my shoulder and led Masao and I away from the disaster. As we neared the front gate, the ringing in my ears finally subsided enough that I could hear the simple message spoken by Masao. "We must leave."

I nodded in agreement, and as we drove back toward his home, I remained silent. Perhaps my silence may have been an opportunity for my hearing to be totally restored. Or perhaps it may have given me time to decide what I really need to say. As we pulled into Masao's driveway, I leaned forward and asked,"How many miners?"

"I don't know," he said quietly. "We'll have a report in the morning." After some thought he added, "This will not make the Army happy. It could set us back many weeks."

"You mean to find the miners sealed in the pit, correct?"

"Hai," he replied.

But I knew in my heart that wasn't the first thing on his mind. I would ultimately find out that close to a thousand miners had died in that disaster.

Sadly, I would also discover the disaster at the mining operation wouldn't be the worst part of the story of the Manchu villagers.

Hiroshima Bay

For the last six months of 1940, the radio had been repeatedly broadcasting the song *2600 Years Since the Foundation*, announcing the arrival of the *Hakko ichiu*, the 2,600th anniversary of the founding of the Empire of Japan.

According to the imperial myth, Emperor Jimmu descended from the Sun Goddess, Amaterasu, thus establishing the unbroken imperial line in 660 BCE on this day, making all five races in Japan brothers and united as one. The government saw an opportunity and fully embraced this holiday after the Prime Minister, Fumimaro Kanoe, referenced it in a speech.

The expression, *All the world under one roof,* referred to the roof that covered all of Asia. It stressed that Asia was the key, and that all Asians needed to fight for every single fellow Asian. Movies were created and songs were written and young people were hypnotized by this grand idea of their all-powerful culture.

The marching song, *2600 Years Since the Foundation* became mandatory in every school, and every student was forced to memorize the lyrics.

During the time of the actual celebration, the streets of Hiroshima were lit with lantern processions and decorated streetcars. The streetcars created a dazzling display of lights as they traveled throughout the city.

But for Hiryo, Yoshi, Connor and Kenji, the real show was in Hiroshima Bay. The boys hurried to the docks early in the morning to await the display of Japanese naval power firing their guns to celebrate the first day of the 2,600th Year.

The four boys lined up alongside thousands of other Hiroshima residents to witness the massive guns of His Imperial Majesty's battleships, cruisers, and destroyers, ring in the New Year.

Uncommon and brutal icy winds swept over the crowd who huddled together for warmth. The cold chill that stung their noses and numbed their fingertips was not going to prevent them from the wonder they were going to observe at nine a.m.

As the clock struck the hour, a great roar of canon fire from the entire fleet erupted in a simultaneous salute. Yoshi and Hiryo danced about in glee at the sight of real warships firing their guns. The explosions boomed in the air and echoed for moments that were long enough to still be resounding as the next shots were fired. The volley of explosions echoed through the frigid sky, lighting the water below and rippling across the waves.

How could something so beautiful and powerful possibly be wrong?

"Japan has a real Navy!" Yoshi exclaimed.

"The world's most powerful Navy!" Hiryo enjoined.

But the magnificent display didn't have the same effect on young Kenji. "If it was a real war," he countered, "the enemy wouldn't just sit still. They'd fire back."

Connor winced at Kenji's loud remark because he knew what would come next.

"Whose side are *you* on anyway?" exclaimed several people standing around the boys. Men, young and old, circled around Kenji.

Hiryo pulled Kenji back from the gathering crowd, and shepherded him and Yoshi away from the docks. Connor kept his head down and quickly followed after his brothers.

As the group of boys walked back home, Connor whispered to Kenji, "You really need to be more careful about what you say. You don't have to agree with it, but you can't say it out loud, at least not in a crowd."

Kenji looked up at his American brother, nodded silently, then squeezed Connor's hand.

Kenji

A few mornings later, as Kenji reluctantly prepared for another day of school, Connor rolled over in his bed and saw the hesitation in Kenji's behavior. The boy fiddled with his shirt, checked in his school bag several times, stood up, then promptly sat back down on the bed.

"What's the matter, squirt," Connor finally asked.

"I don't want to go to school," he said dropping his chin to his chest. "It's not fair. *You* don't have to."

"I have my reasons," Connor replied.

"So do I. I'm scared of those boys from the parade," Kenji said nervously. "Some of them go to my school, and they hate me."

Connor patted the young boy on the shoulder. "I'll walk with you to school. How's that?"

Kenji perked up immediately. "Really? First class, Joe!"

Connor laughed. "Let's get some breakfast first." He leaned over and rubbed Kenji's stomach like a puppy.

After the boys finished their breakfast, they said goodbye to Miyoko and Suki before heading off to Kenji's school. As they walked along the sidewalk, Connor said nothing about his decision of not returning to the British school. Instead, he and Kenji simply enjoyed the fresh morning air, the singing birds in the trees providing a soundtrack to their stroll.

"You know, Joe, we have to be careful now," Kenji finally said.

"Of who? Those kids from the parade?" Connor asked.

"No. The Guidance League. Especially now that you're skipping school."

"Who are they?"

"Vigilantes who look for juvenile delinquents. If they catch you, they tell your parents," Kenji warned.

Connor just shrugged his shoulders. He was pretty adept at dodging the truant officers back in San Diego, so surely it wouldn't be any harder to get away from something called a *league*. After all, he had stolen a plane before and got away with it.

Almost.

Connor looked down at little Kenji and just shook his head. He felt bad for Kenji. He knew the drill. He'd seen it a dozen times in the States. Kids like Kenji were easy targets because they were different. Wedgies in the locker room, pink-bellies after school, cruel notes taped to your back, stealing your books and wrecking your locker. The only thing Kenji could do was keep his head down and run when necessary. Connor had learned the futility of fighting back the hard way.

Connor couldn't help but notice what a beautiful morning it was in Hiroshima. He took another deep breath and thought, *How could such a day bring anything about that isn't good and happy?*

They arrived at the school and toward a tall hedge of bushes that decorated the schoolyard. Kenji had his nose buried between the pages of a *Popeye* comic book and was giggling about a funny joke he was reading when they turned the corner. Kenji abruptly froze in his tracks, and his comic hit the pavement.

"What's the matter," Connor asked.

Kenji pointed a finger toward four boys standing by the front door of the school. "Them," he said in a fearful voice.

As soon as Kenji made the statement, the four boys spotted him and lumbered towards them. They were much older than both Kenji and Connor and looked as if they were almost twenty. Three of them were lean with coal-colored eyes and dark black hair cut in military fashion. The fourth was heftier than the other three

and looked twice as mean. They all wore their school's required military garbs.

"There he is," one of the tall boys sneered. "There's the little coward."

Kenji turned to run, but Connor caught him by arm, then faced the group of boys. "What's your problem?"

"*Problem*? We want to teach that little American want-to-be a lesson in being Japanese," the biggest boy threatened, clenching his fists at his sides. As the boy moved towards Kenji, Connor stepped in front of his little brother.

The hefty boy reached out to grab Kenji, but Connor slapped his hand away.

"Fine. You want to play hero?"

The boy swung a fist at Connor, who intercepted the blow, grabbed his arm, and flipped the startled kid over onto his back with his best judo move.

The burly teen flailed on the ground, his uniform and face covered in dirt, and yelled to his friends. "Don't just stand there... get him!"

On the big boy's command, the other three boys threw themselves at Connor. At first, Connor managed to ward off their attack with what he knew of judo, but he was outnumbered and soon found himself pinned to the ground by one of the boys while another pressed a boot against his neck.

"Hold him still. Let's take care of the American-lover first," the heavy boy ordered and turned his attention to Kenji.

Kenji turned to escape and ran right into the fourth boy, who had snuck up behind him. The tall thug picked Kenji up by the neck, dangling him in the air.

"Let me alone," the little boy gasped. His arms and legs swung frantically but did little to help him escape. As he continued to squirm, his shirt rose up and left his stomach exposed.

The heavy boy seized the opportunity and pulled back his arm to prepare for an excruciating blow to the gut.

Connor struggled to get free of the two boys holding him on

the ground, but they were too strong. He felt his throat close from the pressure of the boot crushing his neck, but he fought anyway.

Not today. Not Kenji.

Blood trickled from the corners of his mouth as he kept struggling to free himself. He'd rather die before letting anyone hurt his brother.

"Drop... him..." Connor rasped.

A voice from behind Connor boomed down the street, "You heard the boy. Drop him!"

The weight of the boot eased off Connor's neck, and as he gasped for air, he watched two boys and a young woman march toward him. The leader, about twenty years old, was shirtless, revealing ornate tattoos covering his upper body except for his face, and was completely covered in colorful ornate art, unaffected by the chill in the air.

The second boy, about Connor's age, wore a shirt, and looked as if he had been in his own share of fights before. Connor could see no discernible tattoos.

But the girl was even more shocking than the two boys. Her entire face was covered with the head of a dragon tattoo that flowed down her tight fitting blouse.

And there was something else, something both striking and shocking. As she approached, Connor could see the need for her face tattoo. The eyes of the dragon covered a hideous scar.

The four school thugs froze, and the stout boy whispered fearfully, "*Yakuza*," and dropped Kenji with a thud to the ground.

"Go," the lead Yakuza commanded the schoolyard thugs, and they promptly fled down the street. "And if you touch this boy again, we'll kill you," he shouted after them.

There was a long moment of silence as the three Yakuza looked over Connor who sat on the ground, still attempting to regain his breath. Connor had no idea what *Yakuza* meant. For all he knew, they could be worse than the boys that were just harassing them.

The boy with the chest of tattoos leaned down and pressed his face within inches of Connor's face. "Ijin," he snarled.

"And you're no different, Goro?" The young dragon-tattooed Yakuza woman countered in a flat monotone voice. "We are all buraku."

Goro pulled back from Connor and continued to sneer at the young American.

"Kodo is right," the second boy added.

The young woman strolled up to Connor with a devious smile. "We, too, are gaishin. Aliens. Outcasts. I am Kodo Tento, and these are Goro Yoshida and Jiro Miyagi." Her deep green eyes sparkled as she stared into Connor's.

Goro noticed the connection between the two, and pulled her away from Connor. "And you, Ijin. Go back to where you came from."

As the trio walked away, Kodo glanced over her shoulder toward Connor, and she smiled. Then they were gone.

Planning for War
Hoping for Peace

I desperately wanted to return to Masao's mining operation to find out if there were any survivors, but I had to file my report. While I pondered what to write, I arranged to meet with representatives of the East Asian Development Company and the Manchuria Colonial Development Company for further interviews.

During this time, the debate in the government over joining the Tripartite Pact with Germany and Italy came to a head in September of 1940. A divided administration guided Japan towards war, even though some in the Diet questioned the strategic problems it posed.

The Navy was much more hesitant to sign the Pact and join what was now called the Axis. The Imperial Navy feared the impressive strength of the American Navy.

Prime Minister Konoe, essentially a peace-loving man, and with the support of Yamamoto, strongly urged against joining the Axis. Minister of War, Hideki Tojo, however, pressed to sign the Pact.

Ultimately, the anti-war faction in the Diet lost the argument, and Saburo Kurusu went to Germany to sign the Pact for Japan.

In response, the American government quickly restricted and eventually cut off exports of oil and other vital resources to Japan. These sanctions swiftly brought events to a head. Yamamoto warned that Japan had no domestic oil production to speak of, and would exhaust its entire stockpile within a year.

Japan needed another source of oil, and its eyes turned towards

Indonesia. The quick victories by Germany against Allied territories and the occupation of Paris emboldened the Army, and their leaders became increasingly more belligerent.

Tojo argued, "Now is the time to strike! The European colonial powers are distracted by the German and Italian victories and are pulling their armies out of Indonesia to support the war effort in Europe. The natural resources of the European colonies in Southeast Asia are an easy target."

Prime Minister Konoe cautioned, "We must remember that there is an American Army in the Philippines. It stands between Indonesia and us."

"That is exactly why we need a plan to remove the American obstacle," Tojo countered. "And we must do it soon while Roosevelt's attention is on Europe."

Yamamoto, realizing he had lost the fight to keep Japan out of war, fell in line with the planning process and returned to his command on the battleship *Nagato* in Hiroshima Bay.

The very next day, Fujiyama entered Yamamoto's wardroom and handed him a recent report. "Sir, Roosevelt has ordered the American Fleet out of San Diego. It's to be stationed in Pearl Harbor."

Yamamoto scanned the report. "So, Roosevelt is rattling his sword. He's brought the United States Navy within striking distance of Japan. He's trying to intimidate us." His eyebrows knitted together. "But what Roosevelt has really done is place his navy within striking distance of *us* putting America in a vulnerable position."

"What do we do?" asked Fujiyama.

"We continue with our planning." The Admiral's mind raced with various scenarios. "What a peculiar position I find myself in. Having been assigned a mission diametrically opposed to my own personal opinion, but with no choice but to push full speed in pursuance of that very mission." He looked up at Fujiyama. "Oi, is that fate?"

Fujiyama didn't respond directly to the query, as he respected the terrible position his Admiral had been placed in. "What about Yoshida? As the new Navy Minister replacing you, can he still oppose the Army?"

"Hai. But I have little confidence in him succeeding."

"There's always the Emperor," Fujiyama replied. "Perhaps he would intervene with a sacred decision against war, abrogate the Tripartite Pact, and pull Japanese troops out of China."

"We can only hope," Yamamoto sadly replied. "We can only hope."

Yakuza

While I was in Manchukuo, Connor's life was about to take a crucial turn. The young boy was unaware of the catastrophic events building around him in the world while trying to find himself at the same time. He had no idea that finding his path and those events building around him might go hand in hand.

Fujiyama and his wife agreed that with the clouds of war gathering, it wouldn't be a good idea to send Connor back to the British School. It would not be safe for him. Unfortunately, Fujiyama wasn't entirely sure that there *was* a place safe for him. And out of Connor's yearning to be part of something Japanese, this *need* would eventually place the young boy, Fujiyama, and his family, directly in harm's way.

It began with an unexpected greeting in late 1940 after one of the intermittent flying lessons with Fujiyama.

"Hey! Ijin," asked a voice walking up from behind Connor. "Where you think you're going?"

Connor turned and saw Jiro Miyagi, one of the boys in the Yakuza group that had defended him and Kenji. Jiro walked with great purpose and confidence. And even though the teen wasn't especially big or menacing looking, the way he carried himself made him stand out in a way that demanded respect. Connor instantly felt the same way for Jiro even though he didn't really know him.

"No place in particular," Connor replied as he walked along the shore of Hiroshima Bay. The ocean breezes blew through his mind and helped clear away his troubles.

As he watched the boy approach, he wasn't sure what Jiro might want. Gratitude? Repayment? To be the harasser now? "Why do you want to know?"

"I saw the way you handled yourself with those nationalist thugs," Jiro smiled. "Damn good. Where'd you learn judo?" Connor felt an instant wave of relief. It appeared that Jiro just wanted to talk, nothing more. "In America. My father taught me." Connor eyed the young boy and added, "And the Code."

Jiro leaned closer to Connor. "The Samurai Code?"

Connor nodded.

"Well, you certainly fought like a Samurai. Courageous, loyal, and with honor."

"What do you know of the Code?"

"My friends and I follow the Code as well," Jiro replied. "And because of that, we are respected."

"But that girl in your group said you were outcasts in Japan. How can you be respected? Code or not?"

Jiro laughed. "A code of honor is a code of honor. Loyalty and respect is our Code."

"I try to live the Code," Connor said almost to himself.

"And you are not respected for living it, because you are not Japanese? Am I correct?"

Connor looked toward the sky for a moment, the clouds swirled overhead like a dream. He had always hoped and prayed there might be a day when someone actually understood how he felt. Did Jiro really understand?

And Jiro was right, of course. No matter how much Connor believed in the Samurai Code, no matter how much he dedicated himself to the code of the martial arts, he would never be respected or accepted as Japanese.

"Would you like to know how people like us practice the Code?" Jiro asked.

Connor nodded.

"Then come with me." Jiro said. He started to walk away from Connor, giving the boy an opportunity to decide if he wanted to follow or not. As Jiro was just about to disappear down an alleyway, Connor caught back up with him. "Come with you *where*?"

Jiro grinned. "To a party."

Birds of a Feather

As the two boys walked together, a heavy rain began to fall, and thunder clapped in the same skies that once held the harmless clouds. They made their way under the overhangs that protected the doors of the alley as water trickled onto them and splashed around their feet like tiny explosions.

Jiro wiped the rain from his face and glanced over at Connor. "You said your *father* taught you judo. I didn't know Americans practiced the martial arts. I thought that was strictly Japanese."

"My father *is* Japanese. My new father." He went on to tell Jiro of how an American boy came to be part of a Japanese family. It was the first time outside the family that Connor had told anyone his story.

Then it was Connor's turn to ask the questions. "Those nationalist thugs said you were *Yakuza*. What does that mean?"

"The word, Yakuza," Jiro replied, "means eight-nine-three. In Japanese, Ya equals eight, ku equals nine, za equals three. Thus, *Yakuza*. It comes from the Japanese version of Black Jack. You know Blackjack?"

Connor nodded. "Played it all the time in the States."

"Well, the main difference between the Japanese version and Western version is that in our version, the goal is to reach nineteen instead of twenty-one."

"But the sum of eight, nine and three, is 20," Connor noted.

"Correct. The sum of twenty is good for nothing. *Yakuza*—good-for-nothing. We don't fit in. We're society's misfits."

Connor could identify with that label. The irony was actually quite poetic. A group of misfits that fit in nowhere, actually fit in with one another. They are good for nothing apart, but together, *that* was something spectacular.

"Over there," Jiro pointed. The alleyway led to an open concrete lot that bordered the water. As their feet splashed through the growing puddles, the drops seemed to announce their arrival.

A few seconds later, Connor found himself standing in the center of an abandoned industrial warehouse near the Hiroshima docks. The building stood two-stories tall, with concrete floors and massive columns. Many of the glass and wire-mesh windows overhead were shattered, and the light from the lamp posts that guarded the shore, streamed through, painting strange and eerie patterns on the floor. The patterns pirouetted up and down as the water from the rains trickled across the existing glass. Other than the constant patter of rain against the roof, silence surrounded them. It definitely didn't seem like there was a party of any kind going on.

Wooden crates lined the walls and a dilapidated staircase hung from the rafters as Jiro lead him through the cavernous hulk to a small door in the back of the warehouse.

"Wait here," he whispered and slipped inside a darkened room. When the door slammed shut behind him, the sound echoed throughout the building.

Connor wiped his blond hair out of his face and dried his blue eyes with his shirt. He wrung the water that had soaked into his sleeves, and was thankful the old building was now keeping him dry. He waited for what felt like an eternity, wondering what he was doing there. Had this been a trick?

After a few more minutes, Jiro finally reappeared. "Come on. I want you to meet some of my friends."

The two boys entered a room inundated with cigarette smoke that hung like gray clouds. Through the haze, Connor noticed several Yakuza boys, some without shirts, showing off their elaborate tattoos. There were several Western style chairs and a long, wooden table with low chairs in the center of the room.

And there was something else about the room. It was cold. Very cold. The windows that lined the walls were wide open to the unseasonable cold and rainy weather that squeezed in from outside. Then Connor spotted a figure sprawled out on top of the long table. A female figure.

As he approached for a better look, Connor could see the girl, laid out as if in a morgue, was completely naked and covered from head to toe with assorted, ornate tattoos. And placed on top of her naked flesh was a wide assortment of sushi.

As Connor watched, men took turns leaning over the human platter, consuming the sushi directly with their mouths instead of chopsticks. Loud guffaws would burst from the crowd of men, followed by clapping, in response to any Yakuza eating his piece of sushi from the woman's groin or breast area.

"Nyotaimori," Jiro noted, pointing to the naked buffet. It was the most decadent thing Connor had ever seen. In his wildest dreams, he had never imagined such beauty would come in this form, but he was not offended or confused, he was quite simply in awe.

As Connor stared through the haze of cigarette smoke, and down at the woman's naked body, he realized it was the young Yakuza girl he met the other day. Now, in her complete nudity, he could see the extent of the woman's tattooing. The ink designs reached all the way down both her legs, right to her ankles, accentuating every delicious curve of her body.

A primitive impulse of desire arose in Connor's belly. One he had never experienced before. Lust. For the first time, he felt sexual longing, and it felt good.

"Recognize her?" asked Jiro. "That's Kodo."

Connor, mesmerized, bent over and stared a little closer. He cocked his head to the side and observed her motionless frame, as she stared into space with almost unblinking eyes.

On closer inspection, he noticed something else. The tip of the pinky on her left hand had been severed off.

The young American teen slowly shook his head, absorbing

everything, his mouth agape. After a moment, he finally found his voice. "You sit around and eat sushi off her body?"

"Hai," a belligerent voice said. "She makes a perfect serving table." Goro Yoshida glared at Connor before looking over to Jiro. "Why is *he* here?"

Goro's tone should have instilled some type of fear in Connor, but he could think of nothing but the girl, her hypnotizing green eyes, and how desperately he wanted to touch her skin.

"On my invitation," Jiro replied.

"He is not Japanese," Goro spat. "Nor is he Yakuza. He does not belong here."

"And neither do I, Goro. But he lives as a Japanese. He was adopted by a Japanese family while in America. His adopted father is a Commander in the Japanese Navy. Commander Fujiyama."

Still, Goro was not impressed. But through the cloud of cigarette smoke in the warehouse, someone cleared his throat off in dark corner of room. Goro glanced over his shoulder, nodded toward the figure in the shadows, then walked off.

Connor, finally breaking the trance that Kodo held over him, turned and looked toward a tall man in a dark, expensive business suit.

Connor tried not to stare at the man in the suit, then spoke to Jiro. "You told Goro you were not Yakuza."

"Hai. I am *not* a member. I wear no tattoos."

"Why do they let you stay?"

"That girl," he said pointing to Kodo, "is my half-sister." He placed a hand on Connor's shoulder. "You can practice the Code with me. With us, if you choose."

Connor's thoughts kept turning back to Kodo. "Tell me about your half-sister."

Jiro smiled. "You find her interesting?"

Connor nodded. "That scar on her face. How did she get it?"

"From an abusive client. He cut her for not performing properly."

"Client? You mean she's a prostitute?"

"*Was* a prostitute," Jiro replied. "A hinin. Considered subhuman." Jiro's mood darkened. "Kodo was forced to cover the permanent scars with Yakuza tattoos. Before Kodo, it was unheard of for the Yakuza to tattoo their faces."

Connor realized that his discrimination didn't hold a candle to what Kodo or what the Yakuza had experienced.

"And what happened to her finger?"

"Oi. She cut it off."

"Why?"

"She cut the tip off of her pinky with a short sword in a ritual called *Yubizume*," Jiro said. "My step-sister is a bit of a wild one. She disobeyed an order from a head Yakuza. To regain his graces, she had to perform this act of contrition."

Courage and sacrifice, thought Connor. Then he wondered out loud, "Why aren't you a Yakuza?"

"I'm happy where I am," he replied. "And so should you be."

Yes, Jiro was right. Connor would be content just being an accepted part of something.

A few moments later, the feast of Nyotaimori finished, Kodo arose from the table, giving Connor a full frontal view of her naked body, and then slipped on a robe. As she draped it over her shoulders, she didn't bother to tie the material in the front, leaving herself exposed. She moved with such grace and elegance, as though she had emerged from a Japanese fairy tale and had the ability to walk an inch above the ground.

"I noticed that you didn't eat. You don't like sushi," she asked with a shameless smile. She walked around them, allowing the silk of her robe to rub across the skin on Connors arm.

Connor wanted to say something clever, *do* something impressive, but all he could do was stare at the semi-nude, beautiful young woman who stood brazenly before him. It was not only her body that mesmerized him. Her inner-strength and presence was unmatched by any woman he had ever met, especially any Japanese woman.

"No appetite?" she flirted. "Or maybe not for *food?*" Kodo gave Connor a final *come-hither* smirk, then walked off as slowly as she possibly could.

This was too much for Goro, who was standing next to the well-dressed man in the back of the room. "Leave it be," the well-dressed man ordered. "Bring the American over to me."

Goro marched over and pulled on Connor's arm. "Come with me."

Connor resisted, but gave in when Jiro nodded to him that it was okay.

Goro ushered Connor over to where the man was standing. "This is Colonel Sato of the Japanese Imperial Army," Goro said.

Connor stared at the man, getting a close-up view of the nasty scar that ran from his half-closed eye to the bottom of his cheek.

"You are called Connor? Correct?" Sato said pleasantly, his voice in direct contrast to his ominous looks.

"Hai."

"I overheard you with Jiro. You speak Japanese very well. Taught to you by your Japanese parents?"

"Hai. My adopted father is a fighter pilot in the Japanese Imperial Navy. Fujiyama."

"Oi. I know of Commander Fujiyama. A true war hero." Sato rubbed at the whiskers on his chin. "You have many questions about the Yakuza, no?"

Connor relaxed a bit and nodded.

"Many think the Yakuza are criminals," Sato stated. "And I guess there is a certain amount of truth to that. But they do very import-ant things for our country as well."

"How?" Connor asked.

"You understand Japan is being threatened on all sides, both from within and without. There are those who would have Japan submit to the European powers. Some call them appeasers. In reality, they are *traitors*." He almost spit the word out.

Connor reflected upon recent conversations he had with Yoshi and Hiryo and his experience with the Brits and American students at the International school. It was all coming together. He was starting to understand.

"The Yakuza seek out these traitors and enlighten them of the error of their ways and thinking." Sato stared at Connor with unchecked intensity. "Let me ask you, would you allow anyone to bring harm to your family?"

Connor shook his head. "Never. I'd rather die first."

Sato smiled. Then took on a serious tone. "Those that seek to harm Japan will harm the Japanese nation *and* its families."

What Sato didn't tell him, was that the Yakuza were not just a criminal gang. In fact, the government found a use for the Yakuza as an aid to the ultranationalists. In the past, the Yakuza were used by the Kempeitai for assassinations and blackmail of two prime ministers and two finance ministers and repeated attacks on other politicians and certain industrialists.

Connor pondered the logic of Sato's last statement. He thought for a moment and then said, "Jiro says he and the Yakuza are *buraku*."

"Hai," Sato replied. "Nearly sixty percent of the Yakuza are buraku. Very little is open to the buraku in Japan. They are outcasts at the bottom of the Japanese social order. Because of that, the buraku have been the victims of severe discrimination and banishment in Japanese society." He took a step closer to Connor, and his one eye seemed to stare directly into Connor's soul. "They are *eta*. The *unwashed*. The filthy masses."

Sato saw the alienated expression in Connor's eyes as he described the buraku and the teen's reaction to the word *eta*. He could read Connor, and that was a skill more powerful than any other.

Sato could see how the Yakuza enticed the young American, and he knew there was potential use for him, especially since he was so closely connected to Fujiyama.

Jiro approached and asked Connor if he wanted to try a little sake.

Sato nodded. "Good. Go with Jiro. We'll talk again later, Connor-san."

After the two boys went to the table and poured themselves

some sake, Sato turned to Goro. "We can use the American." Goro nodded his head in agreement. He wasn't about to question Sato. Not now. Not ever.

Flight Training

In February of 1941, Hiryo, who entered flight training six months before, studied at the Imperial Japanese Naval Academy in Etajima, Hiroshima, a small island in Hiroshima Bay. The island, blessed with large quantities of oranges, and situated nearly five miles out to sea, was a perfect training ground.

Hiryo had finished his intermediate training and was ready to proceed to carrier flight school.

Though he sailed through basic flight training because of the flying experience that he learned while he was young, he made a few mistakes during his intermediate training. Due to his miscalculations, he experienced the harsh discipline that was meted out to all pilot trainees that performed poorly during an exercise.

A pilot trainee would be struck across the chest by their superiors if they failed to land their aircraft properly or failed to perform a maneuver correctly. There was another aspect to the discipline system. If one person in a group did something wrong, everyone in the group was physically punished. It was considered that this form of discipline encouraged each candidate to take responsibility to work as a group.

In one instance, Hiryo made a mistake performing a combat maneuver. The instructor situated in the cockpit behind him hit the back of his head with a wooden stick. After that, Hiryo would wear a towel under his leather flying helmet to lessen the blow. This worked for a while until his instructor caught on, and once they landed, Hiryo was ordered to take off his flying cap, and the instructor hit him with his stick several times across the head.

Punishment aside, Hiryo happily learned aerial maneuvers appropriate for dogfights such as the *hineri-komi* or *turning-in* maneuver that many Allied pilots would soon describe as a *falling-leaf* maneuver. The pilot trainees were trained to work in the three-plane *shōtai* that helped create a sixth sense in the pilot trainees. The sixth sense was the ability to predict each other's reactions.

With his intermediate flight training complete, it was graduation time.

Hiryo, dressed in full, regal uniform, fingered a sharp dagger in a gold-trimmed sheath on his hip while he sat on the reviewing stand above his fellow students. On the platform, and there to celebrate the graduating fighter pilots, were Academy instructors and honored guests. Hiryo, dressed in his waist-length uniform jacket with gold bars on the collars signifying his semi-officer cadet rank, was to be honored as the top-flying student in his graduating class. A great honor, indeed.

He sat steadfast, proud and erect, and Hiryo flashed a broad smile at his father, who sat in the front row of the audience. In spite of the reservations that Fujiyama had of Hiryo joining the military, he returned a proud smile to his accomplished son. It was a smile that concealed his fear, premonitions, and heartache.

The Commander of the Academy, Commander Iko Ishikawa, stood front and center, giving a formal opening speech. Ishikawa was well known in naval air circles as he had earned several citations in the China War, and even a commendation from the Emperor himself.

When his introduction was complete, he turned to a surprise guest. "I'd like to introduce Captain Minoru Genda, who will give the commencement address."

There was a perceptible gasp of astonishment from the graduating students, and for a moment, excited whispers rippled amongst the crowd. But that moment of enthusiasm was quelled almost immediately by the understanding of the expected decorum of accepted behavior, rules, and regulations in the presence of someone as formidable as Genda.

Anyone even remotely connected to military aviation knew of Genda. Genda was a staunch believer in naval air power, and in 1932 he formed a demonstration team of biplanes, leading them around the country conducting aerobatic demonstrations. It was famously known as Genda's Flying Circus.

Genda took his place at the podium and commanded the audience's rapt attention. "I am not an orator. I'm a combat pilot." He straightened his coat and stood like a statue in front of the graduates. "But at the request of Commander Ishikawa, I will give you newly appointed fighter pilots a few brief words." He paused a moment, the wind from the sea blew across his face, pushing one strand of hair over his forehead, making him look almost human for that split second. He left the rogue hair in place and continued to speak in his statuette manner. "As many of you may know, I believe in the power of naval aviation. And I believe in the potential of massing aircraft carriers to project that air power. But please understand that the carrier should not be used merely as air cover for our ships."

He became more animated, and his stoic façade disappeared as he slowly came to life. "Those who believe in the battleship as the primary weapon of the Navy are living the last war." He breathed more deeply, passion exuding from his every word. "They will become scrap metal. The aircraft carrier carrying dive-bombers, torpedo planes, and fighters piloted by *you,* will be the decisive naval weapon of the future."

There was a buzz of excitement throughout the graduates by Genda's words. The Captain took a moment to glance behind him to see what effect, if any, his speech had on the dignitaries, especially on Admiral Chūichi Nagumo.

Although he seemed to be curious of their reactions, his body language told a different story. Genda didn't care what they thought. He had said his piece.

"Thank you Captain Genda," Ishikawa said. After Genda returned to his seat, Ishikawa proceeded to hand out the various class awards.

Fujiyama watched as Hiryo was called up to the podium and presented with the Distinction of Merit for being the top pilot in his graduating class. Hiryo proudly accepted the award and practically strutted back to his seat, a model soldier head to toe.

After the ceremony concluded, Fujiyama congratulated his young son. Few words were exchanged between the father and son, and as Fujiyama hugged Hiryo goodbye, he prayed that he would be given an opportunity to have that same hug again very soon.

As they were about to leave, Genda approached them both.

The Captain saluted Fujiyama, then peered down at Hiryo. "Congratulations, son. I was told you knew how to fly before even attending the Academy. Where did you learn to fly so well?"

Hiryo smiled and looked at Fujiyama. "My father, sir. He taught me to fly from an early age."

"Indeed. Well done, sir," Genda said to Fujiyama. "A Great War hero. A great fighter pilot." A hint of a smile nearly cracked his lips as he looked back to Hiryo. "And you want to follow in that family tradition?"

"Yes, sir," Hiryo said proudly. "Being a fighter pilot is my dream. After my leave, I attend the Yokaren Naval Preparatory Flight School for carrier flight training."

"Nnnnnnnn!" Genda grunted, a polite manner to indicate he was in agreement with Hiryo. He slapped the boy on the back. "Perhaps we will meet on a carrier someday."

"Genda," Fujiyama said, "I was truly impressed with your speech."

The Captain smiled. "Well, at least one line officer here appreciated the importance of my message."

A voice of authority sounded behind them. "Captain." The three turned to see Admiral Nagumo approach.

Genda stiffened and offered the Admiral a formal salute, as did both Fujiyama and Hiryo.

"Captain," Admiral Nagumo stated with a sour tone. "I was not pleased with your references to our battleships," Nagumo stated bluntly. "Our battleships are among the most powerful in the world. Soon we will have the Yamato, the biggest battleship afloat. 72,000 tons of impenetrable steel, equipped with eight eighteen-inch guns."

The three men stood at attention and said nothing, not knowing what would come next. To what extent did Genda's speech displease the Admiral? Would he take some kind of disciplinary action for Genda's obvious distaste for Nagumo's position? Both Fujiyama and Genda were well aware that Nagumo stood as one of the biggest advocates of the Fleet Faction.

The Admiral continued. "Nnnnnnnn " he replied in another of those guttural grunts. "The next war will be decided by engagements between battleships. *A decisive battle from the outset.* The airplane will only be used for scouting purposes. It's battleships, not carriers, that will project naval power."

Genda held his tongue. He didn't want to get into a debate with someone of such authority and superiority. But in the same token, he wanted to respectively counter what Nagumo argued.

"Sir," he began at attention, "I truly believe in the potential of massed air raids launched from multiple aircraft carriers working together. Aircraft carriers supported by submarines, fast cruisers and destroyers. Not slow moving battleships."

"Oi." Nagumo abruptly replied. "We will see." He then stood erect and the three officers took that as the end of the conversation. They each saluted Nagumo before he marched away.

"You have great tenacity, Genda," Fujiyama smiled.

"Perhaps. But he's probably correct. My views do not stand a chance in the current naval strategy. My rank as Captain is too low to gain any real strategic influence." He paused in thought. "If I could only reach those who would understand, and who plan our military future..."

Fujiyama smiled. "I think that can be arranged."

Genda seemed taken back. "Oi. How?"

"I am on Vice-Admiral Yamamoto's staff. *War Planning*. I believe he would enjoy speaking with you." Fujiyama placed a hand on the Captain's shoulder. "He's right here in Hiroshima on his flagship the *Nagato*. Would you like to meet him?"

"Hai. When?"

"How about today?"

The Assignment

That afternoon, after sending Hiryo home on his leave, Fujiyama escorted Genda to the 32,000 ton *Nagato* to meet Yamamoto. Black smoke wafted out of the top of the immense ship, leaving a dark, ominous cloud drifting in the sky. The pagoda mast haunted the sea air with an authority like no other. She was truly magnificent and projected utter power.

Their shoes tapped loudly on the immaculate deck as they boarded the vessel and marched down a long narrow staircase.

"The admiral is expecting us. When I told him who you were, he said he was already acquainted with you."

"Yes. I met the Admiral back in 1933, when I served aboard the carrier *Ryujo*."

"Ah. A small world," Fujiyama replied.

They entered a small meeting chamber and waited for their appointment. A few minutes later, the two officers were ushered directly into Yamamoto's quarters.

"Genda, nice to see you again," Yamamoto said after returning the two officers' salutes.

"I'm honored you remember me, sir."

"Still a thorn in the Navy's side, I hear. Oi. And taking on Nagumo no less. Courage or stupidity?" The Vice-Admiral chuckled at his old acquaintance.

"I'm afraid a little of both, sir. But I am getting little attention for my ideas."

"That could change," Yamamoto replied. "Please, have a seat." He pointed to the two chairs besides his desk. "I'd like to hear your frank opinions. I've been thinking about the various implications if war with America becomes inevitable." He leaned toward Genda. "You are aware of the British attack on Taranto harbor?" "Hai," Genda replied. "The Royal Navy launched the first all-aircraft ship-to-ship naval attack in history, flying a small number of obsolete biplane torpedo bombers from one of their aircraft carriers in the Mediterranean Sea."

Yamamoto then shocked the two officers by bluntly asking, "Can an attack on the American Fleet at Pearl Harbor succeed?"

"I considered such an attack in 1934," Genda admitted. "And I had discussed the possibility with Admiral Takijirō Onishi."

"Oi. And your opinion?" Fujiyama pressed.

"Such an attack is surely difficult, but not impossible." Genda responded. "The harbor in Taranto is shallow like Pearl Harbor, but the torpedoes succeeded in sinking the Italian battleships." He paused a beat. "Secrecy and surprise is the primary factor. If we could achieve those, then I believe it can succeed."

The two officers waited for Yamamoto to respond. When he did, Fujiyama and Genda were stunned by what they heard. "I've already spoken about such a plan with the Naval General Staff."

"And...?" Genda said in anticipation.

Yamamoto laughed. "I received the same exact response that you did from Nagumo. The Naval General Staff believed it to be too risky, and unanimously rejected my idea due to its radical revision of Japanese naval strategy. As you both know, the NGS consists primarily of Fleet officers, and they have their assumptions on how America would respond in the case of war."

Yamamoto leaned back in his desk chair. "The NGS war plan assumes that we would attack the Philippines. America would respond by sending their fleet from San Diego. We would then respond with light surface forces, submarines and land-based air units, whittling down the American Fleet as it advanced across the

Pacific, until the Japanese Navy engaged it in a climactic decisive battle in the northern Philippine Sea."

The Admiral stood up. "The Imperial Navy would fight a war of attrition near the Marianas and there would be a decisive battle of the two fleets. And, I believe the Americans would lose."

"The same type of war planning prevalent for years at the Naval General Staff," Genda noted.

"Oi," the Admiral replied as he peered out his porthole, running his finger around the circular window. "The NGS is a smug society in that all its ideas on strategy conform to this Fleet orthodoxy. If you disagree with their philosophies, you are quickly branded a heretic and ignorant of tactics."

He turned back to his two officers. "I pointed out that their traditional plan did not even succeed in war games. I proposed instead to first reduce their forces with a preventive strike, and then follow it with the decisive battle, but fought *offensively*, rather than defensively, in the hopes that a massive blow to their fleet would force the Americans to negotiate an end to any further conflict."

Yamamoto stood still. The ship smelled of sushi and cigarette smoke, and in addition to the way it was secured to the docks, he knew it hadn't seen the real sea in quite some time. Was this the kind of boat that would win wars? *No*. However, if he did not have this room, this porthole to stare out of, where would he be? Who would protect the coast?

Yamamoto finally broke the silence. "A decisive blow to the American Fleet would leave their west coast defenseless. We could then expand our Empire into the Pacific, thereby gaining control of the natural resources, and solidifying our position. At that point we would press the United States for peace. But the NGS envisioned only one opponent: the United States of America. But I differed, stating that we would certainly face a future conflict with Great Britain, the Netherlands and Australia, and stressed that new operational thinking was imperative."

He drew his attention back to his two officers. "The NGS

believes that the role of the Imperial Navy is to move and protect the Army as they conquered South East Asia, believing the pacifists in the West would not oppose our occupation. I felt the real threat was from the might of the United States." He paused in thought. "We need to take out the United States Navy early in the war to remove their strike capability."

"And Nagumo opposed your position?" Fujiyama asked.

"Hai. But I demanded to have my plan be accepted and, if not, I would immediately tender my resignation."

Stunned, the two officers said almost in unison, "*Resign?*"

Yamamoto dismissed their concern with a laugh. "They took my threat seriously. They knew of my abilities and didn't want to lose my strategic thinking."

"Bluffed," Fujiyama stated with a smile.

"So they conceded?" Genda said.

"Hai," Yamamoto replied. "So, Genda, I want you to work out the details with Commander Fujiyama and report back to me." He turned to gaze out the porthole once again. "We don't have much time. The Army and certain people in the Palace are pressing hard for war." He turned back to the two officers and said solemnly. "I believe we will be at war with America by the end of the year."

47 Ronin

It was late afternoon, and Connor was enjoying some warm sake at the Yakuza warehouse with Jiro, and the boy could feel the numbing effects of the alcohol on his brain. He was learning to love the way the warm sake ran through his body, relaxing him, giving him confidence, taking away his inhabitations. He wondered why he hadn't indulged in it before.

He peered at Jiro and pressed the Japanese boy for more information about the Yakuza Code.

"Have you ever heard of the Forty-Seven Ronin?" Jiro asked.

"No," Connor replied. "What's a Ronin?"

"*Us*. Vagrants. Homeless," he replied, then added, "Ronin are Samurai that serve no Master."

"And the number forty-seven?"

"The Forty-Seven Ronin were samurai who were left leaderless after their lord was compelled to commit seppuku for assaulting a court official."

"Suicide," Connor stated."

"Correct," Jiro laughed, pouring Connor another drink. "The Forty-Seven avenged their master's honor by killing a court official and then eventually killing themselves. It was the ultimate expression of the samurai code of honor. Bushido." He placed his hand on Connor's shoulder. "For sacrifice and honor. The loyalty of the Samurai. The Yakuza hold *that* Code of Honor."

Connor was impressed with everything Jiro shared with him.

He wanted to belong, but even more, he *needed* to belong to such a group that would let him live the Code.

Connor's thoughts turned once again to Kodo. He couldn't get the young woman's eyes out of his mind. "Tell me more about your step-sister."

"Hai. A wild one she is. She had a turbulent childhood, but perhaps turbulent is too soft a word for it. Her father was a kingpin in the Yakuza. A very evil man. He would return home drunk in the middle of the night and tear the house apart in a drunken rage and beat Kodo and her mother."

Connor flashed back to the memories of the beatings his father would give his mother. Beatings that existed in another life, another world that he tried to forget.

"As a teenager, she fell into a rough crowd and became a *yanki*, or what you Americans call a juvenile delinquent."

Connor was beginning to identify with this exotic girl more and more as Jiro spoke. He remembered her silk robe stroking the skin of his arm. Her exotic eyes. Her enticing smile.

"Eventually, like many yanki, she turned to drugs, skipping school, and having sex with married men. All of this before she even turned fourteen. She threw herself into a hell-raising lifestyle, losing her virginity, and then slept with a series of boyfriends who would beat her on a regular basis. One even raped her."

Connor hated the thought of Kodo being hurt and humiliated. "Did she ever have a real boyfriend?"

"Once. A good man who wanted to protect her. But she turned him away, fearing her other boyfriend at the time would split his head open with his sword."

Connor detected no emotion in Jiro's narrative. He just stated the truth as simple fact. They both drank more, and Connor became even more uninhibited. "And why just the tip of her pinky?"

"As I said, the Yakuza consider themselves holders of the Samurai Code. The origin of severing the pinky tip comes from the traditional way of holding a Japanese Samurai sword." He pointed to his hand. "The bottom three fingers of each hand are used to grip the sword tightly, with the thumb and index fingers slightly loose. The removal of digits, starting with the little finger moving up the hand to the index finger, progressively weakens a person's sword grip. The person with a weak sword grip then has to rely more on the group for protection, which reduces the desire for individual action."

Of everything Jiro said, all Connor heard was the word sword. "The Yakuza use Samurai swords?"

"Hai. They use them on occasion. Their use by the Yakuza goes back hundreds of years. But, unfortunately, guns have pretty much replaced them now."

"Do you know how to use the sword?" Connor asked.

"No. I'm not Yakuza. But my sister knows. She's pretty skilled at it. Goro taught her the techniques."

Connor caught a whiff of a pleasant fragrance. A scent of sweet persimmon reminding him of the tree outside the Fujiyama home. He followed the scent and looked up to see Kodo approached. Through the enticing cloud of her perfume, she gave Connor a devious smile from painted lips that made him almost blush.

"Would you like me to teach you how to use a sword?" She took Connor's hand, examined his fingers, and caressed them one by one. She took his other hand and did the same, tracing her finger all the way up to his shoulder. "Would you like me to teach you?"

"Yes," Connor managed to squeeze from his throat.

"Come with me, then," she instructed.

Connor followed her to an anteroom of the warehouse. As they walked inside, their breathing echoed in the concrete chamber. A skylight from above lit the floor, and cigarette smoke hung in the air, creating shapeless designs in the dim light.

Kodo walked towards a group of four-foot-long bamboo swords resting in the corner. She chose two and returned to Connor. "For you," she said, thrusting the handle of one of the bamboo swords into his hands. "This is called a *Shinai*."

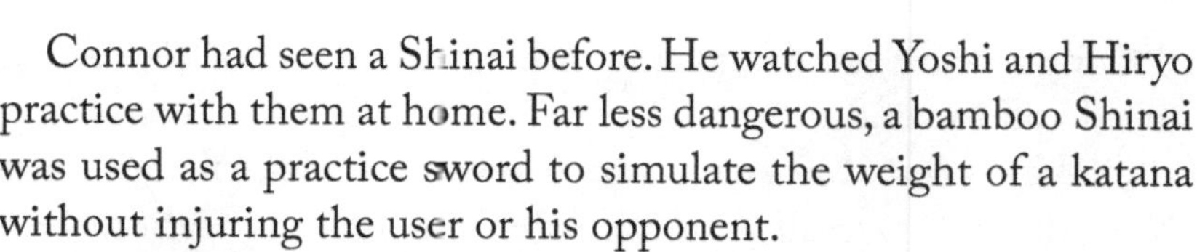

Connor had seen a Shinai before. He watched Yoshi and Hiryo practice with them at home. Far less dangerous, a bamboo Shinai was used as a practice sword to simulate the weight of a katana without injuring the user or his opponent.

Kodo proceeded to demonstrate to Connor the proper way to handle a sword. "First, stand with your body squared. Like this."

She held her hand out for Connor to imitate her pose. He tried, but failed. "Iie. No! Stand like you're standing with friends, but your shoulders need to be square and in line with your hips. Keep your back straight. And your feet need to be shoulder-width apart." Kodo positioned his frame with her hands, grasping his shoulders and pressing his knees apart and strong.

Connor followed her instructions without question.

"Now, grasp, don't grab, the hilt right below the hand guard." She held the bamboo out and wrapped her fingers around it loosely, then handed it to Connor to try.

Connor complied, trying his best to mimic her handling of the bamboo.

"Now pull straight out as though you were using the hilt to strike your opponent's stomach. You are imitating drawing your sword with this movement." Her body language was pure magic. She slowly extended the rod in front of her, disturbing a waft of smoke that drifted in front of her face for a moment. "Now you try."

Connor did so.

"Good. Now with your sword drawn, make your first cut." She demonstrated with her Shinai. "Lead with your right foot, raise the sword over your head, swing it down, and bring the handle to your center." Kodo's movements swept in front of her, and she made it look so simple.

Connor followed her lead, believing it would be easy, but it wasn't, and he nearly fell over.

"Spread your legs more," she coaxed. "You need to find your center of balance." She placed the Shinai on the ground and dropped to her knees, adjusting his legs into the correct position.

Connor tried again, and this time his cut was much more balanced and forceful.

"Oi. Very good." She stepped back and assumed the first position. "Now, defend yourself, Connor," she said, coming right at him, never breaking eye contact. Her gaze was like a lion, determined, ready to eat him alive.

Connor, surprised at her aggression, was caught off balance. He raised his sword to counter the blow coming his way from Kodo, stepped back, and tripped over his own feet.

Kodo swung her sword towards Connor's head and just as the blade of the bamboo was to make contact, she stopped herself, leaned down, and stared at him. She cocked her head the same way Connor had done the day that she lay naked on the table. The emeralds in her eyes twinkled as she took a breath, and then closed her eyes and met his lips with her own.

She finally pulled away. "Lesson done for the day, Connor-san." And with that, she walked towards the door.

Laughter arose from outside the anteroom, and Jiro entered grinning at Connor. "My sister, like they say in America, kicked your ass!"

Connor laughed as well. "Yeah. But I think I still won," he said, wiping the red lipstick from his mouth.

"Kodo can teach you more at another time." Jiro replied, winking at his half-sister. "We have work to do."

As the three stepped out of anteroom, they were immediately joined by Goro and five other Yakuza. Colonel Sato was among them. He said nothing, letting Goro do the talking.

Goro paced back and forth while he spoke, "We are going to teach some peace appeasers here in Hiroshima what we do to traitors." His eyes settled on Connor. "Cowards. Cowards with no honor."

Appeasers

As dusk approached, Connor, Goro, Jiro, Kodo, and a group of other members of the Yakuza, walked the back alleys and streets until they reached a poor sector of the city. Small, ramshackle homes and decrepit shops lined both sides of the streets, and the oppressive stench of rotting trash and human waste filled every molecule they inhaled.

The Yakuza moved as a well-tuned unit, all well armed with automatic pistols. In addition to a sidearm, Goro carried a sledge-hammer slung over his shoulder.

Connor thought a sword would be more appropriate or honorable, but he didn't question what he didn't understand. And he wasn't surprised that Kodo was participating in the raid. He would have been more surprised if she *wasn't* present. In fact, there was very little that would surprise him about this strong Japanese woman.

"Oi," sniffed Goro, pointing to a squat two-story building off to their right. "Upstairs," he ordered. Everyone followed his instruction without hesitation.

As they approached the front of the building, Connor spotted a faded red and white sign over the door. It read *Japanese Communist Party of Hiroshima.*

Connor nudged Kodo and motioned to the sign. "Appeasers?" he whispered.

"Against the Emperor and our military," she whispered back. She gave him a wink. "And now the fun begins." Kodo deliberately brushed her hand against Connor's before she headed up the stairs, taking two steps at a time. Connor followed behind her, trying to keep his thoughts focused on the task at hand.

"Urusai!" Goro snarled as he led five Yakuza members up the set of stairs with Jiro bringing up the rear. Their footsteps should have been loud against the old wooden stairs, but instead, they moved in silence, like an entity that never actually touched the ground.

When they reached the first landing, Goro leaned back and swung the sledgehammer against the small door. The wood shattered easily, and the Yakuza stormed into the room, taking three Japanese men by surprise.

Two of the men wore white smocks etched in black ink, and were hunched over a printing press, as the third, shorter man sat behind a small desk. All three men started jabbering in Japanese, and all Connor could make out in their panicked speech were demands for the Yakuza to leave immediately.

Goro handed the sledgehammer to the biggest of the Yakuza, walked over to the man behind the desk, and yanked him to his feet by the nape of his neck. Paperwork scattered across the floor as the little man was tossed to the ground at Goro's feet.

Two Yakuza wrenched the other men away from the printing press, and began to beat them mercilessly. Blows to the face. Kicks to the stomach. Fingers broken. Heads slashed open.

As Connor and Jiro watched, the brutal Yakuza attack continued. The communist men were tossed to the ground and hammered in their skulls with the butts of pistols. The other three Yakuza ripped apart the office, overturning file cabinets, destroying furniture, and strewing papers and handbills everywhere.

Suddenly, out of a side-room, an older woman came rushing at them, flashing a knife high above her head.

"Kutabare! Die," she screamed and lunged straight for Goro.

Without hesitating, Connor moved towards the woman, but was shoved aside by Kodo. Connor glanced over to see Kodo grab the woman's arm, slam her to the floor, then beat her in the face with closed fists until her nose and mouth oozed red.

Kodo continued her assault. The sound of breaking cartilage in the woman's nose was muffled by the blood gurgling in her throat. Kodo finally stopped her attack and let the woman roll in front of Goro's feet, but he gave no acknowledgment of Kodo's defense.

Kodo sucked for air, her body emotionally charged, eyes wide in exhilaration. From the look on her face, Connor believed she actually enjoyed beating the poor woman.

"Destroy it," uttered Goro, and pointed to the printing press. "Rip it to pieces."

The large Yakuza clutching the sledgehammer nodded, and proceeded to smash the printing press into tiny chunks of crumpled steel.

When Goro was satisfied with the Yakuza's destruction, he turned to Connor, sucked mucus into his throat and spat on the woman at his feet. "*This* is what happens to traitors."

Yoshi

With Hiryo enrolled in flight school, Fujiyama working on his war plans, and Connor being drawn further into the Yakuza, Yoshi pursued his decision to enlist in the Imperial Army.

His first weeks as a raw recruit were not what he imagined them to be. Expecting glorious pomp and circumstance, what he got in instead was harsh training and even harsher discipline that pushed him to his limits. He was now expected to be a *gunjin*—a life devoted to his new profession, his sole purpose to be a Japanese military man.

Intense training began every morning as soon as reveille sounded, and today was no different.

"Get up," Yoshi shouted at his bespectacled bunkmate, Kuro Kobayashi. The two boys would forever be war comrades. "This is not your home in Kobe," Yoshi said as he kicked the bunk above him.

Kuro reluctantly rolled off his bunk and landed on his bare feet. He, in turn, kicked at Taka Onado lying in the bunk next to them. "Taka, it's reveille."

"Get lost," Taka mumbled as he rolled over and pulled the covers over his head.

Suddenly, the barracks door banged opened, and the platoon sergeant, Nakada, stormed inside. "Out!" Nakada ordered, kicking the legs of bunks with his perfectly polished boots while marching down the aisle. When he arrived at Taka's bunk, Nakada reached down and overturned it in one fluid movement.

Taka landed square on his face with a dull yelp.

"Up! You Koitsu!"

Taka stood up on shaky legs but did not rise for long. The sergeant's arm swung back in one fell swoop as he beat Taka with a heavy stick across the back. Taka dropped and rose, and the sergeant swung and beat once again. They created their own reveille until Taka's bruised body finally stood in the proper line.

With the platoon finally assembled outside the barracks, Taka whispered a veiled threat to Yoshi. "Bullets come from behind too," he said motioning toward the sergeant.

The wind blew across Taka's face, and he winced as the cool air stung at a small cut on his forehead. The crisp air should have been welcomed, but instead, cut like a knife on this wretched morning.

Nakada's strong voice bellowed over the recruits. "Face the Emperor's Palace in Tokyo."

With power and grace, the young men turned in order, like toy soldiers in a cartoon. Nakada began to read a portion of the Imperial Prescript. "Be resolved that honor is heavier than a mountain. Death, however, is lighter than a feather."

By now, all the new recruits knew the meaning of that quote. *You were not to be taken prisoner.*

To be taken prisoner would bring utter disgrace to your name. Not only would it bring disgrace to each soldier, but to their families as well. A Japanese soldier was taught that he should die fighting, and only cowards surrendered. Cowards are to be killed. A soldier's only duty was to be willing to die for the Emperor. The Japanese army was not an army for the people of Japan, but rather the Emperor's army, an army of obedient soldiers who served the Emperor's every interest.

This was their Samurai Code. This was *Bushido*.

The recruits were instructed that if they were taken prisoner, it brought great shame to not only the Emperor, but to the soldier's entire country. A soldier needed to be willing to kill himself in order to remove the dishonor, and so that his spirit may enter the hero's Yasukuni Shrine in Tokyo. The golden arches and dangling lights would welcome such an honorable soldier's death.

"Who will recite this morning?" Nakada asked. Part of the daily training exercises was to choose a passage from the Imperial Rescript, and recite it from memory. Each morning one recruit was chosen.

But today, the group stood in silence. No volunteers raised their arms. No voices requested the opportunity to recite.

Nakada scanned the group of recruits until his eyes settled on Eiji Yamaguchi. Yoshi and Kuro knew something about this diminutive former art student through conversations with him. He was branded a bad soldier because he was a member and sympathizer of the Leftist peace movement, and a violator of the Peace Preservation Law. The choice to become a soldier was not his. Instead, he was arrested, and his only hope of avoiding jail was to enlist in the Army.

Yamaguchi was an intellectual, thus an easy target for bullying by both the sergeants and officers. Any physical abuse from sergeants and even the recruits themselves was met with tacit approval.

"Yamaguchi," Nakada ordered, "Come forward and recite your passage."

Yamaguchi complied, quickly taking up the proper position in front of the platoon, and began to recite his passage with a feeble voice.

"The soldier and sailor should make simplicity their... in their... If you do not make simplicity your... you will become effeminate and frivolous and acquire fondness for luxurious and extravagant ways. You will finally grow selfish and sordid, and sink to the last degree of, of... so that neither loyalty nor valor will avail to save you from the... of the world."

It did not go well. He had forgotten many of the words.

Nakada approached him, his face red in anger, and shouted, "Unacceptable!" The sergeant slammed his stick across Yamagu-chi's legs, and the boy dropped to the ground like a sack of rice, writhing in pain.

"Taka Onado," the sergeant shouted. "Front and center." Taka hurried to the front of the platoon with Yamaguchi huddled and moaning at his feet.

Nakada nodded an unspoken command at Taka, who in turn, looked down at the pathetic Yamaguchi.

"Hai," Taka responded and proceeded to kick Yamaguchi in the face with his heavy boot. Yamaguchi's chin cracked and blood flew from his mouth. The boy snorted in an attempt to catch his breath, then began to choke on his own blood as he fell face first onto the ground.

"You have *Nippon seishin*, Onado. A good Japanese spirit," Nakada commented.

Nakada turned to face the rest of the platoon recruits. He grunted and pointed to the unconscious Yamaguchi. "Fujiyama and Kobayashi. Come forward and take this coward to the hospital."

The two obeyed and approached Yamaguchi's bloodied body. They heaved as they lifted the dead weight that was once their intellectual equal.

The harsh training and discipline became a common every day event, and if it were *not* to occur, then something far worse must be looming on the horizon.

The abuses by officers and non-commissioned officers alike were termed *lessons*. Yoshi himself was punished for the slightest infraction. During his physical discipline, Yoshi would attempt to stand strong, trying to remember his life before this, the things he loved, trying to forget the dreams that he once held close to his heart. He would focus on these memories and dreams as the green bamboo poles slapped across his once innocent skin, and leather straps followed the sting of the bamboo.

Focus. That was his only hope.

His fellow recruits fared even worse.

Kuro was made to present arms in a half-erect posture beneath his kit shelf for the better part of an hour. He would try to find the same focus that Yoshi held on to, but failed in this endeavor. When he could no longer stand the pain in his arms, his weapon dipped.

"Take off your glasses and hold still," Nakada ordered, but before Kuro could remove the lenses, Nakada swung his stick, knocking the glasses from his face and across the ground. The sergeant swung again and again, striking Kuro in the face several times, each one followed by roaring laughter, like that of a demon.

The beatings became so frequent and severe, that Kuro could not even drink his miso soup the following morning because his mouth and throat were too swollen.

One day, several senior soldiers entered Yoshi's barracks and ordered the recruits outside.

"Form a single line," a senior soldier ordered.

When Yoshi and the others complied, the senior officer instructed them to clench their teeth. Then, without warning, the other senior soldiers commenced hitting each of the recruits with closed fists.

"These lessons will imbue in you the military man's spirit," they sneered as they beat each defenseless recruit. Like iron cauldrons being thrown into a frozen pond, their punches shattered far more than the bones in the faces of the young men that they were pounding.

The recruits would soon learn that this method of inflicting punishment destroyed their power to think independently, and transformed them into nothing less than zombies that would carry out any order from a superior as sheer reflex. The constant beatings bled the young men of individual conscience, thus stealing their very souls.

This brutal training slowly disillusioned Yoshi. He considered quitting, but giving up would only bring Yoshi dishonor. Although he did not want to live without honor, that was not his primary concern. He feared bringing dishonor to his family, and that thought was unbearable.

War Clouds

In the fall of 1941, I was preparing to return to Japan and file a detailed report of what I had witnessed and experienced in Manchukuo. I had already informed Sakura by phone of the mine explosion and my brush with death and even asked if he was going to publish the event.

"What explosion?" His response dripped with irony. "The Army said no such event has happened. End of subject. Come home. Things are heating up here."

"What things?" I asked.

"The war clouds are gathering. My sources in the military are hearing of a big war conference."

I knew what that meant, and I was not afraid to admit it. "War with America and Britain," I stated flatly.

"Hai," Sakura replied. "Very likely. America completely cut off Japan's oil supply when we occupied Indo-China this summer. We have less than a year's reserve, and Roosevelt is rattling his sword. The U.S. Pacific Fleet has moved to Hawaii." He paused a moment. "If the worst happens, I want you there in the thick of it."

Deep inside, I wanted to raise the issue of Unit 731 and the stolen gold again, but knew it was no use. The mystery of Unit 731 haunted me, but I had no choice but to obey my boss. "I'll be back in Tokyo as soon as I can hitch a ride with the military."

"Hai. Make it soon."

Suki

It certainly wasn't easy securing a flight home in the middle of an impending war zone and on a planet that was a ticking time bomb, but I eventually finagled a flight back to Tokyo.

As I struggled through customs, Suki was with her mother in Kobe, doing weekly volunteer work at the Kobe International Hospital, which had its hands full treating soldiers that had been wounded in the China War. This was a war that was celebrated by most Japanese citizens, including Suki. But her enthusiasm had quickly dampened once she was exposed to the brutal realities of war.

Kobe, with its protected harbor, sat west of Osaka on the Inland Sea in Honshu. It stood as the largest of the four islands that make up Japan, and the surrounding hills, nearby beaches and temperate climate made life for its residents very pleasant and much like a resort.

Kobe was a thriving port city built on the side of hill, with only its port and main downtown area relatively flat. The scenery was worthy of a postcard, and its peaceful serenity held an aura that seemed impenetrable. The remainder of the city stretched up the steep hill with wooden houses clustered around narrow streets.

Besides commerce, industry boomed with the Kawasaki Shipyards that resided there, and soon Kobe would become a major embarkation point for troops and weapons supplied to the war front. Unfortunately, the heartache that Kobe would soon be noted for was quite another characteristic—a characteristic not so pleasant and all too appalling.

The daily trauma of the Kobe International Hospital was emotionally draining for those caring for the wounded. Simple head wounds and shrapnel were seen on the easy days, but on a normal day, the severely wounded that entered Kobe as the result of the war in China became the root of many nightmares. And for the doctors and nurses alike, it proved to be a fatal mistake to expose themselves to crossing the line of developing a personal relationship with those they cared for.

One such patient that Suki grew fond of was Captain Soji Okada, a soldier in the Imperial Infantry. Okada had nearly lost an arm fighting in Nanking.

The weeks that he was at the hospital gave Suki time to get to know him better. He was from Hiroshima as well. Okada's family was in the construction industry, but he wanted to become an officer and make a career in the Army. He was a gentle man, much more interested in photography and painting as a hobby, than in the profession of arms. As Suki came to know Okada, she wondered how such a gentle, kind man, with his pale and vulnerable face, would want to subject himself to the realities of war.

"You're looking much better," Suki commented to Okada when checking the bandages on his arm one morning. "They'll be discharging you from the hospital soon."

Okada squeezed Suki's hand as she took his pulse. "Yes. I already have my orders. I'm assigned to the 9th Regiment, 16th Division, out of Kyoto."

Suki's heart quickened when she heard the news. "My brother Yoshi will be assigned to that same unit after he completes training."

"It's a good unit," Okada replied. "Well led, I'm told. I'll look for your brother when I report there."

Suki was unable to avoid her eyes filling with tears. "Will you look out for him? He's so young."

"Hai. I will."

Okada began to squeeze her hand, but she quickly released his touch as she heard someone walk up behind her.

Miyoko approached, brushing against her arm. "Suki. The doctor wants to see you. There is a patient in—'

Screams filled the hospital corridors, cutting her off.

Suki and Miyoko turned to see a soldier running into the ward, and he was heading directly toward them. His eyes were those of a crazed man.

"I'm not going back," the soldier professed. "We killed—*I killed.*" His desperate eyes begged them for some kind of retribution.

Suki attempted to calm the distraught soldier down. "It's okay. I understand. Take my hand."

"Don't touch me," he screamed. "I didn't want to kill anyone, but they said the Chinese were nothing but pigs! They *made* me kill a woman! An old woman. I shot her in the head." Tears streamed down the man's face. "After that, I killed a child…"

Suki's soul wept for the young soldier. She was about to speak when the young soldier grabbed a scalpel on a table near him and leapt at her grabbing her from behind. He held her in front of him with one arm firm around her chest, and the other with the scalpel pressed at her throat.

"I'm *not* going back!" he screamed.

Suki's heart pounded as she silently begged for him to give her grace.

An armed guard came into the ward and rushed to where the women and Okada stood.

Okada motioned to the soldier to stand down. He turned to the distraught soldier. "Corporal. You are an Imperial soldier of his Majesty. Think of your honor. Think of your family's honor. Die in battle. Not here."

A tense silence filled the ward for several moments, with only Suki's shallow breaths echoing in her ears.

The young corporal stood with his head bowed, tears running down his weathered cheeks. His mind made up, he threw Suki at the armed guard, then jumped at the soldier. He punched the guard in the face and quickly disarmed him.

The young corporal managed to wave the guard's pistol. "Stay where you are."

He then became very quiet. By the look on his face, it was clear that a critical decision had been made.

The distressed soldier then stood at attention, put the pistol to his temple and squeezed the trigger. The anguish on his face disappeared as his brains exploded from the back of his head. Pieces of bone flew across the room, covering Suki as she stood in silent horror.

Suki's eyes filled with tears as she stared down at the dead soldier, so young and such a senseless death. And the same thought played in her mind, over and over again.

This is a bad war. A very bad war.

Six Months

While I was on my way back to Tokyo in the Fall of 1941, Fujiyama and Genda, working under Yamamoto's orders, were finalizing some kind of strategic plan.

"Here's a draft of the plan, sir," Fujiyama said as Yamamoto entered his cabin on the *Nagato*.

Yamamoto took the thick portfolio marked *TOP SECRET* and sat behind his desk. He scanned the document, summarizing parts of it out loud as he read. "Attack on a weekend. A Sunday morning when their defense preparations will be at a low level. Approach Hawaii on a circuitous route from the north to avoid detection as long as possible by American reconnaissance patrols and merchant shipping. Refuel in mid-ocean. Use the new torpedoes. Use six of our best aircraft carriers and supporting vessels. Use highly skilled aircrews, fighters, dive-bombers, torpedo planes, and high-level bombers in multiple waves of attacks."

"And above all else," Genda added, "we will use the element of complete surprise."

The Admiral paused a moment, then finally admitted, "Very thorough." His eyes turned to look at Genda. "I want you to be responsible for training the torpedo crews. Especially in the new tactics of shallow-water torpedo use. Train them to the point of absolute efficiency on the use of level-bombing by tactical aircraft."

"Hai," Genda replied.

"And choose someone you trust to lead the air attack," Yamamoto added. "Someone that you would place the lives of your family with."

"Mitsuo Fuchida, sir," Genda quickly replied. "He was my classmate at the Naval Academy. He is an excellent pilot and a respected leader as well."

"Oi. In expectation of your finalized plan, I arranged to meet with the NGS this afternoon." Yamamoto stood, and the two officers saluted. "Excellent work. I feel as if this strategy can not fail."

Even though the plan to attack Pearl Harbor was approved by the Naval General Staff, the Combined Fleet Command remained obstinate, the NGS cautious, and the leaders of the task force assigned to go to Hawaii had a negative attitude in regards to the plan.

Yamamoto expected this, but the NGS placed a caveat on Yamamoto that he did *not* expect.

"We've assigned Admiral Nagumo to lead the attack force," Admiral Fushimi Hiroyasu, Chief of Staff of the Imperial Japanese Navy stated flatly.

Yamamoto couldn't mask his disappointment.

"You disagree?" Hiroyasu asked.

Yamamoto was unhappy with that decision. He knew that as the commander of the main strike force, Nagumo and the officers that worked under him were clearly not loyal to Yamamoto and did not respect Yamamoto's views. If he agreed with the NGS on this matter, Yamamoto would be burdened with officers that he could not fully trust to do as he ordered.

He could fight the NGS' decision, but such an action would demoralize the attack force at this late date. Yamamoto figured that he could keep Nagumo in check if he was carefully instructed on his responsibilities. So he agreed to the NGS decision.

It was a decision that would come back to haunt Yamamoto.

"Tell me?" asked Hiroyasu. "In your best estimate, what do you think our chances are against the Americans?"

Yamamoto gravely replied, "I can run wild against them and gain victories for six months. After that, I can promise nothing."

There was silence in the room until Hiroyasu spoke. "Let's go over the details of your attack plan."

The Gozen Kaigi

"This is the last of it," Fujiyama said, handing the secretive document to Hiyakawa.

The Assistant to the Lord Keeper of the Privy Seal of Japan appeared tired and beaten, as if the weight of the world were placed squarely on his shoulders.

"I hope this report on the failures of our Army in China will sway the Emperor from expanding the war with the West." Hiyakawa placed his hand on Fujiyama's shoulder. "Of course I will not reveal where I obtained this information."

Fujiyama nodded.

"Be safe, my friend," Hiyakawa said softly.

Hiyakawa decided to try one last time to influence the court through Marquis Kōichi Kido. Kido was the Lord Keeper of the Privy Seal. But Kido told Hiyakawa that he counseled the Emperor for restraint. He feared that if the Emperor became involved in divisive conflicts over national policy, this would undermine the transcendental authority of the imperial house and the principle of ministerial responsibility. So, up to now, he had withheld information from the Emperor at key junctures.

"So you are deliberately keeping the Emperor misinformed?" asked Hiyakawa in shock.

Kido looked at his despondent assistant. "It is not necessary to lie, but rather, tell the Emperor things that will please him in order to ease his mind."

Seeing that his efforts had gone unheeded with Kido, the day before the Gozen Kaigi, Hiyakawa requested and received a private audience with Emperor Hirohito, where he proceeded to give the Emperor Fujiyama's redacted notes.

The Gozen Kaigi—literally the conference before the noble face—was an extra-constitutional conference of matters of grave national importance in foreign affairs that was convened by the government in the presence of the Emperor.

Hirohito brooded over the notes and shook his head. "The military has made a point of concealing its intentions from me, and has acted unilaterally, in total defiance of the government. When I think of all these problems, I cannot sleep at night. The indiscipline and violence of the military and their meddling in domestic and foreign affairs are something which, for the welfare of the nation, must be viewed with apprehension."

Hiyakawa looked again at the notes in his hand and pondered his next move. "But I will do my best," he responded softly.

When Hiyakawa arrived at the Gozen Kaigi the next morning, he was accompanied by high-ranking ministers and military officers. In attendance were the Chief of Staff of the Army, Hajime Sugiyama, Chief of Staff of the Navy, Fushimi Hiroyasu, and Prime Minister Konoe, among others.

They all stood with pride and distinction as they waited patiently for the Emperor to arrive. They were seated behind long tables covered in red decorated cloth, dangling ropes entwined across them, uniting them on each side of the room and leaving them facing one another. In the center, on one end, stood an orator's desk in front of a folded rice paper shield. The high-ranking officials talked amongst themselves in regards to diplomacy with the Western powers or military action.

Several minutes passed until the doors to the conference room swung open, and the Emperor emerged. Everyone stood and bowed while Hirohito took his seat at the head of the table.

Hirohito appeared astonished by those who were present and addressed the officials personally. In breaking the tradition of Imperial silence, he left his advisors struck with awe.

Hirohito held a draft from Konoe in his hand. The draft informed him of the attendees' decision to choose war over diplomacy with the West. Expecting nothing more than the usual passivity from the Emperor and his formal decision to implement the draft, the attendees were shocked by Hirohito's response.

For a moment, it was hard to decipher what Hirohito was preparing to say. Then, with a somber attitude, he glanced at Hiyakawa, then stared directly at Sugiyama.

He asked, "What are the chances of success of an open war with the Occident?"

Sugiyama responded in the positive.

It was Hirohito's reply that stunned the room.

"General Sugiyama, at the time of the China incident, I was told that we could make the army of Chiang Kai-shek surrender after three months. Still today, at this very moment, you have yet to defeat him."

Sugiyama was struck dumbfounded. His eyes widened in disbelief as he searched for an appropriate response to his Emperor. "The interior of China, your Majesty, is huge," was his feeble response before hanging his head in shame.

"And isn't the Pacific Ocean even bigger than China? Didn't I caution you each time about those matters? Sugiyama, are you lying to me?" Hirohito then listed a series of military actions in the China war from Hiyakawa's report that reflected poorly on the Army.

The conference attendees were silent. Then, after a long uncomfortable pause, Hirohito spoke once again. He began reciting a poem that was written by his grandfather, Emperor Meiji.

"In a world
Where all the seas
Are brethren
Why then do wind and wave
So stridently clash?"

Recovering from their shock, the attendees hastened to express their profound wish to explore all possible peaceful avenues before going to war.

At that point, the Emperor stood abruptly and left the room in silence.

Yamamoto
Needs to be Removed

Outside of the chambers, Prince Chichibu and Colonel Sato stood waiting for the answer they hoped for.

Sato did not hesitate before he asked, "Did we get the Emperor's permission for war?"

Sugiyama shook his head. "I have never seen the Emperor reprimand us in such a manner." He paused a moment in reflection. "He seemed well versed on our problems in China. I don't know where or how he could have acquired such information."

But Sato had an idea who had been feeding the Emperor information. He and Chichibu left Sugiyama and walked outside to the Palace grounds. Their feet crunched along the rocky path as the two walked in silence. And although the rising sun bathed the palace grounds with warmth, it did little to alleviate the air thick with tension. The two turned a corner that opened to a secluded courtyard. In the center of the courtyard was a decorated bench underneath a cherry blossom tree. They sat, and Sato took one last look around the area before he spoke. "Hiyakawa gave the China war information to the Emperor."

"How do you know that?" demanded Chichibu.

"My sources said that Hiyakawa was granted a private meeting with the Emperor yesterday evening. And I'm quite certain who gave that information to Hiyakawa."

"Tell me," Chichibu replied.

"Hiyakawa has been meeting with Fujiyama, a naval officer on Yamamoto's staff." He nodded his head in a knowing way. "That should tell you something."

"Are you saying Fujiyama has been feeding information on China to Hiyakawa?" Sato reached down, picked up a cherry blossom, and held it in his hand.

"Hai," Sato replied. "They've been seen together on several occasions. And if we don't put a stop to this act of treason, people like Hiyakawa and Fujiyama will be an impediment to the war effort."

"Oi. What do we do?" asked Chichibu.

"Deal with both Fujiyama and Hiyakawa." Sato crushed the cherry blossom petals in his palm and let them fall to the ground near his feet.

"Hiyakawa is the Assistant to the Lord Keeper of the Privy Seal and a favorite of the Emperor," Chichibu countered. "He can't be touched. And Fujiyama is protected by Yamamoto."

"Perhaps. But there is a way to neuter Hiyakawa's influence." Sato replied. "And there are ways to reach Fujiyama."

They stood, and Sato followed behind the Prince. After a moment, he leaned over Chichibu's shoulder and whispered in his ear.

"Yamamoto needs to be removed."

The Poem

I met with Hiyakawa and Fujiyama the day after the Gozen Kaigi. A black mood hung over the two men, and the light that once gleamed in their eyes had turned to a clouded gray. "What happened at the conference? Bad news?"

"The Emperor recited a Tanka poem." Hiyakawa responded bluntly, seating himself around a small conference table with his two friends.

"A poem?" I replied.

Hiyakawa recited it to me.

"What does it mean?" I asked. "Is he for or against a war with the West?"

"The Emperor wants peace," Hiyakawa replied, "but he does not have the courage to face down the militarists and those in his Cabinet like Prince Chichibu, who wants war so badly that he can taste it."

Hiyakawa made a sigh of lament. "Reciting a poem was scarcely a bold intervention on the Emperor's part, but it was an incredible act of courage on his part. After the conference, he and his advisors at court feared this might trigger another attempted military coup and perhaps his replacement on the throne by his brother, Prince Chichibu."

"Really?" I asked, stunned.

"I believe," Hiyakawa sighed, "if the Emperor stands up to the militarists, there will be a great rebellion within the country, and the men whom he trusts around him would be killed, and his own life would not be guaranteed."

"So what's next?" I sat down and ran my fingers through my hair, trying to process all the various implications. "In a few weeks," Fujiyama began, "Admiral Nagano will take Yamamoto's plan to attack Pearl Harbor to the Emperor. I am sure he will approve it. For practical purposes, his signature is a mere formality. The Cabinet makes all decisions as to war now."

"But will Prime Minister Konoe continue to oppose it?"

"Rumor has it," Hiyakawa said sadly, "that Konoe will be replaced as Prime Minister."

Startled, I asked, "With whom?"

"With General Hideki Tojo," the little diplomat replied.

Fujiyama and I were stunned. "Will Konoe fight this?"

Hiyakawa shook his head. "Very doubtful. I once thought Konoe was a man of vision. But he lacked perseverance and consistency. It appears he has no strong opinions of his own."

"Then that seals it," I said. "The militarists will have their war. Any civilian opposition now will be mute."

"And the Army will lead the Navy into war," Fujiyama replied sadly.

"What about Yamamoto?" I asked. "Surely he was a voice of reason. What was his response?"

"I'm told," Fujiyama replied, "that he expressed to Tojo that should hostilities break out between Japan and the United States, it would not be enough that we take Guam and the Philippines, nor even Hawaii and San Francisco. We would have to march into Washington and dictate the terms of peace in the White House. Yamamoto said he wondered if the military and our politicians, who speak so lightly of a Japanese-American war, have confidence as to the final outcome and are prepared to make the necessary sacrifices."

"That should have made Tojo and the militarists think," I stated.

"Not really," Hiyakawa replied. "In fact Tojo seemed pleased."

"Pleased?" I said.

"Hai. He used Yamamoto's quote against him, and even spread it around the militarists, minus the last sentence, of course. I can only believe that it was interpreted in America as a boast that Japan would conquer the entire continental United States."

"Then there's this," Hiyakawa warned. "Several days ago, the United States delivered a note from U.S. Secretary of State, Cordell Hull, to our envoys demanding the immediate and complete withdrawal of our troops from China and Indo-China.

"And...?" I asked

The little diplomat's mood turned even bleaker. "And if a political settlement is not reached by November 29..." His voice trailed off.

"That deadline sounds ominous," I replied. I looked over at Fujiyama for his reaction. The clouds in the room had turned to a black, empty hole of hopelessness. It gave me the distinct impression that he knew what that deadline meant.

"Your Excellency," Fujiyama added, "You have little time. If that November 29th date passes, certain things are going to happen automatically."

"This is what I'm walking into in Washington," Hiyakawa said. "Japan has been at war for four years. When a nation has a war mentality, it can no longer think straight."

Hiyakawa hung his head then said with a glimmer of optimism, "There is still a small chance to avert war with America. I am being sent to Washington to assist our diplomats, Kichisaburō Nomura and Saburō Kurusu in the ongoing negotiations. I sail tomorrow."

"Good luck," both Fujiyama and I said in unison.

"Luck is when preparation meets opportunity." Hiyakawa replied. "But I'm afraid there may be little opportunity here."

Hiryo

As the war clouds gathered over Japan and strategies were coming into place across the nation, my editor already had his own plans for me. He had received a call from the Ministry of War, as did other news outlets, asking for war correspondents to report to troop ships gathering in ports of departure—destination unknown.

Meanwhile, Hiryo, fresh out of carrier school, was given his first assignment on the *Akagi*. Yoshi was set to leave on his first assignment with an infantry regiment, and Hiyakawa was working with Nomora and Kurusu for a diplomatic breakthrough in Washington. While the diplomats hoped for a peaceful settlement, *Certain things were automatically happening*, as Fujiyama had so ominously warned.

Hiryo proudly walked across the flight deck of the *Akagi*.

Akagi was the empress of all of the Japanese aircraft carriers. Although the ship had originally been designed as a battle cruiser, her unique flattop made the *Akagi* one of Japan's most modern carriers. As Hiryo contemplated his future, staring across the vast ocean that eventually reached America, a voice came up behind him.

"Lieutenant Fujiyama!"

Hiryo turned to see Genda and another officer approach. His face brightened as he recognized Genda. He threw both men a salute and stood at attention.

"This is the pilot I told you about, Mitsuo," Genda said, speaking to the officer accompanying him. "Hiryo, this is Commander Fuchida."

Fuchida gave Hiryo a broad smile, his eagerness to greet Hiryo was astounding. "I've heard a lot about you from Genda here. Seems you have the makings of quite a fighter pilot."

"Hai, sir," Hiryo replied loudly.

Fuchida laughed. "Oi. I want you in my air group."

Hiryo was overjoyed at such an honor. Like Genda, Fuchida was well known by Japanese pilots. "I would be honored, sir."

Brothers Off to War

Fresh off of his leave at home, Yoshi said goodbye to Suki, Kenji, and Connor, and set off with his parents to the embarkation station. Their goodbye embraces were those of pride, doubt, fear, and hope all mixed together.

He and the other recruits were given a public send-off by cheering families, the general public, and high-ranking officials.

Yoshi kept a small Japanese flag with him that his mother had bought him. Thoughts and well-wishes had been written on it by his family, neighbors, and friends, as well as others in his community. Known as a bayonet flag, he would carry that small banner with him into combat. It would be attached to his bayonet and placed onto his rifle.

The send-offs were an important ritual in Hiroshima. Like other cities, members of the recruit's immediate family and others from surrounding neighborhoods participated in the celebration.

The recruits went to a local Shinto shrine where they prayed for their safety and success on the battlefield. After that, they walked to the closest train station to rousing cheers and the waving of small national flags. It was a parade of soldiers surrounded by those whose hearts were full of pride for their saviors, but along with the bayonet flag, each soldier carried the weight of those same loved ones' hopes, and each one knew that those lives rested heavily on their shoulders.

Fujiyama and his wife were there in support of Yoshi, but could not bring themselves to participate in the celebrating.

Yoshi's mother gave him one last tender kiss and a loving hug at the train station while Fujiyama stood by stoically. Deep inside, Fujiyama was sure this was the last goodbye he would say to his heir.

Miyoko prayed that she would get the opportunity to see her little boy again soon, and her fingers trembled as she touched his cheek one last time. A tear ran down her own cheek, and she tightly clutched her *o-juzu* tightly in her fist. She had counted these prayer beads daily in the weeks approaching Yoshi's departure.

"May you have *happiness*. May you be *healthy*. May you be *peaceful*," Miyoko repeated to herself again and again as she watched her son disappear into the herd of soldiers.

✳ ✳ ✳

Shortly after Hiryo's arrival on the aircraft carrier *Akagi*, located in the Hitokappu Bay, attack planes were put aboard the magnificent ship. There were dive-bombers, high altitude bombers, torpedo planes, and fighter planes. Watching the collection of powerful aircraft being stowed on board gave Hiryo a deep sense of pride and enthusiasm for whatever was to come next.

He looked out over the expanse of sea and saw five other carriers join up with the *Akagi*. First was the *Kaga*, followed by the *Soryu, Hiryu, Shokaku,* and finally, the *Zuikaku*. Each of these vessels were followed by a mighty destroyer, the decks of which were covered by training planes from several airfields in Kyushu, which continued to broadcast radio waves similar to those made by carrier planes while exercising. The purpose of this was to camouflage any sudden change in direction when the fleet left the Bay.

The ships were soon joined by the light cruiser *Abukuma*, and nine various destroyers. In addition, there was a supporting unit that consisted of the battleships *Hiei* and *Kirishima*, and the heavy cruisers *Tone* and *Chikuma*, along with three submarines. A supply unit of eight fuel tankers sailed with the fleet as well.

At 6 a.m. on November 26, the fleet steamed into the rising sun of Hitokappu Bay, passing eastward through the stormy North

Pacific Ocean, careful to keep away from the merchant ship routes. As the fleet charted a path east, Hiryo rode aboard, but not fully recognizing its march into destiny.

The Wait

Fujiyama sat inside Yamamoto's cabin on the Battleship *Nagato*, stationed in Hiroshima Bay. Both men sat in silence, each in the privacy of their own dour thoughts, each breathing a knowing air. War was certain. Both men knew it to be an undisputable fact. The classic Japanese virtues of the group loyalties, the solidarity, the patience, the willingness to accept hardships in the hope of future gain, were now turned inside out.

Fujiyama tapped his foot quietly as he waited for his Admiral to speak first.

"Status?" Yamamoto finally asked.

"Hai. Units of the Pearl Harbor Task Force have sailed from Hitokappu Bay. Another large contingent will move south along the Malayan peninsula."

He paused to gather his thoughts for a moment. "Admiral Nagumo is instructed to turn back if a diplomatic solution is agreed upon in Washington. If no diplomatic solution is reached by December 2nd, the Pearl Harbor Task Force will proceed with their attack." He looked at his notes. "The code word to attack will be *Climb Mount Niitaka*."

Yamamoto said nothing in response. The time for debate had passed, and his staff had done an exemplary job to ready themselves for the pending conflict. It was now in the hands of the young pilots.

—THE STORM BREAKS—

December 1941

Into the Maelstrom

Japan, in its belief as the crown of the world with an unbroken line of emperors and confidence in its own superiority, slipped quietly towards the inevitable war, irreversible by the Emperor's power alone. Like a thief in the night, their decisions had been made for them without them even knowing.

In late 1941, it was a matter of course to go to war. *Banzai to the Emperor* was the common war cry, with everyone marching towards imminent disaster. Due to the uncritical patriotism and nationalist fervor, that most dangerous mixture of delusions soon swept the land into an uproar.

Adding to the *Daitoa Senso*, the Greater East Asia War, was now the *Taiheiyo Senso*, the War in the Pacific.

Fujiyama stood helpless as his two sons would be placed in harm's way. One pursued the glory he expected, whereas the other would persevere to uphold the loyalty he was taught. That unquestionable loyalty would soon be tested in the cauldron of brutal combat.

Many Japanese families, just like the Fujiyamas, would soon experience the suffering their country had imposed its citizenry. And Connor would be forced to make a cruel choice between loyalty and family.

The lives of this family unfolded as a country began to crumble against the backdrop of vicious plots of murder and unjust persecution involving family and friends and even the Emperor himself.

And where did I stand in this sad state of affairs? My blinding obsession with the looted gold, combined with my status as a Japanese raised in America, would place my life in more danger than I could ever predict.

A Troubled Sea Cruise

As November came to an end, the chill in the air foreshadowed much more than the pending winter. It was a cold morning when I boarded the troop ship *Tohuku-Maru* out of Osaka. Fujiyama informed me that his two sons had received their assignments and had gone off to serve the Emperor.

To the rest of his family, Connor was simply living the typical life of a teenager. But what his Japanese parents did not know was that moment by moment and breath by breath, Connor was being drawn deeper into the activities of the Yakuza, and farther away from the family ideals that he held so dear at one time.

At breakfast, I found myself in a sea of yellowish, mustard colored Army uniforms that were filled with friendly banter, playfully arguing over their ultimate destination. Many of these troops were seasoned and had come straight out of Manchuria.

"We're being sent to China," one young private enthusiastically predicted. His thick round glasses amplified his small, black eyes that peered out below his canvas field cap.

"And I guess you have the ear of Army Headquarters?" the private to his right responded and snorted a laugh.

"Then why have we been issued these light cotton uniforms, and masks and gloves made of mosquito netting?" a burley corporal chimed in. "We're headed to the jungle, I tell you. I don't know of any jungles in China."

As we steamed south, the air became hotter and hotter with

each passing day. It held a thickness to it and a heavy moisture I had never experienced. I figured we were in the Taiwan Straits by the looks of the irregular Chinese coastline dotted with mountains and hills that extended gradually down to the ocean. Maybe we *were* going to China after all.

But one morning, after another fitful night's sleep despite the gentle rhythm of the waves beneath the massive ship, I awoke to a clatter on deck. A small group of soldiers were pointing out to sea and chanting, "*Banzai! Banzai!*"

I joined them at the railing. As I hung on to the rails, my eyes began squinting through the rising sun and saw an imposing fleet. It was our naval vessels. There were battleships, cruisers and destroyers, along with more ships carrying platoons of troops.

I knew at that moment, that we were part of an invasion fleet, but the question that evaded me was *where?*

After the ships were refueled, we set out again. Traveling south the air became heavier with humidity along with a strong tropical breeze. The salt was infiltrating our lungs, and the beauty of the coast was breathtaking. In spite of the growing discomfort of the ship and the cramped sleeping quarters, whatever our destination, the naval escort and warplanes overhead gave us a feeling of safety.

A Final Plea for Peace

While I resigned myself to this unusual sea cruise, Hiyakawa was on his way to Washington, D.C. to help Nomora and Kurusu search for a diplomatic breakthrough for peace between America and Japan. Over the next week or so, Nomora and Kurusu continued to confer with Secretary of State Hull, carrying the Emperor's sincere message of hope that the evil of a war could be prevented.

When Hiyakawa finally arrived in Washington on December 5th, he took no time in asking the question that had been pressing on his mind while he steamed across the Pacific. "What are our hopes for peace?"

Nomora shook his head. "The American statesmen are arrogant and think that they are the greatest people in the world, and nothing can shake their belief. I suppose, therefore, in spite of our attempts to prevent war, there is little hope of a peaceful settlement." He bowed his head. "Secretary Hull's note for Japan to immediately leave China infuriated Tojo, which he read as an ultimatum."

"But we must continue to try," Hiyakawa pleaded.

"My repeated inquiries have been ignored in Japan, and I received no response to Mr. Hull's compromise proposals. I've asked repeatedly to resign my position here, but have been denied. The war I have feared for so long may be upon us."

"But you must continue to try," Hiyakawa pressed. "War *must* be averted."

"Perhaps something will come of the personal telegram from President Roosevelt to the Emperor, requesting a one-on-one, heart-to-heart meeting. It is a last appeal for peace," Nomora stated.

"That could re-open negotiations anew," Hiyakawa replied eagerly.

"By the way, I have a letter for you that came in the diplomatic pouch, just before you arrived." Nomora went to his desk and pulled out a sealed envelope, and handed it to Hiyakawa.

The diminutive diplomat took the envelope and opened it. It took no time for his face to drain of all color.

Seeing Hiyakawa's shocking expression, Nomora asked, "What is it?"

Hiyakawa lowered the letter and shook his head, "My wife. She was arrested by the Kempeitai."

Taka

"This is correct," noted Taka Onaco, slapping a page from a small handbook he was reading with the back of his fingers. The pamphlet was titled *Read This and the War is Won,* together with the *Collection of Imperial Rescripts* that was being used as material for the practical strengthening of morale in the field.

Taka wiped the sweat from his brow that had accumulated in the hot sleeping quarters of the military transport. "Asia is for *Asians,*" he slapped his hand again against the pamphlet. "Not for Europeans and Americans. They took Asia and Japan as if it belonged to them by natural right. Millions of Asians have suffered constant exploitation and persecution at their bloody hands."

Yoshi rolled over in his hammock that was suspended from the ceiling of the sleeping bay of the transport. "Take a break from the propaganda, Taka. I'm trying to sleep."

Taka bristled at the word *propaganda.* "If the Captain heard you say that—"

"Hai," Kuro Kobayashi added, kicking at Yoshi's hammock above him. "We'd all get a good beating. Now turn off that light and let us sleep."

"Where do you think we're headed, anyway?" Taka asked his fellow soldiers.

"We'll know when we get there," Yoshi replied. "Now go to sleep."

Taka grunted, dropped the pamphlet in his lap, and turned off his small flashlight.

Yoshi stared up into the semi-darkness for the longest time, thinking over the last few months and about his family. He and his Sen'yu had been properly trained and would soon be in combat. He was *Hetai,* the Emperor's foot soldier now, and he pondered how he would react when he was placed under life or death pressure.

The little pamphlet did contain a part that struck Yoshi as important. It acknowledged that the bodies of dead soldiers might not be recovered. In that event, Yoshi had a small box in his pocket. He opened it, looked at a lock of his hair and some fingernail clippings so, at the very least, some small part of him could be sent home to his family if he was killed.

Panic

Hiyakawa was in a panic.

He had been unsuccessful in reaching Fujiyama, who had sent him the communiqué about his wife, Barbara. He couldn't delay leaving Washington any longer, and within the hour, was lucky to arrange a commercial fight cross-country to Los Angeles.

On his arrival at LAX, he tried calling again at Fujiyama's home, and this time he had more luck. Miyoko, answered the phone. "Hai?"

"Oh, Miyoko. This is Kenta Hiyakawa. I need to reach your husband urgently. It concerns my wife."

"Hai," she replied. "So sad."

Hiyakawa felt his heart drop. "Do you know what happened? Do you know where she is," he stammered.

"I only know that she was taken away after she sent an anti-war letter to the Prime Minister. Her neighbors said that the Kempeitai came to her home and seized her at three in the morning."

She paused a moment before blurting out in frustration," Gangsters! Nothing more than common gangsters. They searched the house, rummaged through her belongings until they found a diary she kept filled with criticism of the government. Then she was rushed into a car and taken away."

Miyoko was still a moment, her gentle voice shaking. "And I don't know where they took her."

Hiyakawa thought he might vomit, his mind spinning. "I must speak to your husband. Where can I reach him?"

"That's not possible right now. He's secluded with Admiral Yamamoto on the *Negato*."

"But I must try," he pleaded. "I must find out where they took Barbara."

Miyoko gave him a phone number that she claimed *may* help him reach her husband. "Good luck," she said softly. "I will be praying for your wife."

Hiyakawa hung up and frantically dialed the number. When he reached Naval Command in Hiroshima, no one would forward his call to Fujiyama.

At that moment, his flight to Hawaii was announced for boarding. He would have to wait until arriving in Oahu to try again.

Flight Into Destiny

Before dawn on December 7th, Hiryo joined the other pilots in a purification ritual. First, he bathed in order to clean the impurities from his body, then he put on a clean, white pair of undershorts and wrapped his waist with his senninbari, a thousand stitch belt of cloth, approximately one meter in length. Each stitch was normally made by a different woman in order to complete the belt before giving them to soldiers in route to war. Hiryo's mother had canvassed their neighborhood asking the women in the area to place a small red stitch upon the senninbari for her son's good luck.

As the other young fighter pilots around Hiryo dressed in their muddy brown flying suits, they talked with great enthusiasm about the coming attack. After all the soldiers had properly adjusted their uniforms, they reported to the flight deck and boarded their planes.

The attack fleet was now only 200 miles from Oahu and preparing to launch the air assault. Hiryo was to be in the first wave of the attack. This was an honor given to him by Commander Fuchida.

Hiryo climbed into his *Mitsubishi Zero* and seated himself behind the controls. He looked above him at the tip of the mast of *Akagi*. There, hoisted above his flagship and snapping in the wind, was the infamous *Z* flag flown by Admiral Heihachiro Togo at the Battle of Tsushima Strait during the Russo-Japanese War, the same war in which his own father had won his honors thirty-six years ago.

Hiryo looked over to a Nakajima B5N2 attack bomber and noticed Fuchida seated in the cockpit. Fuchida was the commander of the First Air Fleet, the air group that would soon attack Pearl Harbor. He wore a white *hachimaki*, a cloth headband given to him by the maintenance crew for good luck. Commander Fuchida's plane displayed distinctive red and yellow stripes around the tail that designated Fuchida as aerial commander of the attack.

Fuchida threw a salute to Genda, Air Operations Officer of the First Fleet, standing on the bridge of the *Akagi* and gave him a confident nod.

Genda nodded back. Their plan was coming to fruition. Today was a day of immeasurable honor.

The roar of the plane engines idling combined with the brisk wind that swept over the deck. Dust flew through the air leaving a trail of golden flecks that created the illusion that the ship itself was magical. The vessel pitched and rolled against the waves that crashed over the bow of the flight deck, forcing the flight crews to cling desperately to the planes.

Hiryo looked out his windshield at the other carriers. They were beehives of activity. Planes were brought up from the hangars to the flight deck and readied for takeoff. The carriers sailed in parallel columns of three, followed by the tankers. Battleships, cruisers, and destroyers took positions on the outside of the formation.

This was it. The beginning of the end.

At 1:30 AM, thirty minutes before sunrise, hand lamps glowed in the darkness, guiding the planes as they moved into position, one by one. As Hiryo's plane took its place, he watched as hundreds of crewmembers waved the Rising Sun headbands toward the planes.

From the other five carriers, planes roared from the decks of the ships, taking flight into the dawn sky, and quickly falling into formation.

Hiryo's wait to join his fellow pilots arrived as a green lamp signaled him to take off. Hiryo gunned his engine and barreled down the deck, his heart pounding in his chest with indescribable excitement. His plane took off across the bow, circled to the left, and formed up with his group in the orange-tinted sky.

Like a well-rehearsed ballet, the planes flew in unison, dancing towards their ultimate destination. Hiryo checked his instruments and test fired his guns that chattered in response, as if eager for the pending fight. Adrenaline pumped through his veins, and he experienced a rush of power that he had never known.

The dawn clouds began to part, and a ray of golden light pierced the sky in front of him, inviting him forward.

The formation flew for about two hours when the telltale signs of blue and white breakers appeared on the horizon. It was the north shore of Oahu, and the waves looked like fingers, gentle sirens, beckoning them.

Hiryo thought of his father and what he must have felt at the Siege of Tsingtao when the Japanese Navy seized the German naval base. Would he repeat his father's courage? Would he make him proud?

Ahead of him, Hiryo could see the basket and tripod masts of the battleships *Nevada, Arizona, Tennessee, West Virginia, Oklahoma, California,* and *Maryland* appear through the haze. Every battleship of the U.S. Pacific Fleet was in the harbor except for the aircraft carriers.

And noticeably absent was anti-aircraft fire. As his group drew near to the American fleet, all was quiet below. Not a shot was fired, and there were no enemy planes over the harbor.

Everything appeared to be asleep.

At that particular moment, it felt like a normal training exercise for Hiryo, and this eased his sense of uneven nervousness.

Then, in front of Hiryo's *Zero,* Fuchida fired his flare pistol and propelled a *black dragon* into the sky, ordering the commencement of the attack. On this command, Hiryo watched the dive-bombers immediately climb to 4,000 feet, and the torpedo planes dropped to sea level, their wings skimming the waves of the harbor.

Over his radio, Hiryo heard Fuchida cry, *"Tora! Tora! Tora!"*

The bombing began with unrelenting fury.

No Way Home

When Hiyakawa arrived in Honolulu early the next morning, he quickly checked into the coral-colored Royal Hawaiian Hotel and made his way to his room located on the top floor.

He tossed his luggage on the bed, rushed to the phone and dialed the Naval Command number again.

This time he had a plan.

An enlisted man answered, and Hiyakawa, in his most official voice, barked, "This is His Excellency Kenta Hiyakawa of the Japanese-American diplomatic mission calling from Washington, D.C. It's imperative that I speak with Commander Akihito Fujiyama on Vice-Admiral Yamamoto's Staff immediately. I have crucial news concerning the negotiations in Washington."

"Yamamoto and his staff are in an important meeting," the enlisted man replied, "and only essential communications are to be sent through."

Hiyakawa raised his voice to a commanding level. "This *is* an essential communication. One that can possibly prevent war."

The enlisted man was silent for a few moments. "Let me see what I can do, sir."

It felt like an eternity before Hiyakawa's call was transferred.

"This is Commander Fujiyama."

The frantic diplomat wasted no time. "Akihito, this is Kenta Hiyakawa. I need to know where they took Barbara."

"Kenta, I can't talk now," Fujiyama sighed wearily.

"Please," Hiyakawa pleaded to his friend.

Fujiyama lowered his voice, and it sounded as if he was cupping the phone. "She was taken by Colonel Sato. I don't know where, but I've been trying to find out. And getting information from the Kempeitai is near impossible." He paused a moment. "Are you in Washington?"

"No. I am at the Royal Hawaiian Hotel in Oahu. I'm going to fly back to Tokyo on the next flight out."

There was a long pause on Fujiyama's end. "There will *not* be a next flight out."

"What do you mean?" Hiyakawa asked.

There was a long moment of dead silence from Fujiyama, then he continued. "I am sorry my friend. Look out your window."

Hiyakawa walked to his window and looked out over Pearl Harbor. Giant balls of fire emanated from the harbor, and thick, black smoke had begun to obscure his view of the warships anchored there.

Through boiling clouds of smoke, a fighter-bomber with the symbol of the Rising Sun of Japan on its wings, streaked from overhead toward Pearl Harbor before disappearing into ebony clouds of smoke that rose above the harbor.

Hiyakawa watched as a bomb was released from somewhere above a large battleship moored in the harbor below. A moment of quiet before impact, then another mighty fireball blistered the sky followed by a plume of dark obsidian smoke shooting straight up into the air, quaking the hotel's windows.

Hiyakawa dropped the phone from his ear and murmured, "Dear, God... what have we done?"

The Attack

Hiryo flew toward the American battleships. Black smoke rose above Hickam Field and Ford Island as dive-bombers pressed the attack. These were followed by waterspouts that appeared besides some of the battleships, indicating the torpedo attack had begun.

Hiryo put his *Zero* into a dive toward Hickam Field and checked for responding enemy planes.

There were none.

As he continued to drop in altitude, he could see line after line of American planes sitting wingtip to wingtip on the tarmac, easy targets to zero in on and destroy. He let loose with his 20mm guns and strafed the line of parked planes. Tracer bullets helped him focus on the targets as his machine gun and cannon fire shredded several planes into balls of fire. He felt a fire inside of his own soul as he watched the planes explode at his hands.

Soldiers on the ground scattered like panicked ants, scrambling to avoid Hiryo's tracer bullets and the aircraft exploding around them.

Hiryo pulled up on his stick, taking advantage of the *Zero's* superior climbing ability, and positioned himself above the field for another attack.

He came around again and peppered the hangers and vehicles that tried to escape. Behind him was another line of *Zeros* that were creating the same havoc on the ground.

Satisfied with the results, Hiryo and several other pilots turned their *Zeros* toward Pearl Harbor. The squadron fell into a standard

V formation of three aircraft, flanked by echelons of two, to prepare for any enemy fighters.

Hiryo saw the line of battleships anchored near Ford Island. Some were covered by smoke, and others were bleeding dark brown oil from their sides. Bursts of anti-aircraft fire erupted from their decks in the futile attempt to cease the attack.

The Americans were responding.

Flack was followed by machine gun bullets that buzzed around his *Zero* like a swarm of bees. Some even peppering his wings. But this did not deter Hiryo. He was a warrior. A samurai. A bushido that had drawn blood, and a sense of immense pride in himself, his nation, and his Emperor, surged over his being.

Hiryo pulled his *Zero* straight up to gain altitude and positioned himself for another attack on the ships in the harbor. When he reached proper altitude, he saw the familiar yellow and red striped tail of Fuchida's plane hovering over the battle scene.

Without warning, Fuchida's plane bounced violently across the sky and slid sideways, spinning out of control. Hiryo thought that one of Fuchida's control cables must have been shot away but Fuchida managed to regain control of his craft and maintain its course.

Hiryo marveled at the courage of the man for a moment and then his attention turned to a tall orange and black tower of fire that began to rise from one of the battleships below him. The ball of fire was followed by a jolting shock wave that momentarily disoriented him, and he nearly lost control of *his* aircraft.

It was the *Arizona*, completely engulfed in flames and impenetrable, black clouds. Hiryo looked at downtown Honolulu and watched a high-rise building shake in response to the massive shock wave.

The powder magazine of the battleship must have exploded, Hiryo thought. He winced for a moment, imagining the burning death of the sailors below him, but shook away the images and quickly regained his focus.

The skies were now filled with even more Japanese planes. The second wave of the attack had arrived.

Hiryo wondered why there was no enemy fighter resistance, but that thought was short-lived. The sound of pellets shredding the sides of his *Zero* grabbed his attention. He looked around and saw an American P40 Tomahawk firing directly at him.

True to his training, Hiryo used the speed and turning radius of the light *Zero* to his advantage, and was soon on the tail of the heavier P40 by turning inside its flight pattern.

The P40 tried to escape Hiryo by pulling up, but only succeeded in exposing the belly of his fighter to Hiryo's guns. Hiryo let loose with a barrage of bullets at the lumbering P40.

The P40 started to smoke and flame, but Hiryo was unable to press his attack. Behind him, another burst of machine gun fire hissed by his canopy—a P36 Hawk pressed down on him.

Hiryo once again pulled up on his stick, and his *Zero* responded by quickly gaining altitude. He kept his fighter in a steep climb until it lost some speed, then pulled on through to complete a small loop of high wing-over, which placed him out of reach and in position for another attack on the P36 Hawk, but the plane was gone.

Hiryo frantically searched behind, below, and above him until he noticed the P36 climbing directly towards Fuchida's bomber. Hiryo thrust his *Zero* into a steep climb and quickly closed the distance between him and the enemy plane. He fired fast bursts of 20mm cannon fire at the P36 from a distance of 100 meters. They hit their target, sheering the canopy off of the enemy fighter, and the plane lost control and plummeted towards the ground.

Hiryo checked his fuel gauge just as he received the command to break off the first wave attack and return to the *Akagi*.

After his return, Hiryo climbed from the *Zero*. He felt as if he was in a dazed and faraway state. He returned to his quarters, removed his flying gear, hung them neatly in his locker and sat at his small desk. Adrenaline still coursed through his veins, his hands shook in front of him, but he felt alone. Very alone. He stared down at his desk and picked up an envelope addressed to his father. Inside was a letter to his family and a last will and testament. Not needed. For now.

It was good to be alive.

An hour later, as Hiryo still sat at his desk, replaying the day's events over and over in his mind, he heard that Fuchida was returning to the *Akagi*. He ran up to the flight deck where dozens of flight crewmen were cheering Fuchida's arrival. Hiryo wanted to slap the man's back as well, but before he could get near him, Fuchida broke through the melee and approached Hiryo.

"Thank you," he said with a broad smile. "Your quick actions saved me today."

"Hai." Hiryo said proudly, but Fuchida's attention was diverted as he scanned the flight deck.

Fuchida looked up to the bridge and saw Genda. Their eyes locked and Genda knew right away what Fuchida was asking.

Genda turned to Nagumo, who stood next to him. "Sir, we must launch the third wave. We must destroy the oil tanks and dry docks of the harbor."

"We have been very lucky," Nagumo replied soberly. "We've accomplished our mission." The admiral stared out to sea. "We no longer have the element of surprise. We are in range of enemy land-based bombers and American submarines must now be looking for us. We don't know where the American carriers are and we don't have the fuel to look for them."

"But Admiral..." Genda protested.

Nagumo cut him off. "That is my final decision. We return to Japan."

A Terrible Resolve

"A great victory, sir," Chief of Staff, Rear Admiral Matome Ugaki, said to Yamamoto. He held a detailed report of the attack in his hands. "Five battleships were sunk, three battleships severely damaged, three cruisers and three destroyers suffered serious damage, and nearly two hundred aircraft were completely destroyed. The attack was nearly textbook perfect."

Yamamoto stood and paced the floor of his command center. "But Nagumo didn't press a third wave."

Fujiyama sullenly replied, "The oil tanks and naval facilities still stand at Pearl Harbor."

Yamamoto's worst fears were realized about Nagumo. The admiral didn't follow orders. He was too cautious. Nagumo's loyalty lay with the Fleet Faction and *not* with Admiral Yamamoto.

The members on his staff in the room could see Yamamoto's temper flare. "If Nagumo had followed the plan, *my* plan, the destruction of the remaining naval facilities would have crippled the American war efforts for years. But now, the American Navy can use Pearl Harbor as an operating base against us, instead of having to operate from the west coast." His fist pounded on the table.

The room fell silent as all eyes stared at Yamamoto. In a low voice he said, "I fear all we have done is to awaken a sleeping giant and fill him with a terrible resolve."

Fujiyama knew Yamamoto was correct, and he knew Nagumo's

action would most certainly change the very nature of the war with America.

But Japan had entered the storm. It had sowed the winds of war, and it would ultimately reap whatever whirlwind was to come.

A Message
From the Author

I relished writing this book! If you enjoyed the story of the Fuji-yama family and events leading up to the Second World War, would you consider doing two things?

First, sign up for my newsletter at www.frankfiore.com, and I'll be sure you're the first to get news on the books that will follow in the Ijin Series, in addition to info about my other titles.

Second—and this is a big request—if you liked this story, would you consider leaving a review wherever you bought this book, or on your favorite social media platform? I want as many readers as possible to discover this story, and your voice can help do that. Leave a review and tell a friend! Word-of-mouth is still the best way to introduce this story to other readers.

Lastly, *Thank you!*

Thank you, dear reader, for giving your time to read this book. It means a lot that you trusted me as the author to entertain, and hopefully excite, you with this story. Stories need an audience, and I appreciate you being my audience for just a little while. Thank you.

I know, I know, there are plenty of historical details surrounding World War 2 that are common knowledge, but there are still lots of questions about the lives of our main characters that need answers. Like…

What happened to Kenta Hiyakawas wife?
Does Connor officially join the Yakuza?

255

Will Fujiyama allow his daughter Suki to continue her relationship with the brutal Captain Hidaka Takahashi?
Will Yoshihara Koga survive to report the atrocities he has seen?
And so, dear readers, just for you, here's—

—A SNEAK PEEK AT—

A PYRRHIC VICTORY
Ijin Volume 2

War Fever

On the morning of December 9th, Connor came in for break-fast and immediately noticed Miyoko, Suki, and Kenji gathered around the radio, their faces all drawn with despair. He also felt the absence of the usual morning music, replaced instead with an announcer speaking rapidly and with great urgency much too fast for Connor to understand. The radio then cut to playing *The Warship March*.

He looked at Miyoko, and her face held a look of disbelief. "Miyoko," Connor said. "*Nan desu-ka?* What's going on?"

"*Senso da,*" she replied soulfully. "We are at war with America."

As the news first swept through the country, there was an air of stifling incomprehension amongst the people. Did Japan really go to war? Except for the intermittent blackout drills every day, life seemed ordinary. The only real change was the immediate issu-ance of rationing. Ration books were issued to every household, but the actual distribution of food would be through the various Neighborhood Associations.

But soon, war fever quickly spread like an unchecked brush fire. Pro-war demonstrations and military parades could be seen in almost every major city. Men, women, and even school children marched to martial music, enthusiastically waving little paper Japanese flags.

Several days after the attack on Pearl Harbor, there were a series of huge rallies in Tokyo, including the *Crush America and Britain* rally, the *National Rally on the Propagation of the War Rescript*, and the *Axis Pact Certain Victory Promotion* military rally. Some of the rallies were linked to spiritual mobilization and took place in Shinto shrines. Other victory rallies would follow, maintaining the populace at a high military fervor.

But support for the war was not absolute. Not *all* rallies were in support of the war.

Major Historical Characters
Mentioned In The Book

Michinomiya Hirohito—Emperor of Japan. A peaceful man, but not a politician.

Isoroku Yamamoto—Vice-Admiral in the Imperial Navy and a leading advocate of peace and reason. He was the mastermind behind the attack on Pearl Harbor.

Prince Mikasa Takahito—Youngest brother of Emperor Hirohito. He served as captain in China in 1939 under the name of Wakasugi. During his army career, he was harshly critical of the Japanese military's conduct in China.

Prince Higashikuni Naruhiko—After graduating from Japan's Army Academy and the Army War College, he held several military posts before being named chief of military aviation in 1937. Promoted to full general in 1939, was named general commander of defense three days after the attack on Pearl Harbor.

Prince Nobuhito Takamatsu—Younger brother of Emperor Hirohito. He served as a captain in the Imperial Navy. From the 1930s, Prince Takamatsu expressed grave reservations regarding Japanese aggression in Manchuria and the decision to wage war on the United States.

Prince Yasuhito Chichibu—Emperor Hirohito's younger brother and a general in the Imperial Japanese Army, Prince Chichibu was a vehement ultra-right-wing militarist who increasingly influenced Japanese military policy in the prewar era.

John Rabe—Director of the Siemens AG China Corporation. A German businessman and Nazi Party member, Rabe is best known for his efforts to stop war crimes during the Japanese Nanking Massacre and his work to protect and help Chinese civilians during the massacre that ensued. It is estimated that the Nanking Safety Zone, which he helped to establish, sheltered approximately 250,000 Chinese people from being killed.

Norman Alley—One of two newsreel cameramen who were aboard the USS Panay during the attack on December 12, 1937, Norman Alley of Universal News along with Eric Mayell of Movietone News, were able to film part of the attack and, after reaching shore, the sinking of the ship in the middle of the river.

General Minoru Genda—A Imperial Japanese Navy flight officer, JASDF general and politician. Genda is best known for helping to plan the attack on Pearl Harbor. He was also the third Chief of Staff of the Japan Air Self-Defense Force.

Mitsuo Fuchida—A captain in the Imperial Japanese Navy Air Service and a bomber observer in the Imperial Japanese Navy before and during World War II. Best known for leading the first wave of air attacks on Pearl Harbor, Fuchida was responsible for the coordination of the entire aerial attack.

Field Marshall Hajime Sugiyama—Army Minister in 1937, Sugiyama was a driving force behind the launch of hostilities against China in retaliation for the Marco Polo Bridge Incident. After being named the Army's Chief of Staff in 1940, he became a leading advocate for expansion into Southeast Asia and preventive war against the United States.

Marshal Admiral Prince Fushimi Hiroyasu—Chief of Staff of the Imperial Japanese Navy. Although he supported the southward advance into northern French Indochina and the Dutch East Indies, Hiroyasu expressed reservations about the Tripartite Pact during the Imperial Conference of September 19, 1940. He remained a member of the Supreme War Council throughout the Pacific War.

Prince Fumimaro Konoe—The prime minister of Japan from 1937–1939 and from 1940–1941, Konoe presided over the Japanese invasion of China in 1937 and the breakdown in relations with the United States. He also played a central role in transforming Japan into a totalitarian state by passing the State General Mobilization Law and founding the Imperial Rule Assistance Association by dissolving all other political parties.

General Tomoyuki Yamashita—And general in the Imperial Japanese Army,. Yamashita led Japanese forces during the invasion of Malaya and Battle of Singapore. His accomplishment of conquering Malaya and Singapore in 70 days earned him the sobriquet *The Tiger of Malaya*. Convicted of war crimes after the war and executed in 1946.

Major Fictional Characters
Mentioned In The Book

Yoshihara Koga—A Japanese-American reporter is introduced on page one to tell the story about Connor.

Connor Williams—An American teenager is an innocent soul coming of age against the backdrop of an ill-conceived war.

Akihito Fujiyama—A Commander and fighter pilot in the Imperial Japanese Navy. Fujiyama acts as military attaché to the U.S. Navy. He lives with his wife, Miyoko, their sons, Hiryo and Yoshi, and daughter, Suki.

Kenta Hiyakawa—A diplomat with the Japanese Foreign Office, Kenta is a thorn in the side of the militarists. He is a distant cousin of the emperor, thus a confirmation of the rumors that he has the emperor's ear.

Barbara Hiyakawa—American wife of Hiyakawa; tall, elegant, Caucasian, she is bold and outspoken.

Meiko Nemoto—Connor's Japanese nanny, who cares for him after his father abandons him and his mother dies.

Miyoko Fujiyama—A gentle and loving woman, wife to Fujiyama.

Tomoko Sakura—Yoshihara's editor, who sees himself as an ethical Samurai for truth, like his hero, Edward G. Robinson.

Dr. Shapiro—A counselor on the U.S. Navy base who helps deal with Connor and approves Fujiyama fostering him.

Jack and Charlie—Racist American teenagers.

Haru Sato—A Kempeitai colonel on the Supreme Military Council. Part of the military police arm and leader of the Yakuza.

Russell Brady—A college acquaintance of Yoshihara.

Captain Hidaka Takahashi—A brutal Japanese officer in love with Suki, Fujiyama's daughter. An aide de camp to Colonel Sato.

Kenji—Youngest Fujiyama son, enamored with American culture.

Suki—Fujiyama's only daughter. Connor is enamored with her.

Mai—Miyoko's sister. She has been watching over Suki and Kenji while Fujiyama was on assignment in America.

Father Marquette—Priest who runs the French Catholic mission in Manchuria for the Société des Missions Étrangères de Paris.

Huan Quang—A villager.

Masao Koga—Yoshihara's older brother, presumed to be dead. A member of the Black Ocean Society, an ultra-nationalist organization.

Kodo Tento, Goro Yoshida, and Jiro Miyagi—Members of the Yakuza.

Eiji Yamaguchi—An intellectual and member of the Leftist peace movement. A violator of the Peace Preservation Law, he becomes a soldier against his will.

Taka—A soldier and companion to Yoshi.

Sgt. Gunso—A platoon leader.

Genero Nakatomi—A reporter from a Japanese news service.

Mrs. Ito—An old lady who owned the tobacco store down the street from the Fujiyamas. Head of the local neighborhood association.

Black Patch—close school friend of Kenji's.

Niko Kimura—A former soldier, he is now a civilian prison guard.

About the Author

Frank F. Fiore is a five-star rated author of novels in multiple genres including Contemporary Fiction, Tecno-Thrillers, Action/ Adventures, Sci-Fi, Historical Fiction, and Westerns. He lives in Arizona with his fetching wife, Lynne.

Connect with Frank online at:
www.frankfiore.com

Also Available From

WordCrafts Press

All for the Cause
Gail Kittleson

Plague
Marian Rizzo

The Gift
Cherie Dargan

The Restless Earth
Alan Cockrell

Underground Scouts
Marie Sontag

www.wordcrafts.net